Until Proven Guilty

A Kansas City Legal Thriller

Rachel Sinclair

Also by Rachel Sinclair

For information about upcoming titles in the *Harper Ross Legal Thriller* series, sign up for my mailing list! You'll be the first to know about new releases and you'll be the first to know about any promotions!!!!
http://eepurl.com/hBqhtr

Johnson County Legal Thrillers (Kansas City, Missouri)

Bad Faith

Justice Denied

Hidden Defendant

Injustice for All

LA Defense

The Associate

The Alibi

Reasonable Doubt

The Accused

Secrets and Lies

Until Proven Guilty

Emerson Justice Legal Thrillers (Los Angeles)

Dark Justice

Blind Justice

Southern California Legal Thrillers (San Diego)

Presumption of Guilt

Justice Delayed

By Reason of Insanity

Wrongful Conviction

The Trial

ONE

"Now, what is it that you suggest I do with Nate?" I asked my therapist, whose name was Dr. Betty Jordan. I had managed to talk Nate's school into letting him stay, even after he was caught with a gun in school, on the condition that he completed 40 hours of family therapy with an approved guidance counselor. Nate's school selected Dr. Jordan as the proper counselor, and Nate and I had been seeing her twice a week every week for the past six weeks. Nate had opened up to her, when she saw him individually, about what his teacher had done to him. Mrs. Bowen, his fifth-grade teacher, had pled guilty to molesting Nate and was awaiting sentencing at the moment.

"You really need to spend more time with him. I've spoken at length with both you and Nate, over the past six weeks, and what I'm getting from Nate is that he is a very isolated and lonely child. He feels neglected. He feels like he doesn't have any parents. Losing his mother has been very hard on him. But even more difficult for him is the thought that you don't care about him either. That's been very apparent to me."

I nodded. "I know what you're saying, but I don't realistically know if I can spend as much time with him as what I need to. I've already cut back my hours at work to deal with this, and I've tried to show Nate in every way possible that he's very important to me. I just don't know what more I can do."

Dr. Jordan just watched me. She had to have known what kind of predicament I was in. I was in a stressful position. A stressful profession. I had gone through the ringer myself in the past few years. Between having my wife running off on me, and having her tell my daughter that I was not her biological father, and the fact that I was on trial for my life after my biological father was found murdered and I was accused of it, I had been through it all in the past few years. All sorts of issues came up during my murder trial, including the fact that I had killed my stepfather when I was only 15 years old. I was never prosecuted for it, because he was going to kill either me or my mother or both of us, and he promised this all the time. Even as a kid, I knew it was his life or ours, and I chose his life.

The upshot was that the past few years had been beyond chaotic. My daughter Amelia had beaten cancer, but it was touch and go for a long time. There were years I didn't know if she would live to see her 10th birthday. The bone marrow transplant finally was the thing that put her into remission, but, even now, I felt like her condition was touch and go. Her remission was precarious, as all remissions are, and she was not out of the woods. She was relatively healthy, thank God, but who knew how long that would last? Every time she got as much as a cold, I worried about her.

Amelia's sickness was just one more thing on my plate, and I didn't have the mental energy to really deal with my one healthy child. I was guilty of thinking he would just be okay because there was nothing obviously wrong with him. Of course, I was proved wrong, when he brought a gun into the school and aimed it at a kid who had been teasing him about being gay. He wasn't gay, at least not that I knew, but that was beside the point. That kid thought he was gay, and that was enough for him to bully Nate.

"You can take a leave of absence. Just until we manage to find the proper medication for your son and his signs of depression are lessened."

That was another thing I would have to deal with. The doctor wanted Nate on antidepressants. I was against it, as I was against all forms of medications, yet the doctor had been persistent that Nate needed some kind of antidepressants. She told me that if I didn't go along with her recommendations, she would not sign off to the school that we completed the requisite counseling. Which meant Nate might still end up being expelled from school. In other words, I needed to dance to her tune or Nate would suffer.

The doctor told me that giving anti-depressants to a child as young as Nate, a child who had just turned 11, was tricky, to say the very least. She reviewed all the side effects with me, including the fact that Nate might become suicidal, and I was dead set against it. I had to battle my own bouts of depression over my life and I always managed to get over it without drugs. I wanted Nate to do the same. Yet I gave in, just because of the threat that Nate might be expelled from school if I refused the doctor's recommendations. For a child in such a precarious and unstable position as Nate, being expelled from school would be the last straw for him. It would only be a matter of time before he went the way I went and ended up in prison. Staying in his school was his only hope of beating that scenario. I would do everything in my power to make sure he stayed at Pembroke Hill, the private school he attended.

Now the shrink wanted me to take a leave of absence. I could afford to take one, because I settled a personal injury case case years back that netted me $4 million. So financially, it wasn't a problem to take a long break from work. I just didn't want to leave Harper high and dry, as I had just become a partner in the law firm. She had a lot of cases on her plate and needed my help with them. The only other attorney in her office was named Tammy, an estate attorney who never appeared in court.

"Okay," I said reluctantly. "I guess I could take a small leave of absence. A sabbatical." My plan at that time was to take a leave of absence long enough to be home with Nate while he was going through the early stages of taking his antidepressants. It would apparently take some tweaking to find the right formula for him, as it always took a lot of tweaking to find the right formula for anybody. Because everybody's body chemistry was different, doctors always had to try different dosages and different drugs in different combinations to find out just the right combination and dosage of drugs to alleviate depression in any given person. Then they usually had to do some more tweaking later on, because meds tend to stop working after a certain period, so it would be back to the drawing board. Because Nate was so young, it was even trickier. There was a real chance he could become suicidal because of the antidepressants. That was a known risk. I certainly could not take the chance and leave Nate to his own devices when he was first taking these drugs.

But, as I left Dr. Jordan's office, I got a phone call that changed everything.

"Damien," my mom's voice was on the other end of the line. "I'm in the clink. The hoosegow. Gotta come down."

I rolled my eyes. This was not the first time my mother had been in the jail and it probably wouldn't be the last. My mother was regularly being taken to jail for one reason or another. Unpaid parking tickets, unpaid moving violations, a DUI or two. Always minor things, never anything enormous, unless you consider drunk driving to be enormous. That was just a routine thing for her anymore. I was really in no mood to have to deal with her. Not at that moment, when I was coming out of the therapist's office, with Nate strongly on my mind.

"I'll get there when I get there." That was a game we played. She would go to jail for one reason or another and I would take my own sweet time getting her out. That was my way of saying, in a very passive-aggressive way, that she needed to get her shit together. "What are you charged with this time? How many speeding tickets have you not paid, or maybe you got a DUI?"

"I wouldn't be making so much fun if I were you," she said. "I'm being charged with murder."

TWO

"Come again? Mom, seriously, this isn't funny."

"You think I'm being funny? I'll show you funny. Unless you think the cops coming into my house at 2 o'clock this morning and hauling my candied ass to jail, asking me all kinds of questions for the past 10 hours, if you think that's my idea of a good time, you got another thing coming. Now get down here. I didn't want to call you but the person I usually call to get me out of these things is deader than a doornail. And the cops think I'm the one who killed him."

I took a deep breath. "Mom, you're going to have to slow down. Who do they think you killed, and what –"

"They think I killed my friend Tracy Dunham. He's a guy I screw around with once in a while, good guy. Ain't never been more then a bed buddy, but we hang out too. Tracy, he was taking the drugs, which ain't no concern of mine. I don't get into that crap, but to each his own. Anyhow, turns out he's married. Or he was married, he ain't married now to nobody. He was married and his old lady threw him out of the house."

Mom was rambling, like she does, and I just had to let her do it.

"Last July, he comes over to my house, higher than a kite," Mom went on. "Tells me his bitch wife don't want him no more, can he crash?

I say yeah, sure, why not? So he comes over and sleeps on my couch. I go to bed, I wake up and he's dead. You know, I try to do CPR and shit like that, I don't even know it all that well, but I seen it on TV shows. I try doing what I saw on TV. But he was stiff and cold, there ain't no bringing him back at that point. I didn't know what to do, so I call up the hospital, 911, they send somebody out to pick him up. They send the ambulance over and some woman, she says her job is to comfort the people who wake up to find a stiff in their house. I tell her I didn't need no comforting, I barely knew this guy, I wasn't shedding no tears for him. The cops come next, they question me, they want to do a piss test. I tell them okay, sure, why not? I ain't taking drugs. They're gonna find out I was drinking, but that ain't illegal, and I was sitting in my home, so I'm allowed to drink. They do a piss test, but they're not telling me the results."

She was on a roll, so I let her keep talking.

"They go into my medicine cabinet, I guess they figured out Tracy died of an overdose, they're looking in my medicine cabinet to see if I got some horse in there. I tell them 'have at it, knock yourself out, loser,' then they come out and tell me they're taking one of my BP meds in for testing. They tell me they found a suspicious powder in my BP med bottle.

They take him away, I think that's it, then two cops show up at my door three months later. They're telling me I'm responsible for Terry's death. They're saying they did an autopsy and some kind of test, toxic test or something like that, and-"

"Toxicology test," I said. "It's to find out about the presence of drugs or poison in a dead person's blood at the time of death. Go ahead."

"Yeah, toximology test, or whatever, anyhow, they tell me the toxic test showed Tracy died of a heroin overdose and it's my fault 'cause I gave him the drug. Then they tell me my BP meds weren't BP meds at all, but high-grade heroin. I tell them to go to hell and to fuck right off, in those words, ain't nobody responsible for Tracy's death but Tracy, and I don't know nobody who would sell me that junk and they made a mistake. I don't possess horse and I never have. Well they don't like me telling them off like that, so they haul me down to the station. They're asking me questions for God knows how long, not letting me pee, freezing my nipples off. They're keeping the room colder than a witch's tit, which is bull, if you ask me."

I knew what she was talking about, and I thought it was nonsense as well. I knew why cops did it, but it didn't make it any less ethical. They were trying to get a confession from my mother in any way they could. They deliberately tried to make her uncomfortable to the extreme so she would confess to a crime just to get out of there.

My mother was talking way too fast and I wanted to slow her down.

"Mom, it's okay. You don't have to tell me the entire story right now. I'll be coming down to the jail within the next half-hour."

Nate and Amelia were home with Gretchen. I had arranged for Gretchen to watch the both of them. I needed to speak with the counselor completely alone because I needed her advice for what to do with Nate. Turned out that everything she was telling me about how I needed to slow down, maybe even take a sabbatical, would go right out the window. My mother was charged with murder. As much as my mother and I did not get along over the years, and we didn't get along over the years because of the way she was when I was growing up – drinking all the time, a revolving door of men, just basically being neglectful – I had forgiven her once I found out the reason she always had her own share of mental problems. She was raped by a very wealthy man, Josh Roland, and I was a result of that rape.

Josh Roland was then bludgeoned to death by an oriental lamp in his office and I was charged with his murder. It turned out the person who murdered him was Addison Weston, the First Lady of the State of Missouri. She had hired somebody to actually do the deed, Jaclyn Peterson, who ended up charged with manslaughter and was currently serving 10 years in prison for her role in the murder. As for Addison, she managed to be acquitted on the basis of temporary insanity. She hired the best attorney money could buy, which was why she got that result, while her patsy did the time Addison needed to. It was the best justice money could buy, which unfortunately was the way of the legal system. If you got money, you get away with anything. If you don't, you're going down no matter if you did it or not.

Now my mother was charged with murder. A nonsense charge if

ever there was one. I had heard of people being charged with murder just because they were taking drugs with somebody who happened to die, and also instances where people were charged with murder because they bought drugs for somebody. But in this case, it was none of the above. My mom wasn't doing drugs with him, she just let him sleep on her couch. So she happened to be in the room when he died, and that makes her a murderer? Seriously?

Something was very off about this entire thing. To say the least. I would have to see her in jail and try to figure out what was going on. And then I would have to storm over to the prosecutor's office and find out what the hell they were thinking. How could they possibly charge my mother with murder for something so stupid?

Then I realized something. My mother was probably lying. She said didn't do drugs, but I knew she did. She also drank a lot. It was entirely possible that when they took a urinalysis at her home, after she called 911 about Tracy's death, they found out she had drugs in her system as well. And if they were the same drugs as those found in Tracy Dunham's system, they could charge her with murder. It would still be a baloney charge, but it would be a much more solid charge than if she was just sitting in her house when he came to visit, he passed out on her couch, he died and she had nothing to do with it.

I had a feeling there was more to the story than what she was telling me. He probably came over, the two of them started doing drugs, she went to bed, he did as well, and he was dead when she woke up. If that was the case, her urinalysis would prove that. If the UA showed opium in her system, then the state would have a much better case than if she was sober and just let him sleep on her couch.

I would definitely need to find out the results of my mother's drug test before I spoke with her. If the drug test showed she was clean when she was arrested, it would be no problem getting the case dismissed. I didn't know why they could charge her in this case unless there was something else I didn't know. At any rate, the prosecutors would have to drop the charges against her if she was clean at the time of the death because they couldn't win at trial unless they showed she supplied the drugs to him somehow. It would be an open and shut case and a waste of money for them.

I called Gretchen, told her what was going on, and then immediately headed down to the police station. I would get my mom's records, see what kind of questions they asked her in the interrogation room, and, most importantly, get the results of her urinalysis and see if she had drugs in her system.

I left the office building where I had been talking to Dr. Jordan, opened the door and a blast of cold hit me in the face. When I went to see Dr. Jordan, the weather had started to change from the 70° it had been earlier, dropping to around 50°. That was the one thing people always said about the weather in Missouri – if you don't like it, just wait a minute, and it'll change. And it certainly did on that day. It was early fall, October, and the leaves were just starting to change and fall from the trees.

I hugged my coat closer around my body as I made my way towards my Mercedes SUV in the parking lot. It was a new car for me, the one luxury I bought when I settled a large medical malpractice suit a few years back. In that case, it turned out the doctor who had given my client's son anesthesia that he was allergic to, did so deliberately. He was an angel of mercy, which was what he fashioned himself to be, for he was killing terminal patients. It turned out he had a son who had died slowly of cancer, going through much pain and agony along the way and didn't want anybody else to suffer that. So, when he got the records of his patients and found out they were terminal and were going in for surgery, he would deliberately give them the wrong anesthesia or too much anesthesia and they ended up dead. Everybody was entitled to punitive damages against him because he was doing intentional acts. I was the first in line, so I got a large settlement from him.

Once I got that $4 million settlement, I put most of it away for my kid's college and gave Harper a good percentage of it as well. I bought a new house, close to where Harper lived in the Brookside area, and this new Mercedes SUV. The rest of it, I squirreled away. After growing up poor, in a trailer, with a mother who didn't work and was constantly cycling men in and out of the home, I was constantly insecure that I would be poor again. No matter how much money I had, it would never be enough for me to feel like I would never be on skid row again.

I got to the jail and told the guard that I needed to see my mom's file. They knew me because I was there all the time, so they gave me her file without questioning me or asking me for an ID. I opened it up and immediately saw the results of my mother's blood test – she had tested positive for opiates. Also in the file were the results of the toxicology test they did for Tracy Dunham, and he too, had opiates in his system. Specifically, the results of the toxicology examination showed that the heroin in his system was high-grade and extremely pure.

It also looked like mom's "blood pressure" meds weren't actually blood pressure meds, but were heroin in a pill form. The officers indicated they had probable cause to seize the meds and test them because mom dropped a dirty UA and her companion had died of an apparent overdose. So the label on the pill bottle said Nifedipine, but it was actually heroin, according to the toxicology report on my mother's prescription BP pills.

I looked through the interrogation documents and saw my mom did not admit to doing anything except for what she told me – she told the cops that she was sitting in her trailer home, minding her own business, when Tracy came to her door. According to my mom, Tracy told her that he'd been thrown out by his wife, Priscilla. My mom then went to bed and woke up to find him dead. That's what she told the cops, over and over again. They never told her they knew she was lying and had opiates in her system at the time Tracy died.

It looked like I would have to confront my mother with her lie.

I went back up to the guard station and told them I was there to see Olivia Ward. The guard nodded. "Just a second, I'll let you through."

I went through the first set of double doors into the hallway, took the elevator up to the fifth floor which was where my mother was staying, went down the long corridor door and got to her pod. Once there, I rang the guards, and they let me through. I told the guard inside the waiting area that I was there to see Olivia Ward, the guard nodded her head, and told me to wait just a few minutes.

Mom came out a few minutes later, looking her usual self. She was down to about 100 pounds or less, and her hair, which was usually dark or bleached blonde, was currently pink. Or, rather, it was streaked pink. I could see her usual brunette hair peeking out from underneath the pink streaks, along with a lot of grey roots. She was dressed in an orange jumpsuit that absolutely hung from her skinny frame.

"God, I could use a smoke and a drink." She put her hands on the table, and they were shaking. It looked like she was going through the DTs, and I wouldn't be surprised if that was the case, as much as she drank. "I've been puking in this place. Nobody cares. Got the shakes so bad I feel like I'm going to rattle and roll right out of this joint."

"Mom," I said to her. "You tell me you need a smoke and a drink. And I'll be honest with you, you look like you're worse for the wear."

"I look like something the cat dragged in and I know it. You don't have to rub it in, kiddo."

"I'm not saying this to be mean. I do need to ask you a question, though. You told me over the phone that you weren't doing drugs with this Tracy Dunham person." I stopped my sentence right there, because I wanted to see her reaction to what I was going to say to her. I wanted to see what kind of facial expression and body language she displayed.

To my surprise, she didn't flinch. "Yeah, I told you that, because it's the God's honest truth. I told you I wasn't doing drugs with him, and that's what I mean. I was sitting in my trailer, minding my own damn business, and he came over and crashed on my couch." She narrowed her eyes at me. "Why do I think you think I'm lying? I got the sneaking suspicion that you're over there thinking I told you a tall tale."

I leaned forward. "Mom, I took a peek at your file before I came to see you. According to the file, there were opiates in your system at the time you were arrested. Heroin was also found in the bloodstream of the victim. You care to explain that?"

"Dammit. I told you I wasn't doing drugs with him. I told you I don't do drugs. I drink, I get shit-faced on that, I smoke a lot. I do weed. And that's it. No cocaine, no meth, no heroin, no hillbilly heroin, no nothing. I don't get into that crap. I know, I know, I used to do all that crap. All of it. But I gave it up about 10 years ago and I've never looked back. Drinking, smoking cigarettes, and smoking bud are all I do now."

"Mom, I don't believe you. If it's true what you're saying, why were opiates found in your system?"

"Hell, I don't know. You tell me."

I closed my eyes. "Mom, this is important. If there were not drugs in your system, there would be no way the prosecutor could possibly prove you were doing drugs with your friend Tracy. If they can't prove that, the whole case goes away unless they can prove you supplied Tracy with the heroin that killed him. I mean, they could still try to pursue charges, but it would be so easy to prove to the jury that you had nothing to do with his death that they would have to drop the charges. But if there was really heroin in your system, it'll be a little more difficult to get the charges dismissed."

She shook her head. "What is this bullcrap, anyway? Is that how it's going to be? You're doing drugs, somebody bites it and suddenly you're on the hook? I never heard of that."

"Unfortunately, it's not unheard of. All around the nation, people who were just doing drugs with another person who died are being found guilty, or at least charged, for their death. Usually, however, the charge is a murder only when somebody actually supplies the other person with the drugs. Regardless, it would be helpful if there were not drugs in your system."

"Is sounds like somebody was cooking the books here."

"What's that supposed to mean?"

"Just what it sounds like. Somebody doctored up my damn record and made it look like I was taking drugs when I wasn't. And you know when those pigs found drugs in my house, I knew for sure they're full of crap, because I damn well know I had no drugs at the house. Everything I said to you earlier on the phone is the God's honest truth. I didn't give that man no heroin, I didn't take no heroin with him, I had nothing to do with none of it, and I certainly didn't have no heroin in no prescription bottle."

I made a steeple with my hands, and stared at them for a minute or two. "Did you know Tracy was on drugs?"

"Hell no. I told you, me and him were sex buddies, nothing more, nothing less. We get together, drink and smoke weed, hit the sack, he'd leave. That was all there was to it."

"How did you meet him?"

She rolled her eyes. "At some fancy-schmancy thousand-dollar plate dinner. The governor himself was the guest of honor." She shook her head. "I met him at a dive bar. He asked me to dance, I said yes, we hit it off, he came back to my place, boom boom boom, that was that. No muss, no fuss."

"Do you remember the bar you met him at?"

"Why the hell does that matter? I don't remember which bar it was, probably someplace in Lee's Summit where the fake bikers go. You know the guys I'm talking about, the muckety-mucks who got full-time jobs as executives who like to ride their hogs on the weekends and act tough. A bunch of those fake bikers were hanging out at the bar that night. That's all I remember. I don't remember which bar it was."

I made notes as we spoke. "Was Tracy Dunham one of those fake bikers?"

She shrugged. "I suppose so. I don't really know. All I know is, I get up to go to the little girl's room to take a leak, and when I come back, there's a guy sitting at my barstool. Never seen the guy before in my whole life. It's crowded, there ain't no place to sit, and he's sitting in the one open seat. My seat. I even have my purse on the bar in front of him. I go to take my purse from the bar and try to find some other place to sit. He just looks at me, drags on his cigarette, tells me to sit on his lap. I ain't in the mood for that, I tell him to go to hell. He keeps going, says he wants to buy me a drink because he took my seat. I say why not? Free drink, all I got to do is hang out with the guy. So I did. I hung out with him. Got my free drink. Free drink turned into about six more, next thing I know, we're back in my dump screwing around. He leaves, I figure I'm never gonna see him again, but he pops back in a couple weeks later, and it just kind of went like that. He'd come over like a booty call and I let him come over like a booty call. I didn't know nothing about him, he didn't know nothing about me. That was how I liked it. He liked it too."

"Okay. So you knew nothing about this guy. You don't even know if he was doing drugs on a regular basis."

"Yeah, that's right. Why do you keep asking me these questions like you don't believe what I'm telling you? Listen, you've always been a shit to me. You've never trusted me any further than you can throw me. But I'm telling you the God's honest truth right now. I knew nothing about that guy."

"What else can you tell me?"

She shrugged. "I told you everything I can tell you. Everything I'm gonna tell you. You can either believe me or not, but I'm telling you what I know."

I tapped my fingers on the table, wondering why I had a nagging feeling there was much more to the story than what she was telling me. There was something behind this case. Something I wasn't seeing, and maybe my mother wasn't seeing either. I just wished she knew something more about this guy. I believed her when she said she didn't know anything about him, however. My mother was just that kind of person. She had sex with men she didn't know and didn't always get their backgrounds or histories. She wasn't somebody who would even get a person's last name all the time.

"Okay, then. I guess I'll talk to the prosecutor's office and find out why they're doing this to you. Maybe I can glean something from them. In the meantime, you just sit tight, and I'll try to figure out what's going on. I guess your initial appearance is tomorrow, so I'll try to get a bond for you."

She shrugged. "Do what you gotta do. God knows I'm not going nowhere anytime soon. I'll see you tomorrow."

As I drove home that night, I thought about what my mother was telling me in the jail. I didn't doubt her story, but at the same time, what was up with her file saying she had heroin in her system? Did somebody really falsify that record, and if they did, why would they do something like that? And who would do something like that?

Something was fishy, and I would find out what exactly it was.

THREE

I got home a little bit after 10 PM and went straight to Nate's room to see what he was doing.

He was sitting at his desk, looking at his computer, apparently playing a video game. He didn't look in my direction when I came in the door, so I went over to him and put my hands on his shoulders and squeezed them lightly. "Hey, buddy. How are things going?"

He shrugged and said nothing.

I sat on the bed. I waited for him to turn around and look at me, but he kept on playing his game. I remembered what my therapist, Dr. Jordan, told me – she told me not to be discouraged if Nate didn't want to open up, but to not let him shut me out.

Without turning around, he said "Dad, you were supposed to be home hours ago. You promised you would be home tonight after you talked to our therapist."

I took a deep breath. "Nate, I know what I said this morning. But something came up with your grandmother. She's in trouble. A lot of trouble."

Nate finally turned around, his green eyes looking haunted. "What kind of trouble?"

I debated about how much I wanted to tell him about what was going on with my mother. Nate was very close with my mother and always had been. Even when I went through a period of time when I didn't want to talk to her, he would always ask about her, asking when she would come and visit them. My daughter Amelia felt the same way about her. Both kids would be upset when they found out about my mother being charged with murder.

It was such a precarious time with Nate. I hesitated to say anything to him.

"She's just having a problem. I really wanted to be home tonight with you guys, make you dinner, watch movies with you, just hang out. I had every intention of coming home right at six, and I would have if I didn't have to see my mother."

Nate turned back around and started playing with his video game again. "It's okay, Dad. Really, it's okay."

The way he said that made me know it really wasn't okay. I just had the sinking feeling that I was losing him. I remembered my own childhood, how I was going down the wrong path, stealing cars, smoking and drinking when I was ten, the same age Nate was now, generally getting into trouble and raising hell. Once I got out of prison for a crime I didn't commit, I swore I would turn my life around completely and no child of mine would go the route I did. Yet, here was Nate, shutting me out, shutting out the world, and I didn't know how to reach him. I didn't know what he needed from me. He wasn't telling me.

I felt adrift.

"No, Nate. It's not okay. It's not okay that I told you one thing and then went back on my word. You can tell me, buddy. You can talk to me. You can tell me anything on your mind and I want you to. If you hate me, I want you to tell me that. If you're angry, tell me. Don't be shy."

What was ironic was that his sister, Amelia, was the opposite of him. She told me anything and everything, and if she was mad, I knew it. She didn't mince words, even though she was only 9 years old. She had stared down death and beat it. She told the Grim Reaper *not today asshole*, and that gave her the kind of strength to face anything life threw her way. She was tested by her battle with cancer, and by how close she came to death's door, and she came out the other side.

In a way, Nate was tested along with her. He suffered right along with her. True, he didn't go through all she went through – the infections, the nausea, the pain, the fatigue, the fear. The constant tests, the stays in the hospital. He didn't actually go through those things. But he was a very sensitive boy, so he absorbed her pain. When she hurt, he did as well. I knew that.

He just shrugged. "It's late, Dad. I gotta get to bed."

I stood up and squeezed his shoulders and tousled his hair. "You're right. I'll see you in the morning."

I turned away, closing the door behind me. Before I went to bed, I went to Amelia's room and checked on her. She was fast asleep, so I went down to my own room, sat on the bed, and thought about things.

I thought about what my therapist, Dr. Jordan, told me about how I was supposed to deal with Nate. I realized that was just not possible. Until I got my mom out of this jam, there was nothing I could really do but work her case and make sure she got the best representation possible. I didn't trust her case in anybody else's hands.

I called Harper. It was late, I knew that, but I knew she usually stayed up late working on her cases. I had a feeling she wouldn't be too upset with me if I called her.

She answered on the third ring. She sounded like she had been crying. "What's going on, Damien?"

"Nothing." I took a deep breath. To tell the truth, I didn't know why I was calling her. I guess I just needed someone to talk to, a sounding board. I had been seeing, off and on, Ally Hughes from the prosecutor's office. It wasn't anything serious, and she wasn't necessarily somebody I could call and talk to when I was feeling out of sorts. Yet Harper and I had become close friends and confidants, as well as being partners in our law firm.

She sniffled on the phone. "It's not nothing, the reason why you called. Something must be going on. You don't ever call me this time of night. So tell me what's up."

I took a deep breath. "Are the girls in bed? I'd really like to come over. My kids are asleep, but I can have the neighbor girl, Gretchen, come over and watch them. She does that sometimes when I need her at night." She didn't mind it. There were times when I would go out late at night and she would sleep on the couch or in the guest bedroom. I only had her come over because I didn't entirely trust my two young children to be home alone. And the great thing about Gretchen was that she lived close by so she could come over at just about any time. At a moment's notice. And she liked it, because I paid her a lot more when she came over on an emergency basis.

Harper sniffled again, and coughed. "Yeah, the girls are in bed. Come on over. In fact, I'm glad you called. I really didn't want to be alone tonight."

"Why? Is there something going on?"

She cleared her throat. "Axel and I are not seeing each other anymore. He broke up with me tonight."

Oh, crap. Harper and Axel had been dating for a long time and were very serious and in love. I liked Axel a lot and I knew he was really a part of Harper's family. Harper would no doubt be devastated.

"Oh, I'm so sorry to hear that. What happened?" I asked.

Harper cleared her throat and caught a sob. "He's going back to Australia because he's being deported. I thought he was a permanent resident, even a citizen. I mean, he's been in the states for a long time. He told me he'd tried to become a permanent resident, but his brother Daniel had already been deported to Australia because of his drug problems. Because of his brother's problems, Axel broke the law to make sure his brother didn't go to prison. He covered up his brother's drug problems by taking some evidence out of the evidence room at the police department. His brother would've gone to prison for life, because he was busted with a lot of drugs, and the Feds would have to get involved, so Axel went into the evidence room and destroyed the evidence that would've been used against Daniel. The KCPD had to drop the charges against Daniel after that. I guess Axel finally got caught, so now he's being deported."

I listened to Harper without a word. I knew what she was going through. I had gone through my share of broken hearts myself. My most recent broken heart was when I divorced my wife, Sarah.

Sarah was not a good person. Granted, she had gone through a lot in her life – her father committed suicide, her brother died of cancer when she was young, not six months after her father committed suicide, and her mother had a hard time trying to pick up the pieces with just the two of them. So, in a way, I had a lot of sympathy for her. Even though she abandoned Amelia and me when we needed her the most, when Amelia was on death's door, and I really thought we would have say goodbye to her, I still felt sorry for Sarah. During that time, Sarah was not only not around, she was fighting me every step of the way. She wanted to stop Amelia's treatment. She thought it wasn't doing her any good and our daughter was only suffering on our behalf. I was of the mind that we had to do everything we could to make sure Amelia survived. I felt that if I didn't do everything in my power, I would have a lot of regrets if she ended up dying. Turned out the last thing I did was the thing that actually saved her, so I didn't regret putting Amelia through all those years of torture.

That was bad enough, but when Sarah tried to terminate my parental rights to Amelia, just because she wanted her new boyfriend to get his inheritance money, and he wasn't entitled to it unless he had a child, it was the final straw. Sarah claimed her new boyfriend was Amelia's biological father and doctored up a paternity test to prove it. It turned out I wasn't Amelia's biological father. Yet, I was able to not have my rights severed because the biological father also was not Sarah's boyfriend. It was another guy, a guy who didn't want to be named the biological father of Amelia. Because of that, I beat the case that Sarah filed against me to have my rights terminated to Amelia. It was a long way back, psychologically, for Amelia and me after that.

I couldn't forgive Sarah for doing that to us.

And that, truth be told, was why I was reluctant to get close with Ally. She was a beautiful girl, very smart and capable, and we had a lot of fun together. But I was held back by my general lack of trust in women. If Sarah was capable of doing something like that to me, who knows what somebody else might do to me? I trusted Sarah completely and she burned me in the worst way possible.

I drove over to Harper's house, and she greeted me on her front porch.

"Come on in," she said to me. "I'm glad you came by. I'm glad you could come over and talk. I've been sitting here in a dark room, trying to imagine what's going to happen to me now. Axel was the first man I've been able to be with since my teenage years. He's been the first man I've been able to trust. I've never let a man into my heart until him. Now I just worry that everything will be sown back up. That my heart will be blocked again."

I looked at her glass and saw it had an amber liquid in it. I felt more than a little concerned about it. Harper was a recovering alcoholic and had been off the wagon a time or two in the recent past. I had to hope and pray she was not drinking again.

I sniffed at her glass and smelled the unmistakable odor of bourbon.

I put my arm around her. "Harper," I said, as gently as I could. "Is that whiskey in that glass?"

She shrugged. "What of it?"

I took a deep breath, not knowing how to handle the situation. I had been around my mother as she was trying to quit drinking several times and it never took. But I knew Harper had really wanted to not go back to drinking. I knew how much she struggled. I knew she had gone to AA, and had a sponsor, whose name was Crystal Warner. She had several sponsors over the years and Crystal was her current one.

"I understand you're hurting but you have a couple of children to think about. They'll be affected if you're drinking again. You need to think of them."

She shook her head. "I just don't know, Damien. Sometimes I think I just can't handle life. Just can't face it. I thought that when Axel and I were good, he would always be there for me. Hold me up when I'm down. He was my person. And now he's gone. Deported to Australia. I'm never going to see him again."

Harper was not a woman who felt sorry for herself a lot of the time. She was always somebody, in my eyes, who carried on no matter what happened to her. Yet it seemed she was breaking down.

She shook her head as she took a sip of her bourbon. "It's just one. I can handle it. It's just one."

I was very concerned, because that was what all addicts say. They say it's just the one, they can handle it, they don't really have a problem. But that was a lie. It was a lie all addicts tell themselves and the world. And I didn't really know what to do. I could never stop my mom from drinking. As much as I tried to stop her from drinking when I was younger, she never would.

And now, here my mother was, being charged with murder. And what she did to be charged with murder was a nonsense charge, but that didn't matter. In a way, her drinking led her to where she was at the moment – sitting in a cell. If she wasn't such a drinker, she would have never been at the bar where she met that Tracy Dunham, and if she never would've met Tracy Dunham, she would never have been charged with his murder.

I didn't know what to say to Harper, so I decided to change the subject. "Thanks for seeing me. I was feeling out of sorts because of what's going on with Nate, and my mother –"

She nodded. "After you told me your mother was being charged with murdering Tracy Dunham, I did a little bit of research on him. Bet you didn't know his family is very well-connected and very wealthy. Came as a surprise to me too, because of what you said about him. Sounded to me like he was just kind of a drifter and loser. I don't know, I guess that was just my own prejudice showing. Whenever I hear of people dying of a heroin overdose, I always think they're people on the fringes of society. People who don't have it all together. This guy was not only from a wealthy family, but was a medical doctor."

A medical doctor? His family was rich and powerful? I guessed that made a certain kind of perverse sense to me, considering my mother said she met him in a fake biker bar where professionals hung out and tried to pretend they were hog-riders. It sounded like Tracy Dunham was one of those fakers who probably wore leather jackets and dark sunglasses while hanging out at a biker bar trying to look cool. I doubted he even could find Sturgis on a map, let alone attend an annual rally.

"That's interesting to hear," I said to her. "What kind of medical doctor was he?"

She laughed ruefully and took another sip of her bourbon. "You want one?" she asked me, gesturing with her glass.

I shook my head. "No," I said, not wanting to encourage or enable her. "Thank you."

"Suit yourself,"she said. "It's the good stuff. Pappy Van Winkle 20-year reserve. Smooth as molasses, this one is. The better stuff doesn't give me as much of a hangover, either." She took another sip and seemed to forget the question I just asked her.

"Thanks," I said. "Now..." I cleared my throat. "What kind of doctor was Tracy Dunham?"

She nodded. "Dr. Tracy Dunham was the best kind of doctor there was if you've been in a bad car accident or skiing mishap and are in excruciating pain. His specialty was pain management." She laughed. "Ironic, huh? You would think a guy like that could substitute Hillbilly Heroin for the real thing. I wonder why he got high on street junk like that, let alone take so much that he overdosed."

"Hillbilly Heroin" was the street slang for Oxycodone, a powerful opioid.

A doctor taking heroin made little sense to me, either. Harper was right. A doctor would have access to Oxycontin, Fentanyl, Codeine, Hydrocodone, anything he would want to get high.

Then again, once I thought about it, I realized he probably was trying to hide his drug use and addiction, and there's only so much a doctor can do to legally obtain painkillers. Even a pain management doctor. He couldn't legally use his own scrip pad to write himself a prescription. He would have access to free samples sent by pharmaceutical companies, but not Opioids, which were Schedule III drugs, therefore pharma reps cannot give them out as samples. He no-doubt received drugs his patients might bring to his office for disposal, but he needed to properly dispose of them according to law.

So, unless he was actually diagnosed with a condition that would warrant him being prescribed pain meds, he wouldn't have legal access to them.

"I don't think he could get pain meds legally, even if he was a doctor," I said.

She nodded. "Huh. How naive are you?"

I took a deep breath, not liking where this conversation was going. I didn't like Harper's attitude, either. She seemed colder, more bitter, more cynical than usual. Harper wasn't exactly the warmest woman on the planet, even on a good day, but at the moment she seemed to be just a bit icy. "Harper, maybe this was a mistake, my coming here."

"A mistake?" She shook her head. "I did you a solid, finding out about your victim. I know you didn't know that about him, although you probably should have. Wasn't his occupation in the file you read before you went to see your mother?"

"I don't recall seeing that," I said. "But, then again, I skimmed that file. I was just looking to see if my mother was high at the time he showed up at her door."

"Well, let's see," Harper said. "Something is clearly amiss in this case. I don't know what, but something clearly is. Your mother insisted to you, up and down, that she didn't take a single drug that night. Yet opiates were found in her system. Tracy Dunham wasn't a rando drug user off the street. He was a physician and his family is rich. The cops interrogated your mother as if she were high and Dunham was a rando, but they had to have known at the time that this just wasn't true. It sounds like they never even pressed the issue of Dunham's occupation when they were questioning your mother. Why do you think that's the case? Add to that the fact that they have such a hard-on for poor Olivia in the first place, and I think you can agree something clearly rotten in the state of Denmark on this one."

"Well, that goes without saying," I said. "And I would imagine I'll figure out just what happened in this case. I usually do. And I thank you for doing the research on it."

"Not a problem," she said. "After Axel dumped me, I went looking for something to do to clear my mind and decided to try to solve your mother's case. Because I know you have more important things on your mind and don't need to be worrying about whether or not your mother will end up thrown in the clink."

I rocked in the porch chair for a few minutes, while Harper sipped her bourbon. I looked up at the sky, noticing that it was clear with a visible blanket of stars. A man walking his dog ambled up the sidewalk and the dog lifted his leg on Harper's bush while the man rapidly walked past.

"Harper," I finally said. "I'm concerned about you."

"Why?" she asked. "Because of this?" She lifted her glass of bourbon and then brought it to her lips again. "Most people don't stay on the wagon, you know. It's too difficult. Sometimes you go for so long and then you get triggered and thirsty and you just can't help yourself. It's there, it's a friend, it's always been the one thing that can you make you feel good when you feel worthless. And that's what I feel - worthless. I just can't seem to not screw up my life, no matter what I do. So I drink. I drink to drown out those feelings."

She looked up at the stars and it was her turn to get silent.

"Harper-"

"My rapist is out of prison," she said, not looking at me. She brought her hand to her mouth and wiped it. "His lawyer proved ineffective assistance of counsel, no problem. While he was at it, he almost got my bar license. I had to do some pretty creative maneuvering and butt-kissing to keep my license after what I did to Michael Reynolds." She shook her head. "He lost his first appeal to the Missouri Court of Appeals, and I thought that was that. But it wasn't that. He filed a Rule 29.15, challenging his conviction, and he won on that."

Rule 29.15 in Missouri was what inmates filed after they lost their appeal, and it was used to challenge a conviction, using facts outside the trial record. Where an appeal to the Court of Appeals was based on the trial record, and was based on any errors the court might have made, a Rule 29.15 was filed when there weren't any trial errors but there were grounds for conviction relief because of events that might have happened outside of trial. Rule 29.15 relief was typically where convictions were overturned for ineffective assistance of counsel, as the facts concerning such bases for relief were typically outside the trial record.

I cocked my head. "What did you do to him?"

"I took his case with the express purpose of throwing him under the bus. Dammit, I proved he killed his father-in-law, too. I proved it. I had a pair of his leather gloves, showed that his DNA was on those gloves and then the prosecutor proved those gloves were on the murder weapon. It was all for naught."

"What happened?"

"Well, the bastard managed to show all the ways I screwed him over at trial, including the fact that I secretly sent those leather gloves to the prosecutor. The prosecutor requested documents and I gave her documents and those gloves." She shrugged. "She asked for any objects I planned to introduce at trial, and I sent her the gloves. I mean, obviously, I wasn't going to introduce those gloves at trial. That would be inculpating, to say the very least. But, you know, I wanted her to have those gloves, because I knew they would be the one thing that would nail him to the wall."

I closed my eyes. "And-"

"Well, he lost in the Missouri Court of Appeals, but it was an open and shut case for Rule 29.15 relief. Made even more open-and-shut by all the other things I did, including tricking his girlfriend into confessing all that happened. I told her I could get her a good deal with the prosecutor if she just told me what happened, and she did. Of course, I lied, and she went to the bar, too. By the time that whole crew got through with me, I was on probation, a probation that was almost revoked when I got stopped by a cop who planted pot in my car. Anyhow..."

"Let me guess. Michael Reynolds got a new trial and the prosecutor couldn't introduce the gloves and he walked. How close am I?"

"Bingo. His new lawyer was a much better lawyer than me and managed to keep the gloves out of evidence. Which was a real trick, considering the fact that the gloves were known by the state to exist at the time of his second trial, when they weren't known to have existed in the first. The state wouldn't have even known about them if I didn't send them to the prosecutor. Without the gloves, it was all circumstantial, and the bastard was acquitted." She sighed. "I guess the Postman doesn't always ring twice."

"What do you mean?" I asked.

"Well, in that movie, *The Postman Always Rings Twice*, a guy gets away with murdering somebody. Then he gets sent down for a murder he didn't commit. In this case, Michael got away with raping me and raping many other women. He didn't get punished for that, so I really, really wanted him to be sent away for life for murdering his father-in-law."

"Yeah, but he did it, though. Therein lies the difference between your situation and that movie."

"True. Which makes it even worse. But, truth be told, I wasn't even all that concerned that he pay for murdering his father-in-law, even though his father-in-law was a good man. I mean, he was a terrible husband - he maintained a second family that his wife never knew about - but he was a good, decent judge. Really cared about the common man, always tried to side with the little guy against the big guy. Found for the plaintiff more than any other judge in the circuit. I was devastated when he was murdered, but I really wanted Michael put away because of what he did to me, not necessarily what he did to that poor judge."

I knew the real reason why Harper was drinking was not just because Axel was leaving. It was because Axel was leaving and she was upset that her rapist still hadn't paid for the things he did in his life. He served time in prison after he was convicted for murdering his father-in-law but was currently out and free. He was acquitted after his second trial, and that meant he was at large. His getting out probably served as a trigger for Harper.

I knew something about triggers. Sometimes you're good for a long time. Mentally, physically, emotionally. But there are always scars from any past trauma. And, sometimes, there isn't a scar, just a scab. When there's only a scab over a traumatic mental wound, that scab can be ripped off pretty damned easily, and it can be ripped off by any number of triggers. A certain smell, a certain song, a certain color even - all can be something that can send a recovering trauma victim off the deep end.

She put her head on my shoulder. "When will he ever pay? When? He destroyed so many lives. He killed his own father-in-law. Yet he's free as a bird. I hear he's even gotten back with his rich girlfriend, Kayla Stone. Why is there no justice in this world?"

I took a deep breath and put my arm around her shoulder. "It's because of people like you and me. Us defense attorneys are so adept at pulling rabbits out of hats that sometimes we do our job too well and guilty people go free."

"Yeah, but it's even worse for rape victims. We aren't believed. We see powerful men get away with sexual assault, time after time, and it makes us want to stay silent and in the shadows. Then one of us comes forward and she gets pummeled publicly, and it just makes us think nothing that can be done. They want corroborating evidence before they can convict. Well, guess what? You're not going to get corroborating evidence in a date rape. Period. If that's the standard, men will continue to get away with it."

"Well, it's always going to be he-said-she-said," I said.

"Right. And in cases like that, defense attorneys have eight ways to Sunday to make rape victims look bad. In my case, I was rip-roaring drunk when I met him at a party, and we were dirty dancing for at least an hour. That would be his corroborating evidence to show I willingly had sex with him, and there would be no getting around that so I never even reported it. It ruined my life, made me not want to date anybody for years, made me afraid of my own shadow and turned a drinking problem into an addiction. And he never paid. He never even thought twice about that night. It's haunted me, night and day, ever since, and he just about forgot it happened."

"I'm so sorry, Harper," I said. "I truly am."

"Right," she said, nodding. "You're sorry, but I need to put this glass of bourbon down and get back into rehab. Or AA. Or call my sponsor, Crystal Warner, who told me I can call her any time of the day or night. Well, I don't want to do any of those things. I don't want to. And I'm not going to."

"Think of your kids. Of your career. Of your mom and dad and sisters and brothers who love you. Think about how you're going to feel when you wake up in the morning with a hangover. Think of the puking, the headaches, the DTs, the depression. Just...think."

She shook her head and pointed at me with her drink. "I'll get right on that. In the meantime, you need to figure out exactly what went down with your mother." At that, she stood up, went back into her house, and shut her door.

I was left out on the porch wondering what the hell was going on, and how I was supposed to help her. Because I clearly needed to help her. She was my law partner and friend. She was open and trusting with me and I was grateful for that. I couldn't just watch her fall without a word.

I suddenly realized I had her on my plate, along with Nate and my mother.

I didn't quite know how I would juggle it all, but I certainly would try.

FOUR

T he next day, it was time for my mother's initial appearance, which was just as it sounded - it was my mom's first court appearance. Initial appearances were conducted in docket form by the associate circuit judge, and it was where the charges were read to the defendants and they were given a chance to get a bond.

As per usual, the initial appearance docket was a madhouse with about 50 defendants appearing in front of the judge, along with their lawyers. The defendants in custody were the first ones up, and that included my mother. She was brought into the courtroom wearing a baby blue jumpsuit that positively hung on her skinny frame. She looked at me and shook her head.

"Damien, you have to get me out of this joint. I'm gonna go crazy if you don't. My roommate last night, she was talking all night long about nonsense. Talk, talk, talk, talk, talk, talk talk. She wouldn't shut up. She told me she was manic and had that manic-depressive thing. She told me that if I waited a day, she would be crying in her cell and wouldn't be able to stop. I don't know, Damien, from what she tells me, I think I'm gonna prefer her mania to her depression. But I don't want to deal with either of her weirdo personalities. I just want to go home."

"Don't worry, Mom, I'm sure I can get a bond for you."

"Damien, I ain't got no money for no bond. I ain't talked to no bondman, either. I can't afford no bond. Some of the girls in there, they tell me something about a signature bond. They say that if I can get a signature bond, I just gotta sign my name and that's my bond. No money involved. Try to get me that."

I rolled my eyes. "Mom, you're up for murder. Murder. Sorry, but a signature bond won't be a possibility. Signature bonds are for people who shoplift, not for people who are accused of killing somebody."

"Well, try, Damien. I can't afford no bond."

"Mom, I'll pay your bond, whatever it is."

She shook her head. "No, thank you. No, thanks. You pay my bond, and I gotta do whatever you tell me. I don't want to give you that kind of power."

"Okay, Mom, then I guess you'll have to stay behind bars until trial. You'll just have to live with manic-depression girl and anybody else you're going to be stuck with back there. You'll have to live with freezing cells, hard bunks, clogged toilets and inedible food."

She shook her head. "I guess I will, then, because you ain't bonding me out. Get me a signature bond."

"You're not getting a signature bond."

"Then I guess I'll just stay behind bars." She glared at me.

I decided to remind her of one more thing she would be giving up. My Ace in the hole, as it were.

"Okay. Guess you'll have to live without your best friend Jack Daniels and your other best friend, Mary Jane."

I smiled as I saw her face. It seemingly just dawned on her that she wouldn't have ready access to her pot and alcohol until I said that.

"Okay, okay, go ahead and pay my bond. But I'm warning you, you can't use that to control me."

"I won't."

At that, Judge Rhidenour came on the bench and starting calling the names of the people on the docket. He got to my mother, she approached the bench and I went up there with her.

"Olivia Ward, you've been charged by the state of Missouri with the Class D felony of one count of possession of a controlled substance, the Class C felony of one count of delivery of a controlled substance, and the Class A felony of Murder in the Second Degree. How do you plead?"

"Not guilty," she said.

He nodded his head. "Your bond is set at one million dollars. The conditions of your bond are that you are to submit to random drug tests, you are not to associate with known felons and you are to wear an ankle monitor."

"An ankle monitor?" Mom said. "I don't want no ankle monitor. What kind of nonsense is that?"

"Ms. Ward," I said to my mother. "It's either an ankle monitor or jail. Your choice."

Judge Rhidenour smiled at me sympathetically. He was used to outbursts from clients who had no desire to do this or that, so he paid my mother no mind.

"Dammit, I guess I'll take that ankle monitor, but I'm not happy with it."

I nodded at the judge. "Thank you, your honor."

I escorted my mother over to the bailiff, who was tasked with taking her back to the jail, where she would be processed out as soon as I posted her bail.

I should have let her rot in jail.

FIVE

The next day, I got my answer as to how I could help Harper. There was an article in the newspaper that caught my eye. The headline said that a prominent physician, by the name of Carrie Blackwood, was found dead of a single gunshot wound to the head.

As I read the article I saw that the reason her mother gave for her killing herself, and this was apparently the reason Carrie put into her suicide note, was a viral video posted of her having sex with none other than Michael Reynolds. Her mother told the newspaper that her daughter was being raped on this video, which clearly added to Carrie's pain and anguish. Once the video went viral, it was posted on many X-rated sites, but also was posted to other sites where the general public could see it. Her career was ruined because of it. She was a pediatrician, and, one by one, she lost her practice. The parents of the children she treated did not want her to be treating them any longer. She also lost most of her social group and friends.

I read further to see why Michael Reynolds would rape this woman and post it online. I would have to get ahold of the videotape and see what the deal was. I knew that at the moment, because this was apparently the cause of this woman's suicide, it wouldn't be easy to find the video.

I decided to call Anna, our hacker. Harper used her quite frequently to hack into databases to find information she needed, and I figured Anna could get access to this video.

I had an idea on how to finally bring this guy to some kind of justice. I thought that maybe if I could get some kind of justice and retribution, it would help Harper heal. She was having a tough time with the fact this guy was out of prison, combined with Axel being deported to Australia, so she lost his support.

I never knew how fragile Harper was. I always saw her as a badass – I mean, after all, she was a criminal defense attorney. She defended the worst of the worst. She defended murderers, arsonists, robbers, everybody but sex offenders. She would never do that kind of thing, for the simple reason that defending accused sex offenders would just trigger her too much.

Now I knew that, underneath it all, Harper was really a marshmallow. At least she was when it came to the subject of Michael Reynolds, the man who ruined her life. The man who would apparently keep on ruining her life unless he was brought to justice.

I needed to know what was going on with this Carrie Blackwood case – specifically, I needed to know if any charges were filed against Michael for posting that video online, and if charges were filed for him raping her.

I called Anna, told her I needed the viral video of Carrie Blackwood, and she said she would have it for me within 10 minutes. Ten minutes later, she emailed it to me. "It wasn't hard to find. I mean, it it was hard to find for an ordinary person, because obviously after this poor woman committed suicide, the sites took the video down. But it was still on the dark web. Which means it's still being accessed by people, probably a lot of people. But here you go."

With a heavy heart, I brought up the video. I saw the reason why Michael could evade rape charges. Carrie Blackwood seemed like she was not quite with it. I figured that maybe she was drugged up. She seemed like it, anyway.

I also wondered why this video, of all things, would've gone viral the way it did. Why did anybody really care about a woman who was not quite there having sex with a man? Why was it such an important thing that so many people knew about it?

I decided to call her mother. It would be fairly easy to make Michael Reynolds pay for this – we had grounds for a lawsuit against him on multiple levels. But the most expensive lawsuit for him, by far, would be a lawsuit for wrongful death. That would especially be true if Carrie was making a lot of money with her job as a physician. It appeared she was fairly young – only 32 – when she died. An invasion of privacy lawsuit would be a given. All I had to do was show Michael posted the video without her consent.

The wrongful death lawsuit would be a bit trickier – but I knew I could probably win that one as well. I would have to talk to her mother, get a copy of her suicide note, and, hopefully, show Carrie was vulnerable. If Michael knew Carrie was vulnerable, that would make the wrongful death lawsuit that much stronger.

At any rate, I would have to find out all of this when I spoke with her mother.

I found out who her mother was, I called her, and I told her what I wanted.

"I don't know. I don't know if I want to go through this," Carrie's mother told me when I called her. "My daughter just died. She just died because that man, that bastard, he took everything away from her that she cared about. She had a thriving practice and she lost it. A lot of her social circle started to shun her. She tried to tell anybody that would listen that she did not willingly have sex with this man, went on one date with him, and he apparently put something in her drink. Something happened to her to where she really didn't know what was going on so much. But nobody seemed to really care about that. Everybody seemed to think that somehow or another she was responsible for having that on the Internet. I just don't understand any of it."

I had a feeling the mother would be resistant. "Mrs. Blackwood, here's the thing. This is a man who has hurt a lot of people over the years. He somehow manages to always get away with it. He was imprisoned for killing his father-in-law. The jury found him guilty. But he won on appeal, and now he's out. It seems like nothing can touch him, but you can. I understand he's possibly still married to his sugar mama. That means he has enough money to pay a multimillion dollar lawsuit. That might break him, finally. At any rate, I really need to see this guy pay for something he's done in his life. Even if it's not something that means he has to go to prison. Even if it's just monetary, I want him to pay."

I heard her sigh on the other end of the line. "I just don't think it'll work. She tried to go to the prosecutor's office after it happened. They wouldn't file charges against him. They said they spoke with him and he said it was all consensual and she'd consented to having the video put online. They believed him. I don't know why, but they believed him."

I had a question for Mrs. Blackwood, and it was one I didn't really want to ask, but had to. "Is there any particular reason why this particular video would've gone viral? I mean, not to be too explicit, but couples make amateur porn all the time. They make porn, they put it online, and nobody really cares. I'm trying to figure out why this particular video went viral, when others like it don't. Is there anything special about your daughter that would have caused the Internet to really want to take notice?"

Mrs. Blackwood was quiet on the other end of the line. "My daughter was somewhat famous. She was a minor pop star about 15 years ago, when she was 17 years old. She had one hit. And, over the years, she still maintained a fan base. So I think that's the only thing that caused it to go viral from the very beginning. There was still an interest in her. I don't know, I wish I knew exactly why people were so interested in seeing this video of her and this guy." I could hear her sniffling on the on the other end of the line. "I would do anything to have her back in my life."

"Mrs. Blackwood, you have to believe one thing. Nothing can ever bring your daughter back, but there is a way to make Michael Reynolds pay for what he did to her. Even if the prosecutors have declined to file charges against him for invasion of privacy, let alone for raping her, we can still bring a cause of action against him civilly. We can still make him pay."

She was quiet again on the other end of the line. She finally spoke. "I'll come into your office. Just let me know what time I can come in and see you, and I'll be there."

I thought about Harper. I didn't want her to know what I was doing. I wanted it to be a secret. I didn't know why I wanted to keep it from her, except that I thought that if she knew about it, she probably would be upset with me.

Then again, maybe she would be all for it, but I just didn't want to reopen the old wound. I didn't want her to know Michael Reynolds was responsible for yet another life ruined.

This ruined life ended in a suicide.

"I'll come to you. If you don't mind," I told her.

She sounded surprised. "An attorney who makes house calls? I never heard of that."

"I don't usually make house calls, but in this case I'll make an exception. Just give me your address and I can see you whenever you want me to."

She gave me her address, which was in Lawrence, Kansas, about 45 minutes away. I wrote it down.

"Thank you, Mr. Harrington," she said to me. "No amount of money can ever bring her back. No amount of money can ever fill the hole in my heart. But if there is a way to make sure that bastard pays for what he did to her, I'm all for it."

As I hung up the phone, I realized no amount of money would ever be adequate to bring this guy to justice. But that didn't really matter. If I could possibly make his life just a bit more difficult, I'd done my job.

Six

Before I went to see Mrs. Blackwood, Carrie's mom, I decided to do some research on Tracy Dunham. As Harper indicated, he was a part of a wealthy family. The Dunhams were old money. Tracy Dunham's great-great grandfather was one of the early investors in the railroad and made his fortune there. The Dunham family had diversified into shipping and bootlegging, before branching out even further into the pharmaceutical industry. All the Dunhams in Tracy's father's generation were billionaires, and Tracy himself was an heir to a vast fortune of a diversified portfolio that included everything from shipping and lumber to green technology.

Apparently, Tracy had not yet come into his inheritance, for reasons unknown. At least, that was what I understood from what I found out on the Internet about him.

I wondered about that. How come Tracy Dunham couldn't come into his inheritance just yet? That was a strange thing because from what I understood, all the kids in his generation in the Dunham family had already come into their inheritance. At least, that was what I could see from quick research online with court records and basic news articles about the family.

I wrote that down on a piece of paper. I made a note to myself to figure out exactly why Tracy was denied his inheritance, or at least, that the inheritance had not yet come to him. Not that he was never going to get the inheritance, but there was something holding it up and he died without laying claim to it.

I also did a quick background check on his credentials to be a pain management doctor and ascertained that he graduated from the University of Missouri with a degree in science, and then went to medical school in UMKC, which was the University of Missouri branch located here in Kansas City. From there, it was an internship at the Kansas University hospital that was also located in Kansas City, in the midtown area. He had been in practice for the past 10 years, treating people suffering from chronic pain. His website indicated that he specialized in individuals who had recurring migraines and neurological disorders, but he had a proficiency in treating all pain.

He emphasized on his website that he treated patients with alternatives to opioids. Apparently, according to his website, he prescribed a method of pain management that combined elements of acupuncture, acupressure, and a technique he invented that had a patent pending.

I read the reviews of the people who had seen him at his office and they were truly glowing. A lot of times those reviews could be manipulated, so I had to bear that in mind. But it seemed like patient after patient stated that they had gone to him as a last resort. They were prescribed opiates by other doctors, became addicted, would have to get off them but would still have their pain. So they would see Dr. Dunham and would have relief from their pain without any drugs. According to the reviews I read online, he had changed more than one person's life for the better. Completely.

Review after review talked about how effective he was. There was more than one person who said that if Dr. Dunham's pain management method could become the standard of care for all doctors, the opioid crisis would be solved, simply because people would not have to rely on addicting drugs to get pain relief.

While I thought that was slightly hyperbolic – one doctor in Kansas City, Missouri solving the opioid crisis – I did come to know after reading these reviews that this doctor was very much loved. His patients swore by him. He had an almost cult-like following.

I decided to make it a point with the prosecutor to ask them why they were going at my mother in such a way. I had a feeling there was something behind the prosecutor's decision to charge it in the matter it was charged. I also wondered about whether or not it was possible that my mother's drug test result was somehow altered. My mother swore up and down that she had not taken heroin at the time this guy died. Yet her blood tests showed she clearly had opioids in her system.

I knew enough not to believe my mother when she was giving me a story, because she was not known to be the most honest person in the entire world.

Yet, at the same time, there was a little voice inside me that said she wasn't lying about this. She really wasn't taking opioids when this guy died. And if this was the case, what was the deal with the UA saying she was high?

But before I went to the prosecutor, I would have to see Mrs. Blackwood. I hated that I would have to see her, just because I didn't do so well with people in mourning, as this woman clearly was.

I decided to call Nate, knowing he was probably home from school. He could probably use some time out of the house, so I decided to see if he wanted to go along with me to this woman's house. Well, not necessarily to her house, but I knew her neighborhood and there was a basketball court on the way to where she lived, and there were usually people playing there. Nate was good at basketball and could probably use the exercise and the social camaraderie. I figured some fresh air would do him some good, and I really wanted to take him out to dinner afterwards, just him and me.

I felt guilty about taking on yet another case during his crisis period. It was bad enough that I had to take my mother's case, but now I apparently would be taking the case of Carrie Blackwood. Not that I really wanted to do that, but at the same time, I knew it would somehow help Harper if I did.

I got in the car and called Nate. "Buddy, I'm coming to get you. I'm going to see somebody in Lawrence and thought you and I can talk on the way to her house. There's a basketball court by where she lives, I've been by there several times, in that area, and I figured you could play some games while I'm talking to her." I was really interested in the talk on the way to Lawrence, which was where the University of Kansas was and about a 45-minute drive from my house. Assuming traffic. I had to be realistic about the fact that sometimes I would have to just fit in time when I could and hoped and prayed it would be enough.

"What about Amelia?" he asked me.

"Gretchen can watch her. I really just need a little bit of quality time with you because I want you to keep on talking to me. I want you and I to keep having conversations. And I know things are stressful, and difficult, because your grandmother is in trouble. And I wish I could rely upon someone to take her case, and I could just spend time with you, but I don't trust anybody. It's too important to trust another person to take her case. There are just some real oddities cropping up that I have to get to the bottom of in this case. I hope you don't mind."

Truth be told, if Harper was not having some kind of a mental breakdown, I probably would've asked her to take the case. Harper was somebody I could trust. She was somebody who would do a really good job with my mom's case. But, at the moment, she was dealing with her own emotional problems, and I just knew there was no way to rely upon her to do my mom's case justice.

"Okay, Dad. I've got nothing going on at the moment. I got a little bit of homework, but I could just get that done later. I'd like to go with you." And he was quiet for several minutes. "I'd like that, Dad. I'd like to keep talking to you about what's going on with me."

I felt a sense of relief as I put on my coat and started to head out the door.

As I was coming out, Harper was coming in. She was wearing a pair of dark sunglasses and was walking extremely slowly. She had a cup of coffee in her hand and was dressed in a heavy coat, scarf, hat, and gloves. It was a somewhat odd get up, considering the fact that it was 50° outside. Chilly, but not that cold. Not cold enough for all she was wearing.

"Harper," I said to her. "How are you feeling?"

She shook her head and said nothing. I could see that the hand holding the coffee cup was shaking. She bowed her head and walked right past me.

I followed her into her office. I looked at the clock, seeing it was

3:30, and this was the first time she had made an appearance at her own office. This was unusual – she was never in the office past 8 o'clock in the morning.

"Harper," I said. "How are you feeling?"

She threw her bag down on her desk, and took off her hat, gloves, and coat. She did not, however, take off her dark sunglasses. "How does it look like I feel?" She shook her head. "I feel like crap. Mentally, physically, I feel like crap. I feel like every single cell in my body is filled with alcohol, and my head is pounding like you would not believe. I'm nauseated, I'm tired, yet I'm here. I was supposed to be in small-claims court this morning. Somehow, I overslept and missed it. Now my client is pissed-off, to say the least, because I was supposed to be there and because I wasn't, the guy got a default judgment against him. Which means I'm going to have to do an appeal for him for free, to say the very least."

"Harper, you need to tell me when you need me to cover for you."

She took a deep breath. "I suppose you didn't hear the part where I said I overslept. In other words, I didn't know at the time that I needed for you to cover for me. If I would've known that, I would've asked you to cover for me. As it is, I have to work on this motion to set aside the judgment and hope I can get it vacated. Not that that's necessarily going to be easy to do."

I looked at my watch, knowing there was only a short period of time I could go and get Nate and see my new client by 5 o'clock, which was the time we set up for the meeting. "I'd like to still talk to you more, but I have to go see my new client."

"You're going to see a client? A new client? Since when do you make house calls for someone like that?"

She was right about that. While I didn't mind seeing existing clients at their house, I didn't usually like to go chasing after clients and going to their home. Especially not a client who lived out in Lawrence, Kansas. That was a bit of a drive, and I really should've had her come see me. But I didn't know what to say to Harper as to why I wanted Mrs. Blackwood to not come to the office.

"I made an exception here. Besides, I'm going to have Nate come with me. He and I need some guy talk, so I figured the drive to

Lawrence and back would be a good time for some one on one. I also would like to take him out to dinner in Lawrence. I guess it's just a good excuse for me to bond with Nate."

Harper nodded. "You better be careful. He's at an age where things could go either way. You could either reach him, and things will be okay, or you may not be able to reach him, and things might be devastating. I know, I went through something with Abby last year. Don't forget, she was trying drugs herself. Not that Nate will experiment with drugs, but you certainly don't want to risk that. So stay on top of it. That's the only thing I can say."

I bit my tongue. I didn't want to tell Harper that she needed to tend to her own garden before giving me advice. Yet, I knew her advice was sound and it would be nothing but mean for me to throw in her face that she was having her own problems with addiction at the moment.

"Thanks for the advice, Harper." I looked at my watch again. "I'll see you later."

At that, I went to my car.

SEVEN

I went home and got Nate, and the two of us got in the car and drove towards Lawrence. Nate looked better than he did the previous day. He was smiling and looked happy to be going with me.

"Thanks, Dad." He looked kind of shy. His hands were clasped together on his lap and his head was bowed. "I really wanted to talk to you today. I thought about it all day. I talked to a teacher, a guy this time. I don't trust the women teachers in my schools anymore."

I felt sad that that was the case. I knew some of Nate's teachers, the female teachers, and they would be good confidants for him. Yet I knew that after the incident with Mrs. Bowen, there was just no way he would ever trust a female teacher again. At least not for a long, long time.

I drove along and put my hand on Nate's shoulder. "What did you want to talk to me about?"

He shrugged his shoulders. "I just wanted to talk to you about how things were going. I feel like talking." Then he looked at his hands again. "You know how the counselor, Dr. Jordan, tells us that we need to tell each other things that are bothering us? You know how she says that to us?"

"Of course I remember that. That's probably been the most important thing."

He nodded his head. "There are some kids at school, they're telling me they can see I'm sad and they have a way of making me feel better. They're trying to get me to take drugs. Trying to sell me drugs, Dad. I've been telling them no, but it's been hard. They keep telling me that if I take these drugs I won't feel pain anymore. I won't feel like I am." He shook his head. "I'll do anything Dad, anything to stop this pain."

I drew a breath. Nate was on the verge of taking drugs, and I didn't really know what to do about that. I certainly could get the names of the boys who had been harassing him at school, trying to sell him drugs. I could turn them into the cops, tell the principal about what was going on, any number of things. But that would not be getting to the root of the problem. The root of the problem was that Nate wanted to take drugs because he was in so much mental pain. So much emotional turmoil.

"Thank you for telling me about this. I think there is a better way for you. Dr. Jordan has advised me that she wants you on an antidepressant, a kind of prescription drug that will hopefully make you feel better. Dr. Jordan thinks you might have a problem with the chemicals in your brain." I didn't really think Nate would understand what I was saying. It was difficult for most people to understand about norepinephrine, serotonin and the other chemicals that are supposed to be in balance in your brain, but are not in certain people's brains.

Nate just nodded. "You know best, Dad. Does a doctor think that if I take these drugs, I won't be so sad all the time?"

"That's the goal, buddy." I was still so apprehensive, however, because I knew that one of the side effects of this drug was suicidal thoughts. And that a kid as young as Nate was at risk of committing suicide if he took this drug. Yet, from what he was telling me, he needed something. We were already going to counseling, twice a week, and he was still talking about how he wanted to take drugs because he was still in so much pain. The antidepressants would be a last resort, but I felt I needed to at least try it.

Nate decided to change the subject. "We're going to go see a woman, or you are. She's got to be somebody you're going to be taking on? What did she do?"

"She didn't do anything wrong. Her daughter was hurting just like you are. Then something happened and she died. I'm going to try to file a lawsuit against the person who hurt her."

Nate didn't say anything but just stared at his hands. "Are you going to file a lawsuit against Mrs. Bowen?" He said that in a tiny voice, so tiny that I could barely hear it.

"Is that something you would like me to do?"

He shrugged. "No. She's going to jail. She's sad, Dad, just like I am. I feel sorry for her. She doesn't have a good life. She cries a lot. I don't want her to be more sad than she already is."

I was struck by how compassionate he was. This was a woman who hurt him very badly, and he was concerned about how depressed she was. "Okay, Nate."

I felt justice was done with Mrs. Bowen, because Nate was right – she would go to prison for a long time. Filing a lawsuit against her would be something that might make Nate feel better, but, at the same time, I didn't think there was much potential for it. She didn't have a lot of extra money or property, so it would have been a Pyrrhic victory if I would've filed a lawsuit against her and won.

"Nate, what makes you most sad? Mrs. Bowen? Amelia being so sick? Your mother taking off? Or is it something else?"

He shrugged and didn't say a word. He looked out the window, at the trees with their yellow and red leaves. He was quiet for quite a long time, as we drove along for a good 20 minutes without him saying a word.

We got to the basketball court where I would drop him off. "Here you go, buddy. There's a bunch of kids already playing a pickup game, so go on over there and get into it. I'll come get you when I'm done with my new client."

He got his ball and zipped up his hoodie. He nodded. "I'll see you, Dad." He ran towards the court, and I saw him get in with the other guys.

It was a short drive to Mrs. Blackwood's house. It was a smallish ranch that was probably built around 1980, maybe before. It was white with green shutters, and there was an enormous oak tree in her front yard that had dumped a thick blanket of leaves that needed to be raked. It was 5 o'clock, so it was almost completely dark, but there was still a little bit of light.

Mrs. Blackwood apparently saw my headlights, because she opened the door before I ever got to her stoop. She was an attractive woman in her mid-to-late 50s. Her hair was greying slightly and she wore it short. She wore glasses that were thick framed and was dressed in a hot pink jacket and black pants. She looked like she had kept in shape over the years, for she was slim and muscular. She wore no makeup, but she really didn't need to. Her skin was unwrinkled and smooth.

"Mrs. Blackwood, it's a pleasure to meet you," I said as I shook her hand.

"Please, don't call me Mrs. Blackwood. I should have told you that over the phone. My name is Audrey. I'm actually excited to meet you as well."

I was definitely encouraged by the fact that she was excited to meet me. Specifically, I was encouraged because she used the word *excited*. "Okay, Audrey. And you can go ahead and call me Damien."

"Damien, please step into my humble home."

Inside the home was a small living room with hardwood floors, a big screen TV, and several small red couches. I could smell the scent of burning incense, some kind of patchouli. There was a small cage in the corner of the living room and a green and yellow parakeet chirped excitedly when I walked in the door. Also greeting me at the door were a pair of yellow labs, both of them female. They came up to me and wagged their tails and sniffed my crotch, and Audrey shooed them away.

"I'm so sorry, I've been trying to train them not to do that, but you know how they are."

I laughed. "Not a problem. Not a problem at all. I happen to love dogs. I don't mind when they sniff me. They're just trying to make sure I'm not a bad guy. I guess they can tell that from my scent, although I don't know how that's possible."

"Well, I don't know if they can tell if you're a good guy or not by your scent, but they certainly can tell by your body language and other signals. Dogs are good like that. They can always tell if you're friend or foe. And I hope you're a friend. I could certainly use a friend right now."

I sat down on one of the red couches and she sat down on the other end of it. She poured me a glass of cucumber water and handed it to me. I sipped it and got out my notepad.

"Now where do you want to begin?" she asked me.

I cleared my throat. "You told me quite a bit over the phone, but I'm interested in knowing a few more things. One of the things that a judge or jury's going to look for in a wrongful death case is whether or not it was foreseeable that your daughter would have killed herself over the actions that Michael Reynolds took against her. Once we can establish that her killing herself was foreseeable, it'll be a matter of damages. That is if the jury believes his actions were the proximate cause of her committing suicide. It's a complicated issue, I won't lie. Many times when people commit suicide, there are a lot of reasons why they do it, not just one. But, in this case, his act against her was so egregious that I think we have a good chance to prevail."

"What would the jury be looking for when they award damages?"

"They can award damages on the basis of pain and suffering, and also they can award damages based upon the value of her life. In other words, they can extrapolate how much she would've made over the course of her life, and that could be how they would calculate damages. Also, in this case, since it was an intentional act, we can get punitive damages, which can be many millions of dollars. Of course, that all hinges upon whether or not we can prove the proximate cause issue, as well as the foreseeability issue. The proximate cause issue is probably more important than the foreseeability issue, but they're both important."

At that, she handed me a copy of her daughter's suicide note. "You can see it here in this note. She said she felt humiliated and degraded and felt she'd lost everything because this video was made public. She talks about how ashamed she was about the video. She talks about how her pediatric practice was her life. It was her calling. She really cared about those kids she treated, and it wasn't just a paycheck. When she lost her practice, she felt she was losing herself. Her identity. She didn't know who she was anymore. She wrote all of that in this note. It's all there."

She gave me about 10 minutes while I read through the entire note. It was a good note, for the sake of establishing causation, because there was nothing in the note that talked about anything other than how she felt about the video. There was nothing about her wanting to kill herself because of other reasons, such as failed love affairs, or lifelong depression, or anything like that. It was pretty clear the video and what happened after it made her feel that life was not worth living, that when she lost her practice she lost herself, and she was full of shame and humiliation.

"This suicide note is tragic. And I'm very sorry for your loss," I said. "If I can be absolutely cold about it, I will say that it provides good evidence of her mental state at the time she killed herself. Now, you knew her well. What kind of person was she before this incident happened?"

Audrey took a deep breath and hung her head. "That's another thing. My daughter was a shy person. She really couldn't come out of her shell with most people. That was the reason she liked her kids so much – the kids she cared for at her practice. She related much better to them than she did to most adults. She was a beautiful girl, but I will have to say that she always had a bit of a sadness about her. I don't know exactly why she was so sad over the years, but she was. I tried to have her treated for clinical depression over the years, but nothing ever really took."

Somehow, the words she was speaking to me hit home. I wondered if it would be the same thing with Nate. Was he always going to be just a depressed guy, isolating himself away from other people his age, never making a meaningful connection? Would he end up with the same fate as poor Carrie Blackwood, killing himself at the age of 32?

"Has it always just been you and Carrie?"

Audrey nodded her head. "Her dad was around for the first six months of her life, then he took off. He went for the proverbial pack of cigarettes and never came back. I never got child support out of him, even though I had orders against him for years. He never saw her after he left, either. I heard he ended up in Wyoming, living out in the woods like some kind of crazy suicide bomber. At least, that's what his sister told me. But I don't personally know what happened to him, because I haven't talked to him since she was a baby."

I felt so sad for this woman. Carrie was probably her pride and joy. She became a physician, and I was sure Audrey was very proud of her daughter. It was evident that Carrie was all this woman really had in her life.

"Do you know how Carrie managed to meet up with Michael Reynolds?"

"No. I don't really know. As far as I knew, Carrie didn't date a whole lot. She was more into her practice than socializing. She never talked about any men. We were close, she came over at least twice a week for dinner. She would stay around and we'd chat, or watched movies together. But she never talked about Michael Reynolds or any other man."

"What about suicide, did she ever talk to you about that sort of thing? That she wanted to kill herself?"

Audrey shook her head. "No. She never said anything like that. She never told me she wanted to kill herself. In fact, I never saw any signs she was that depressed. I mean, I know she always had kind of sadness about her, but I never thought for a second it was that far gone. Believe me, if I would've known it was, I would've tried to do something to intervene. Anything." She looked down at her hands. "I've been seeing a therapist about this because I blame myself for not seeing how far gone she was. About not seeing how devastated she was to find this videotape going viral. My therapist told me I'm not to blame for her killing herself, but I feel like I am. I feel like I am."

Once again, I thought of Nate. He was going down the road to where he was tempted to try drugs. And there was the warning that the antidepressants I would put him on might cause him to be suicidal. Would I be able to see the signs on time? Could I stop it? If something ever happened to him, I didn't think I could forgive myself. I'd have a hole in my heart so huge that I couldn't recover. Yet, people who are on the edge of killing themselves don't always reach out to their loved ones and tell them so. Carrie Blackwood apparently never told her mother. I had talked to other people who've lost their children through suicide, and they usually said the same thing – they had no idea their loved one was so depressed that they were on the verge of killing themselves.

I had to comfort myself with the thought that maybe Carrie Blackwood killed herself exclusively because of this videotape, and Nate obviously didn't have something like that going on. But he did have the molestation of his teacher to contend with, not to mention all the other crazy things that had happened to him in his life the past few years. Was my son on the verge of getting to the point of no return? Could I stop it? Those unanswered questions scared the living crap out of me.

"So what do you think about this case?" Audrey asked me. "Do you think we can hold this guy responsible for my daughter's death?"

I took a deep breath. "I'm going to file a lawsuit and get him in for a deposition. I can ask him a lot of questions about his relationship with Carrie and how he knew her, and whether or not he understood she was depressed and vulnerable. Now I don't necessarily think he'll tell the truth, but I have a way of asking questions to where I can get at the truth without the person even knowing it. Even if he comes across as somebody who clearly didn't know Carrie was suicidal, he had to have known that what he was doing was not just wrong but illegal."

"What I can't really understand, however, was why he posted that video online," I said. "Usually in these things, it's revenge porn – that means that when one person breaks up with another person or does something that makes that person mad, that person will post a humiliating video online as a way of getting back at the person who wronged them. There are a lot of unanswered questions I have in this entire scenario. Why would he post the video online? How did they meet? Did he know she was in such a state that she would do something like this?"

I didn't want to tell her I had another unanswered question - that maybe she didn't know her daughter as well as she thought. I could not discount the possibility that there was more to the story than what Audrey realized.

However, I couldn't lose sight of the fact that the main reason why I was doing this was to get some justice for Harper. This Michael Reynolds might be so slippery that he could get out of criminal charges for everything he'd done to hurt people, but I was determined to hold him to account for some of his wrongdoing. Maybe this was just a small thing, but if I could get a judgment against him for millions of dollars, especially if that ruined his life, I would feel some modicum of justice was done.

I left Audrey's home and went and picked up Nate. He saw me pull up to the basketball court, and he grinned a grin bigger than anything I had seen from him in a long time.

"Hey Dad," he said as he turned around and waved at the other guys on the court. They all waved back, and smiled, and some of them shouted they hoped to see him around again.

"Buddy," I said to him. "How did things go?"

"Good," he said. "All those other guys were a little bit older than me, but they let me play. They all said I was pretty good. I actually feel good right now, Dad. I think I feel better than I've felt in a long time."

This gave me encouragement. I knew Nate enjoyed basketball, but it never dawned on me that maybe that was something he should really get involved with. He was a little young to be on the team at school, but at the same time, I knew there were leagues where he could play. If I could just get him really involved in the sport, maybe, just maybe, that could be something to get him out of his depression. That would be the best thing – get him involved in something that brought him out of his shell, and maybe I wouldn't have to put him on the antidepressants.

We got in the car, and Nate sat next to me with the ball on his lap. He chatted to me excitedly about all the points he scored, and how he actually managed to make a three-pointer from the middle of the court. "I never knew I was so good at this, Dad. The other guys were a lot bigger than me, but they were really liking me. I'd like to keep playing, Dad."

I tousled his hair, wondering if it was as simple as that. Growing up, I never had the opportunity to play organized sports. I was in reform school by the age of 13, because I was already committing crimes. Already running with a bad crowd. And the school I went to didn't really offer sports that much. The middle school did, but I was never in a real middle school, just the reform school. I wondered if I had a chance to play a sport that maybe I would not have turned out as bad as I did.

"I'll see about getting you into a league for kids your age. Would you like that?"

Nate beamed. "I'd love that Dad. Do you have time for that? Do you have time to get me to the practices and games and everything?"

"For you, buddy, I'll make the time. No matter what."

"What about grandma? What's going on with her case? Aren't you going to be taking a lot of time out for that?"

"I'll make the time to make sure that you can play basketball. I have to make you a priority in my life. You and your sister. It's just the three of us. And the two of you mean more to me than anything else in the entire world."

I thought about Audrey Blackwood, and about how devastated she was. How empty she was. How I looked around her house, and I saw all the evidence of her love for her daughter, and now her daughter was no more. She had nobody else in the world. And I wondered how I would be if something like that happened to me – I lost my two kids. How broken I would be. I would be just as broken as Audrey Blackwood appeared to be.

I would do everything in my power to make sure both my kids were safe and sound.

Eight

The first thing I did the next day was my due diligence on the Tracy Dunham case. There were just a few things nagging at me. A few things not sitting well.

I wondered how a pain management doctor could become addicted to opioids. And I really wondered why he would've taken street drugs and not prescription drugs. Harper accused me of being naïve when I said Tracy couldn't get prescription drugs unless he had some kind of a diagnosable condition, even if he was a pain management doctor. After she accused me of being naïve, I realized she was probably right. There were ways Tracy could've gotten ahold of opioids.

One of the main ways was to form close relationships with pharmaceutical reps who typically gave out drug samples to doctors when they would get a new drug in. The doctors could then give the samples to their patients. They were not supposed to take them themselves, but my research showed me that quite a few addicted doctors would take those samples for themselves, whether or not they needed them.

Addicted doctors also had access to pharmaceuticals because patients would turn over leftover pills to them for disposal. Doctors would then take those pills and pocket them. Sometimes, a particularly resourceful nurse or doctor would sell them on the black market.

Doctors would also use their own prescription pad to write out a prescription to themselves and get it fulfilled at a pharmacy. That was clearly illegal, but doctors did it anyhow.

Granted, it was illegal for a doctor to pilfer pills in these ways. Doctors were not supposed to take advantage of any of these avenues to get pain pills. Yet it seemed to be a common problem in the medical profession. That was how they got ahold of prescription drugs, which meant they didn't necessarily have to go on the black market and get actual heroin from a dealer.

Yet, Dr. Dunham apparently bought heroin from a street dealer. That was also illegal. So I wondered why Tracy didn't go the more safe, albeit still illegal, route of getting prescription drugs for his problem. I knew something about street drugs and knew it was always a crapshoot when you got them. You never knew what was cut with those drugs – sometimes rat poisoning, sometimes Fentanyl, a drug that is 30-50 times more potent than heroin and is deadly to touch in its purest form. Other times, the dealer would sell drugs that weren't very pure, and then another another dealer might sell drugs that were much more pure. That was a reason for a lot of overdoses according to my research – a user might be used to a certain level of purity, which meant that if they got a more pure batch than what they were used to, it was too strong for them, and they overdosed.

I would have to find out who sold these drugs to Dr. Dunham. And, from his office manager, I would have to get some kind of a background about why he thought he needed to get them from the street.

I made an appointment with his office manager to see her, and, if I thought she would be a viable witness, I would probably bring her in for a deposition. That would get her statement under oath, which would be valuable for me at trial.

I made an appointment to see her at 3 o'clock in the afternoon. "I'll do anything to help you out. I don't know what I can tell you, but I'll do anything I can to give you whatever information you need," she told me over the phone.

I went to my office and looked at my notes to get prepared for my interview. After a few minutes, Harper appeared in my doorway. My door was open, but she knocked lightly on it.

"Do you mind if I come in and talk to you?" she asked in a timid voice.

I kind of did mind, because I was hot into looking at my notes and doing my research, but at the same time, I wouldn't turn her away.

She looked a lot better than she did the previous day. She wasn't wearing dark glasses, and her eyes looked focused and bright. She didn't look tired. She wasn't shaking like she was the previous day.

I nodded and gestured to the chair. "Have a seat. You know you're always welcome to talk to me about anything. And I do mean anything."

She nodded. "Thank you. I knew you would be willing to talk to me." She sat down and then picked up my paperweight and looked at it apprehensively. "I'm really sorry about the other night. I don't know what got into me. It just seemed like everything was falling around me at once. I mean, I found out about Michael being acquitted in his second trial on the same day that Axel told me he was being deported and we wouldn't see each other ever again. I don't know, I guess I just lost it."

I nodded. "Harper, I won't lie to you. I'm worried. I know some-thing about addiction and alcoholism. My mother has been an alcoholic my entire life. In fact, I think she's been an alcoholic for *her* entire life. Well, not her entire life, but pretty far back. Growing up with her was not fun. Having her as a mother was why I became the person I became when I was young, somebody out-of-control and committing crimes. I went to prison for something I didn't do, but there was plenty I did do in my life. Things I'm not proud of. And a lot of that was because my mother was an alcoholic, she had a revolving door of men, and she just didn't have time for me. She didn't want me around so she let me do whatever I wanted. I was desperate for attention. All I wanted was for her to show she cared about me, but she was too busy drinking and getting with men to make me feel I was a priority in her life."

Harper's eyes still didn't meet mine, and her shame was palpable. "I know what you're saying," she said, "and you're worried that because my two girls rely on me and only me that they'll become messed just like you were. And I worry about that, too." She sat back in her chair and looked out my window. "But I don't really know what to do right now. I'm seeing my therapist again and she's helping me. And I'm back to not drinking, but it's only been a couple of days. I went to several AA meet-ings yesterday and I've been calling my sponsor almost every hour. So, I'm working my steps again, starting at step one. But I don't really know what to do about my depression."

I thought about Nate, and how he would possibly be helped by playing basketball. I didn't think Harper could find the same type of distraction. I knew she was taking antidepressants, as well as other meds, because she had been diagnosed with bipolar disorder a few years back. I had to assume she was still taking her meds. She was also seeing a thera-pist, so that was good.

"Harper, do you have any cases you're really focused on these days?" I asked her. "Do you have anything occupying your mind? Anything challenging?"

She sighed. "I've been dry these days. I mean, I have your usual robberies, burglaries, stealing cases, DUIs, cases I'm working with the prosecutor to plead out. Frankly, I'm bored with all of it. What I wouldn't give for a juicy murder case these days."

Just what I needed to hear. "Now, I don't know if this will help you in all you're dealing with, but if you need a distraction from what's going on in your life, I would love for you to work on my mom's case with me. At this point, she could use all the help she could get."

Her face lit up when I said that. "I was hoping you would invite me onto the case. To tell you the truth, I was kind of angling for that, when I did all that research on Tracy Dunham before you could get to it. I know you're afraid that maybe I would drop the ball because I'm drinking again, but I think that giving me a purpose, such as saving Olivia from prison, would really help me. So I thank you for that."

I had to smile. I didn't even think about the angle that she was doing research on Dr. Dunham because she wanted on the case. "Well, you're my second chair. We can work this case together, 50-50. And, even though I'm calling you my second chair, I think we should be co-first chairs. We'll split the duties on this one, if you don't mind doing that."

"I'd love that, Damien."

I nodded. "Okay, then. Let's divide and conquer this case. I need to find out a lot more information about Dr. Dunham. I have a feeling that once I find out more about him, everything will fall into place. What I know about him is what I've read from his website. Basically, he's a pain management doctor who relies upon alternatives to pain meds in treating his patients. Acupuncture, acupressure, meditation, things like that. But I also read he was pioneering a new method of dealing with pain and was to be seeking a patent for it. I read the reviews, and the patients seemed to really like him. A lot of his patients were on pain meds to begin with, got addicted to them and still had pain, so they came to him."

Harper looked confused. "Okay, then. It seems like this guy would have access to a lot of pain meds, probably more than other doctors. So it's still confusing to me as to why he would turn to street drugs, when he could get as many pain meds as he needed."

"I wonder about the same thing. If he was seeing a lot of people who were trying to get off pain meds, it would follow they probably would turn their leftover meds into him. That makes a lot of sense. So, you're right – he would have access to a lot of surrendered meds which would help him with whatever issue he was dealing with. But, then again, I need to do a lot more research on the whole issue of heroin versus prescription drugs. I know heroin provides different benefits to people than your average pain meds. And by benefits, I mean that term loosely, of course. I guess that's a good place to start – do what we can to get some kind of patient list from him. Although I don't think we can do that without resorting to Anna hacking his database. But I would like to get a handle on the kinds of people he was treating."

I liked bouncing ideas off Harper. When she and I would brainstorm, we often came upon the right solution. I also liked the fact that she generally got along with my mom, who was definitely an acquired taste. Mom wasn't somebody who was necessarily easy to love or get to know, but Harper always got along with her.

Harper didn't come from the kind of weird background I did. She had a mother and father who stayed married for many years, and she had a lot of brothers and sisters. She was close to one sister in particular, Albany. Her father came out as gay recently and was married to a Russian man. Her father and his Russian husband seemed to be happy enough, and Harper was happy for him.

So, even though Harper did not have firsthand experience with dealing with someone like my mother, that didn't really matter. She still accepted my mother for who she was. In fact, Harper even found my mother to be funny. A hoot, as she said.

"Okay, Harper. There are two lines of inquiry with this, to start," I said. "Number one, I need to find out who was the dealer who gave him that heroin. Number two, I'd like to somehow get information about the number of patients who surrendered their drugs to him. We also need to talk to his assistant and find out if he was following the protocol for disposing of these surrendered drugs. Third, I would like to get a listing of all the pharmaceutical reps who had visited him over the years. Especially the ones who visited him recently. I'm curious as to what drugs these reps supplied him with and how much. I need to find out how his office was run - if it was loosely run, or if he had a really good assistant who stayed on top of everything. And I wonder who was supervising him, if anybody. If it was known he was having a problem with addiction, then he was probably supervised by somebody. I also would like to know if there were any complaints against him. I know a lot of physicians have addictions they can cover up, but I would also like to know about the system in place to try to catch them."

"Where do you want me to begin?"Harper asked. She was making notes as I was talking, a mile a minute, to her. I was brainstorming, just throwing ideas out at the top of my head, as fast as I could go. She was keeping up with me, and I could see the light in her eyes coming back. I felt a sense of relief when I saw that light in her eyes. The last couple of times I'd seen her, she looked so down and depressed. I was afraid she would go back into depression, so I was happy to keep her busy.

"Why don't you talk to his office manager?" I asked Harper. That might not be a bad idea - instead of my interviewing the office manager, I could get Harper to do it. "I understand he was in private practice, but had an office manager and also had another physician in his suite. His office manager might be invaluable. She would know what kind of patients were coming to see him, although she can't supply any of the names, and she could give you some information about if he was super-vised by anybody. She might be forthcoming in telling you if there were any complaints against him from the AMA or from other patients. If you talk to the office manager, we could probably get a handle on whether his addiction was affecting his practice. If he had many days he didn't come into the office and canceled all appointments, the office manager would know that. If he had complaints against him, she would know that, too. And I think, even more importantly, she would have a name of all the pharmaceutical reps who had visited him. I think if we got a handle on how he interacted in his day-to-day practice, we could glean clues about what was going on with him."

"Thanks for giving me this assignment." Harper looked at her hands. "I was wondering if you could come along with me to talk to these people." She rolled her eyes and took a deep breath. "God, this is so embarrassing." Another deep breath. "I'm just going to say it. I need support right now. I'm really happy to sink my teeth into your mother's case, but I don't really want to be alone. So, for right now, it's kind of a bad, crucial time. And I know going to his office and doing the research on him are things I can do alone, but...."

I knew what she was getting at. "Harper, do you have bottles of liquor stashed in your car, by any chance? Do you have a thermos of coffee spiked with alcohol? Is that what's going on?" I knew the alcoholic's game too well. My mother had liquor bottles stashed in her car at all times, and, as for taking a thermos full of alcohol, mixed in with a little bit of soft drink for color...that was Mom's MO. She used to take just such a thermos to work at Wal-Mart, stashing it in her locker and drinking it during her breaks, before she got caught and her job was threatened. After she was given a warning, she just went to her car during her breaks and boozed it up there.

Harper hung her head. "Yes. That's what's going on. I'm just afraid 'll go to Dr. Dunham's office and sit in my car in the parking lot and drink." She had tears in her eyes. "It's bad, Damien. I don't think I've been through a crisis like this for a long time. I mean, I fell off the wagon a few years back, but there was nothing bugging me at that time. This time, I'm scared. I'm really frightened I can't find my way back. So I'm reaching out to you. I'm telling you I need a little hand up. I know you would like me to just take one piece of the investigation, and you take another piece, but I would like for us to just do all of it together."

It was then that I realized the main reason Harper was so excited to be working on this case was because she needed to be side-by-side with me. She would need me to supervise her, so to speak. She couldn't come right out and say she needed supervision, but I could read the subtext.

She didn't want to be alone.

"Okay," I said. "We'll go over and talk to his office manager together. That's where I would like to begin this investigative process."

She looked embarrassed. "It's hard for me to ask for help. It's always been difficult to admit I have a problem. For most of my life, I've always tried to put a face to the world that there was nothing wrong with me. That I had it all together, was strong enough and didn't need help. It's taken a lot of therapy, a lot of talking, for me to realize my strength can't always come from within. Sometimes I have to look outside myself and hope that other people can give me strength. At least, during times like this, when I feel very weak."

I put my hand on her hand. "Harper, you don't have to explain things to me. Sometimes everybody needs a person to be there for them, to reinforce them. To give them strength, like you say. We don't always have that internal fortitude to stay on track with our lives. That's true for everybody, even me. I mean, just look at me – I was in prison for something I didn't do. I relied upon The Innocence Project to bring me out of that situation. And then I relied on my public defender who tried my second trial for that robbery and murder. Without them, I would still be in prison. And, I'll never forget that you represented me on my own murder charge. You did an awesome job figuring out what really happened to my father. You took control of that investigation, and that trial, when I needed you. Now, you need me, and I'll be there for you no matter what."

She took a deep breath and hung her head. "Thank you."

That was all she said. But nothing else needed to be said. Those two words, and the way she said them, spoke volumes.

NINE

Before I went to see Dr. Dunham's office manager, I wanted to talk to Mom. She was back at her house, playing Bunco with her friends and complaining about her ankle monitor. Her sink was still regularly stopped up, she still ran her car tires until they went bald, and she still didn't have a dishwasher. It was October and she had her Christmas lights up, as she did year-round. Her trailer was in its usual state of disrepair – rain coming in through the roof, mold starting on the walls, and she was constantly having to spray some kind of insecticide or another to take care of the spiders and other bugs that constantly were invading her home. Whenever I went to visit, mouse-traps were everywhere.

I never wanted her to live like this, but that was exactly what she wanted for herself. I always tried to do what I could to make repairs around her house, and I always wanted to at least buy her a brand-new trailer. A double wide, preferably. But she always got mad whenever I would even bring the subject up. She was always determined that I wouldn't help her because she always felt that any assistance from me would have too many strings attached. I didn't approve of the way she lived and she knew it. She therefore wouldn't accept my help, because she knew that if she did, I would try to change the way she did things.

I didn't really want to change her. I just wanted her to get off the sauce, stop picking up strange men in bars, and clean up her act. Take some responsibility for her negligent actions, such as her habitual drunk driving and failure to pay tickets on time, and start taking better care of her car and home.

Eh, I guess I really did want to change her, but only for the better.

But she always insisted she was happy, and I guessed she was.

Harper and I went to her trailer that afternoon. I called to tell her what time I was coming and told her Harper was coming with me.

She was excited about seeing Harper.

Me, not so much.

"Good, I'm glad she's coming with you. I've always wondered when the two of you would get together and start doing it. I know she's got that boyfriend but I think you could take him. I met him and he's a handsome cop and all, but I think you can shove him aside and start making it with her."

For some odd reason, I felt embarrassed by what my mom was saying. I didn't bother to correct her and tell her Harper was no longer seeing Axel, because that would just add fuel to the fire. Mom would be on my case more than ever to try to get the two of us into bed. And, at the moment, that was the last thing on my mind. Not that I didn't find Harper attractive. On the contrary, she was objectively attractive. I didn't know anybody who could find Harper physically unattractive or unappealing. She was beautiful, with her thick red hair, green eyes, lean frame, and beautiful skin. And she had a certain combination of grit, determination and vulnerability that was almost intoxicating.

Yet, there was just no way I could possibly make a move on Harper in her state. We were just friends, and I had to set my mother straight about that.

"Mom, we're just friends. Not to mention, she's my law partner. I'm sorry Mom, but I'm not in the habit of crapping where I sleep."

"Whatever. I see the googly-eyes she makes at you and you make at her. You better just admit it. You're going to be hitting the sack with her before we know it. At least, I hope so."

It was time for me to change the subject. "Okay, whatever. Listen, Mom, we're coming to see you in an hour. So be ready for it."

"Okay, see you in a bit."

I got off the phone and saw Harper standing in the doorway. I wondered how much she heard of the conversation I had with my mom. I hoped she didn't hear the part about me talking about how she was my partner and friend and nothing more, because if she heard that part of the conversation, she could ascertain what my mom was saying. I didn't want her getting ideas. I didn't want her to know that my mom had been pressuring me lately about the two of us getting together.

"My mom says she's looking forward to seeing the two of us," I said.

"That's good. I wonder how much we can really get out of her, though."

"Maybe you can talk to her. My mom has always had a bad habit of lying to me. I don't necessarily know why that is. But it seems like she lies to me more than she lies to anybody else. Maybe she'll be straighter with you than me about what she knows about Tracy Dunham. If she knows anything more about him than what she's been telling me, hopefully it'll come out."

Harper nodded. "Let's go."

TEN

We arrived at my mom's trailer in about a half hour. She apparently heard us pull up, because she walked out of the trailer when we got there and came out to give Harper a big hug. "Hey there, Ross. Come on in, don't be shy." She put her arm around Harper, and Harper did the same, as the two women walked arm in arm into the trailer. I brought up the rear.

My mom didn't even say hello to me, but I wasn't offended. I got the impression that Harper was the daughter my mom never had but always wished she did.

When I walked in, Harper and my mom were already sitting on the couch. I took a seat on a chair. My mom had her hand on Harper's knee, and she was leaning very close in to her. It looked like the two of them were talking conspiratorially about whatever women talk about when they get together.

"Harper, don't get me wrong, you look fit as a fiddle. Fitter than a fiddle. But you also look whiter than a *Twilight* vampire and as frightened as a whore in church. Why do I think you're not exactly sitting on top of the world?" Then she narrowed her eyes. "In fact, if I didn't know any better, I think you've been getting drunker than a hoot owl."

Harper laughed nervously. "I've been off the wagon, but I'm really trying hard to get back on. The other night, Damien came over, and I was, as you say, drunker than a hoot owl."

Mom laughed too. "And now you're sober as a judge." Then she got up and brought back a batch of cookies. "Well, here you go. My magic cookies. I call this my Alice B. Toklas mix. Just because you're not hitting the sauce don't mean that you can't have the weed, right?"

I rolled my eyes. "I don't want to be a square, Mom, but we have a job to do. And I'm going to pretend not to see this batch of cookies, because I remind you that one of the conditions of your bail is that you do not indulge in illegal drugs." In Missouri, it was legal to possess up to three ounces of pot, but it was safe to say that Mom had more than that in the house. She always did.

Mom shook her head. "There you go, my convict son, giving me a lecture. Listen, Damien, I might like my bud, but at least I don't like jacking cars, unlike some people I know in this room. If it's good for the goose it's good for the gander, I always say. Sorry, but I'm not having a lecture from somebody who spent most of his years in reform school because of all the crap he did."

I just rolled my eyes. I'd been getting this whataboutism from my mom for years. I cleaned up my act, unlike her, and I think she resented that fact. She liked it when she had me to look down on. And now that I'd gotten straight and gotten on with my life, she felt it was my turn to look down on her. Which I did. I admit it. I never could understand why she didn't try to do something to improve herself. Now, here she was, being accused of murder.

Harper looked uncomfortable when my mom was saying those things to me. "Olivia, Damien's one of the top defense attorneys in the area. He really has it all together. I mean, I know that when he was younger, he was kind of a hell raiser, but he's not anymore."

Mom just shrugged. "I know. But I just don't like him being on my ass constantly the way he always is. Anyhow, let's just change the subject. The two of you are here for a reason, so what is it?"

Harper cleared her throat. "I wanted to talk to you a bit more about Tracy Dunham. Now, I know you told Damien that you didn't know much about him. The two of you were friends with benefits, as you put it. But I wanted to dive a little bit deeper into your relationship with him. Because Damien said you told him something interesting. You told Damien, when he bailed you out of jail, that the person you usually relied on to bail you out was dead and you were accused of killing that person. I zoned in on that comment when Damien said that to me, because it sounded to me like maybe you and Dr. Dunham might've known each other a bit better than what you say."

Mom took a deep breath. "Yeah, yeah, Tracy has bailed me out of jail twice in the past six months. Once because I got stopped for speeding and had parking tickets I hadn't paid. And the other time was because I happened to get nailed for drunk driving." She pointed at me after she told Harper about her pecadilloes. "Not one word from you, Damien. I'm tired of your lectures."

I rolled my eyes. "I wasn't saying a word."

"Yeah, but you were going to, I could tell." She straightened her back on the couch. "Anyhow," she continued, "I called him both times just because he's the only one I know who's got money. Besides Damien, I mean, and there ain't no way I'm calling Damien for nothing. Damien will bail me out and lecture me the whole way. I also don't like going through a bail bondsman, because they charge too damn much money. And, look around, I got lots of friends in this trailer park, but none of them got a pot to piss in. None of them got two nickels to rub together. So Tracy was the only friend I knew who had the money to bail me out. And he didn't mind bailing me out either, because he liked what I did with him in bed."

Harper carefully took notes while she spoke. I knew Harper would get to the meat of what she was trying to get at, which was that my mom probably knew more about Tracy than she let on. "Okay. So he bailed you out whenever you asked him? It sounds like maybe you guys were on slightly different terms than what you say. What time of the night would he come and get you?"

Mom shrugged. "Midnight, usually. He worked at his practice until 6 o'clock in the evening and then went home and pretty much got drunk in front of the television. So he wasn't never doing nothing when I called him, so it wasn't a problem for him to come down to the jail to bail me out. That's all there was to it."

I bit my tongue. Tracy apparently habitually drove drunk to bail my mom out of jail, and that somehow wasn't a problem in my mother's eyes.

"And how did you know how he spent his evenings? How did you know he drank a lot?" Harper asked.

"He'd tell me about it. Listen, he had a bitch wife who always nagged him. He had a big old house over in Leawood and had a man cave. He told me that when he came home from work, he'd go down to that man cave and jack it while drinking Jack. You know, he'd watch porn while drinking a bottle of whiskey, and that was that."

Harper continued to make notes, and I could see by the look on her face that she wasn't quite believing what my mom was saying. "So, when he would bail you out, he was drunk himself. Is that safe to say?"

Mom got up and went into the kitchen. "All this talking about Jack Daniels is making me thirsty. I hate to do this to you, Harper, because Damien's telling me how much you're trying to stay on that wagon, but I really need a drink. Damien, you want one?"

I looked over at Harper, and I knew she wouldn't take Mom up on her whiskey offering. I didn't want Harper to feel left out, and I knew Harper couldn't drink. However, a whiskey on the rocks sounded really good to me at that point. There was something about being around my mom that drove me to drink.

"No, Mom. That's okay."

"Suit yourself." She came back to the living room and sat on the couch, a whiskey and water in her glass. "Yeah, when Tracy came to get me at the jail, he was usually three sheets to the wind. But that don't matter. He always drove like that. He always told me he drove better when he was drunk, because that meant he didn't speed or run lights. You know that guy never did got a DUI in his life? He's that good. Or he was that good."

Harper looked like she was thinking about what mom was saying, and trying to figure out what to ask next. "So, Olivia, are you telling me that every night that Tracy went home, he pretty much spent the evening ignoring his wife and drinking in front of a television in his man cave?"

"No, I didn't say that. I just said that's what he was doing those two nights he bailed me out. I know that a lot of other nights he was busy working on other things. He told me he was hard at work on improving some kind of newfangled pain treatment he was using on his patients. I think he said he was getting close to getting a patent for his idea. I don't really know what it involved, but I know his patients thought that bastard shot the moon. They thought he walked on water."

Harper nodded. "I remember reading that on the website. It said something about him pioneering a pain management technique and there was a patent pending. Are you saying he was perfecting that?"

Mom just shrugged. "I guess so. I don't know what he was talking about. He would come over here, babbling on about it, telling me how he got this letter and that letter from new patients telling him he changed their lives and crap like that. I don't know. I paid no mind. I really didn't care. You know how some people get, just flapping their gums over nonsense. That's the kind of guy he was. I just looked at him, acted like I cared and was listening to him, but I really wasn't. All I know is he said he was working on something he could patent."

"Okay, so you have no idea what this new technique was, correct?"

"Hell, I don't know. Like I told you, he was just babbling on. Flapping his gums. I couldn't care less." She took a sip of her Jack Daniels, and then smiled. "Then again, maybe I should've paid attention to it. My arthritis has been acting up something fierce and my back's been killing me lately. I don't get into all that painkilling crap, I just take some Aleve and bear through it. But Tracy, he swore that what he was working on would be a miracle for people in pain. Maybe I should've listened to him."

Harper glanced at me and I couldn't read what she was thinking. "Tracy's family is very wealthy. So, Tracy had it covered as far as getting a patent. That's the one thing that most patent seekers lack, money, because it costs a lot of money to seek a patent. You have to hire a lawyer, for one thing. Also, I wonder if he would try to franchise his idea in some way."

Mom nodded. "Yeah, yeah. That was another thing he wanted to do. He wanted to charge doctors a lot of money to learn this technique, and he told me he had a ton of those doctors lining up at his door, anxious to take his class for that. He even told me he had magazines lined up, asking about it. Not just medical journals, but he told me he had some guys sniffing around from *Time* magazine and things like that. I don't know, it sounded like it would be some big deal. Some big fat deal."

"What else did he tell you about what he was doing?" Harper asked.

Mom shrugged. "Not much. He told me all about his bitch wife and how she was always hollering at him about this or that and how he just shut her out and drank."

"Now, was it unusual that Tracy would be high on street drugs? You don't happen to know where he would get those drugs, do you?" Harper asked.

Mom took a drink and started to roll a joint. "I'm not waiting around for the two of you. I'm gonna roll this joint and I hope you don't mind if I smoke in front of you. If you guys do, I'll go out on my porch. Don't nobody care about that around here, nobody's gonna turn me in. Anyhow, no, I don't think Tracy got into that kind of stuff. He didn't strike me as a street-drugs type of guy, if you know what I mean. I don't know who might've dealt it to him, but he was rich. At least, that's what you guys tell me. You tell me he was rich. Guess I'm gonna have to take your word for that. Anyhow, those rich guys, they got all kinds of ways to get drugs, don't they?"

"So you don't know who could've given him that heroin, do you?"

"Hell, no. I just told you that. Harper, why do you keep asking me the same questions? I know you lawyers. I know that's what you do. You ask the same question eight ways to Sunday and hope you somehow get a different answer. I told you no. I don't know nobody who would be supplying him heroin."

Harper nodded. I wondered what was going through her mind. I knew she got along with my mom, but at the same time, my mom could be pretty annoying. "Now, you were saying earlier that you could go outside on the porch and smoke a joint, and nobody would say anything about it. Nobody would turn you into the cops. Right?"

"Yeah. That's what I said. Listen, this backward-ass state finally passed legal weed. Ain't nobody can do nothing to me now. Not that anybody around here would do a thing to me about that anyhow."

"Mom, I hate to tell you this, but it's still illegal to possess more than 3 ounces. I'm sure you have a lot more than that," I told her.

"Yeah, I know that," Mom said with a roll of her eyes. "But if I smoke weed on my porch, it's perfectly legal, so lay off me."

I looked over at Harper, who was impatiently clicking her pin on her paper. She was getting sidetracked by this conversation. I couldn't read her mind, but it looked like she was honing in on a specific area of inquiry.

"Olivia," Harper said. "Do you know other people who live around you who have access to heroin?"

"Yeah. Of course. My next-door neighbor, Rosemarie, she's got a son living with her who's on that junk all the time. She's always kicking him out for it, but he always comes back. I got other friends around here who have kids taking that junk, too. Hell, I even got a couple of friends who do it. So yeah, I think people around here know dealers."

"So you also have access to heroin, right? I mean, if you have friends who take it, and other friends whose kids are on it, they could get some for you too, right?"

Mom shook her head adamantly. "No, not right. Listen, the friends I got with kids on it, they want no part of it. No part of it. They ain't going to be getting junk for me if I ask them for it. As for my friends who do it, they're always wanting to get off it themselves. I ask them for a phone number for their dealer, they ain't gonna give it to me. They gonna tell me to kiss their ass." Mom raised her glass of bourbon and gestured towards Harper before taking another sip of her drink. "I know what you're getting at, you're trying to trap me into saying I know somebody who gave me that junk and I took it. Now, I know what that drug test said. It said I had opium in my system. But I can tell you right now, that's wrong. I like my pot, I like my whiskey, I like my cigarettes. But I seen far too many junkies in my life to ever want to go down that road."

"Do you know of anybody who could take heroin and shape it into a pill form that would resemble a Nifedipine pill?" Harper asked, already knowing the answer, but having to ask it anyhow.

Mom rolled her eyes. "Are you trying to piss me off now, Harper, because if you are, you're doing a good job. If I don't know nobody who's gonna sell me heroin, then I wouldn't know nobody who could shape heroin into a pill, now would I?" She shook her head and took a sip of her whiskey. "I'm gonna take a hit. I can't take this. I don't even care if you guys don't want me to or not." At that, she lit up her rolled joint and inhaled, not even coughing a little bit when she blew out the smoke. "There, now I'm relaxed. You can ask me more questions. Go ahead. Ain't nothing gonna bother me now."

Harper glanced over at me and nodded. "Olivia, thanks for seeing us. You've been very helpful, more helpful than you know."

"I'm just telling you what I know, which ain't much. Damien, why does that prosecutor have such a hard-on for me? I don't get it. Tracy, he took the junk, he died. Simple as that, yet here I am, up for murder of the guy. I just don't get it."

"That's what I'm trying to figure out as well, Olivia," Harper said. "I know Damien will speak with the prosecutor within a couple of days, trying to pick their brain on why they charged your case like this. Not that they're going to tell us anything, but it's worth trying to understand what they're thinking."

A kernel of a thought came into my brain about what the endgame was with the prosecutor's office on this case, but it was just that. A kernel. I had to wonder if the guy being rich had anything to do with my mother being on the hook for killing him.

But, that didn't make a lot of sense. So, he was rich, and his family was extremely rich. So what?

Actually, he wasn't rich, come to think of it. He hadn't been given his inheritance, unlike just about everybody else in his generation who was part of the Dunham family. That was still an oddity that stuck out to me.

We chatted with my mom for about another hour, just kind of shooting the breeze. I did my usual amount of fixing up around the house – unclogging her toilet, setting out mousetraps, fixing her washing machine, etc., while Harper and my mom shared a piece of pie.

ELEVEN

The next day, I filed a petition on behalf of of Audrey Blackwood. I knew it would be opening up a big fat can of worms, but I didn't care. All I knew was it was time this guy, Michael Reynolds, paid at least a little bit for what he'd done to so many people.

After I filed that petition, I decided to pay a visit to the prosecutor for my mom's case, Kevin Williams. I knew he didn't have court right at that moment, so there was a good chance he was around.

I got to his office suite, told the receptionist I needed to see him, and she told me to go on back. I went to his office, saw his door was open, so I knocked lightly on the open door.

Kevin looked up from his desk and smiled. Kevin was a handsome black man with a bald head. He was a big guy, having played Division 1 football as a linebacker, but he wasn't fat at all. I had to admit, as a man with a limited amount of fashion sense, I admired the sharp way Kevin dressed. Nothing was ever out of place with him and everything seemed to come together with whatever color combination he chose. He looked the part of a high-dollar attorney from a white-shoe firm, even though he was a prosecutor making around $70,000 a year, if that. Tailored suits, Italian wing-tipped shoes apparently shined every morning, gold cufflinks, and a perfectly folded handkerchief in his pocket. He also had a scent that was a part of his image, for he was known for wearing high-dollar cologne that wasn't overpowering, just woodsy and clean.

He smiled broadly when he saw me. "Damien Harrington, where've you been keeping yourself? I haven't seen you around in awhile."

I smiled back. "Right. Well, I have this serious case with my mother, so I haven't been going to my usual docket calls. I've been getting coverage for my docket calls. Don't have time for those right now."

He shook his head, a broad smile on his face. "Don't I know it. I'm so glad I don't do those things anymore. I'm telling you, the plea docket was the ninth circle of hell. Anyhow, I know why you're here. You want to know why I'm prosecuting your mama. Listen, I'm sorry about that, I really am. When this case was dumped on me, I asked the same damned thing. The only answer I got was that the district attorney wanted her prosecuted. That's all I know, man. Wish I knew more."

That didn't sound right to me. "Kevin, the district attorney personally wants my mom prosecuted?" While that wasn't necessarily unusual - technically, the district attorney wanted everybody prosecuted who was charged with a crime - it seemed unusual that the DA himself was personally involved in prosecuting my mother.

"Yeah, that's what's been coming down the pike on this one. I don't really know what to tell you. You know that our policy, generally, is to speak with the victim's family before dropping a case. Or to the victim, if the victim is alive. And, for some odd reason, Dr. Dunham's brother, Robert, who is Dr. Dunham's closest living relative, is adamant that the charges against your mom not be dropped. And if Robert Dunham speaks in this town, he's listened to. I think you probably know that by now. The guy's got more money and power than the Kauffmans or the Hunts. I'm sorry, man, I wish I had better news for you." The Kauffman family was one of the wealthiest and most prominent in Kansas City, making their money in pharmaceuticals, and so was the Hunt family, who owned the Super Bowl champions, The Chiefs, and made their money in oil. So, if the Dunham family rivaled those two families, that was saying a lot.

I sat down. "Kevin, I think you know the case against my mom is weak tea to begin with. I mean, charging her with murder when your only evidence is that she possibly, maybe, got high with the guy?"

Kevin shrugged. "You shouldn't be so surprised about that. That's the new trend, my man, where've you been? People are being prosecuted all over the country for supplying drugs to a person who overdosed. And if your mom was high on the stuff and Dr. Dunham came over to her house, that's circumstantial evidence right there that she gave him drugs. We can establish a timeline with Dr. Dunham's wife that when he left the house that night, he was sober as a judge. He left the house that night at 9:00, your mother's statement to the police indicated he arrived at your mother's house at around 9:30, his home was almost exactly a half hour away from your mother's home, so the chance that he picked up that heroin in between leaving his house and getting to your mother's house is slim. The jury can ascertain from those facts that your mother supplied the drugs to Dr. Dunham." He unwrapped a pack of gum and popped a stick in his mouth. "Besides, we only have to show the two were getting high together for a murder charge to stick. With your mother's UA, taken the next morning, that won't be hard to do at all."

I crossed my arms in front of me. "Kevin, again, all you have is circumstantial evidence. You can't show my mom supplied Dr. Dunham with anything. For all you know, he could have had the heroin in his pocket when he went to see my mom and he supplied her with the drugs."

"You know, I would almost agree with you, except for the fact that the blood pressure medicine seized at your mother's house tested positive for, you guessed it, high-grade heroin, the same kind of heroin found in the toxicology examination of the good doctor. Sorry, the evidence isn't looking so good for you."

"That was planted, plain and simple. I don't know what the chain of evidence was when those blood pressure drugs were seized. I have no clue. You still don't have anything too solid with which to charge my mother."

"Tell it to the judge," he said. "In the meantime, I can't dismiss this case. I'm really sorry, I don't want to do that to your mama, I know I wouldn't want my own mama done like this, but it is what it is."

"Okay," I said. "I thought I could talk some sense into you, but I guess I can't right now. You're going to end up dismissing this, sooner or later, mark my words. But thanks for your time."

He nodded. "I do have an offer for you. 20 years, plead to man one. I can even talk to my boss about giving your mom 20 years, plead to delivery of a controlled substance, so she won't have a murder on her record. At the moment, we're going for felony murder, as the death occurred during the commission of a felony, the felony being the original delivery of a controlled substance. That's second-degree murder she's facing. You have an opportunity for a plea to man one or simple delivery of a controlled substance. I think you should take it myself."

"Whatever," I said. "I'm not pleading my mom to anything. Nothing. If you don't dismiss the case, prepare to go to trial."

He smiled a disarming smile and a small chuckle came out. "I wish I could, Harrington. Believe me, I wish I could dismiss it. But I can't. Higher-up orders and all that. Sorry, man, I hope we can still be friends even after I put your mama in prison. It's nothing personal, you know."

"Of course, it's nothing personal," I said. "And I hope you don't take it personally when I beat your ass in court."

He nodded, still smiling. "I would expect nothing less. Anyhow, let's exchange our discovery and see where the chips fall." He nodded again, and I got up to walk out.

"Okay," I said. "I'll get you my discovery and my expert witness designation within a couple of weeks. You do the same."

"See you Harrington," Kevin said. "Wish I could have helped you more."

"Be expecting a Motion to Dismiss and a Motion to Suppress. I don't believe there was probable cause to give my client a UA, let alone for the search and seizure of her home."

"File it, and I'll see you in court."

"I will."

I didn't say anything more, but just walked out. I shouldn't have been angry with Kevin, but I was. He was the face of the prosecution, the face of the government, the same government that was trying to put my mom away on a BS charge.

I couldn't get around that.

TWELVE

The next week, I got into court on my Motion to Dismiss and Motion to Suppress. It was a long-shot, but I had to take it. From the evidence, I saw no reason why my mother would've been given a UA. Her dirty UA ostensibly gave the cops a reason to search her home, but even that shouldn't have been the basis for the search and seizure, because it wasn't illegal for her to have been high in her own home. No law against that.

I got into the courtroom and Judge Watkins and Kevin were waiting for me. Judge Watkins smiled at me. "Hello, counselor, I understand you have some motions for me to entertain?"

"Yes I do, your honor. I have a motion to suppress the heroin that was found in my mother's medicine cabinet. As you can read in my motion, the police did not have probable cause to arrest my mother at the time they seized the pills in her cabinet that tested positive for heroin. I also have a motion to suppress the UA given to my client. If these items are suppressed, then I'm going to ask for you to rule on my Motion to Dismiss the case."

I looked over at Kevin. "This is your last chance to not humiliate yourself. You know this case will be an uphill battle for you anyway. It'll be hard to show my client gave Dr. Dunham the drugs that killed him."

"Dream on, Harrington. Sorry, but I'm not buying what you're trying to sell. And I told you once before, I can't possibly move off my offer for this case. 20 years in prison, and I can possibly move the charge down to a 20% charge. That would take some maneuvering, I'm not going to lie, but I can try."

This actually was a different offer than the one he offered before. Before, he simply said 20 years. In the state of Missouri, second degree murder, which was what my mom was being charged with, was an 85% charge. That meant that if you get convicted of second degree murder, you served 85% of your prison time. That was the way it was with what was called the "seven deadly sins" in Missouri – rob one, murder of any kind, voluntary manslaughter, arson one, forcible rape, and forcible sodomy were among the deadly sins in Missouri and the convictions for these crimes necessitated that the perpetrator serve 85% of his sentence.

If Kevin was willing to deal my mom's sentence down to a 20% crime, to where she would only have to serve 20% of her crime, typical for a first-time-down situation, then he must have known his hand was weak.

I felt more confident after he made that offer. I knew I could go for the jugular on this one.

"No thanks," I said to Kevin. "In the meantime, I have my motion to suppress the heroin for the judge to hear."

Judge Watkins nodded his head. "Go ahead, counselor, hit me with your best shot."

I cleared my throat and glanced at my mother, who was sitting at the defense table with Harper by her side. She looked terrified, her rheumy and blood-shot blue eyes wide.

"Okay," I said. "Here are the facts, as Mr. Williams knows, and so do you, your honor. But the officers in this case, Officer Conrad and Officer Black, appeared at Ms. Ward's residence at her behest. She called 911 when she woke up to find her friend, Dr. Tracy Dunham, deceased on her couch. When the paramedics arrived, so did Officers Conrad and Black. At that time, they did not have probable cause to arrest my client. In fact, they didn't have probable cause to give her a UA, either. They didn't know at that time how Dr. Dunham died, and, even assuming my client was high on drugs at that time, which she was not, but assuming she was, the Officers still didn't have probable cause to arrest her because they could not have known that Dr. Dunham had died of a drug overdose. Indeed, my client was not arrested that night, even though her UA returned a result that indicated she was taking opium during that time."

At that, Kevin interrupted me. "Your honor, Mr. Harrington is giving you a false narrative here, all right? The officers had every reason to suspect that Dr. Dunham had died of a drug overdose, which gave them probable cause to take Ms. Ward into custody at that time. When she was given a UA, which indicated Ms. Ward was high on some kind of opium at that time, those officers really had probable cause to arrest her."

I cleared my throat. I was itching for a fight. "With all due respect, what gave those officers the indication that night that Dr. Dunham had died of a drug overdose? There was no way that anybody could know how he died until they autopsied him and did a toxicology examination. For all those officers knew, Dr. Dunham died of a heart attack, which would mean that even if my client was high on heroin, which she wasn't, but even if she was, there wasn't a reason to arrest her that night. You cannot arrest somebody simply for being high in their own home."

Judge Watkins looked at me. "True, you can't arrest somebody for being high, but you can arrest them for drug possession. Once the officers saw your client was possibly high, and they gave her a UA to confirm it, it was incumbent upon them to search your client's home and person to see if she had drugs. You can't very well argue that the officers couldn't arrest your client just because she was high, and then tie their hands to search for the drugs she took that night, drugs that would be the basis for a proper arrest."

I knew what he was getting at, and he wasn't wrong. If the officers suspected my mother was high, that gave them suspicion enough to try to find the drugs that made her that way. But I wasn't having it.

"Your honor, they didn't arrest her that night, and that's the point. They didn't arrest her, because they had no reason to arrest her. All she was doing that night was minding her own business in her home, in her castle, so anything she was doing in the privacy of her own home was not the business of anybody else. And-"

Judge Watkins was stuck on the idea that if there were drugs at my mom's house, that meant the cops had a reason to search. "But counselor, if she was minding her own business in her own home, and that home had contraband, then the police officers were acting within their purview to search. And your client consented to the search."

That was the sticking point, I had to admit. My mother consented to the search. "Your honor, my client is unsophisticated. She didn't know the ramifications of allowing a search of her premises. Moreover, she had no indication that she was in any kind of trouble. She wasn't under arrest. She wasn't in custody. She just saw that two officers showed up at her door, she thought they were there only to question her about how Dr. Dunham died, and the officers never told her they even suspected her of playing a role in his death."

"Yes, but your honor, they did give her a UA. That should have given her reason to believe that something was in the air," Kevin said.

"Again, she wasn't under arrest. In fact, the officers did not arrest her until months later, after Dr. Dunham's post-mortem showed he died of a drug overdose and my client's UA showed she had opiates in her bloodstream at the time he died. No probable cause to arrest means no probable cause to search. If the officers would have told my client they suspected her of playing a role in Dr. Dunham's death or was in custody, she would not have willingly consented to a search of her premises. As it was, she thought there wouldn't be any harm in letting them search, because she had no idea she would be in trouble."

It looked like the judge was considering my argument. He put his hand to his chin and tapped his pen on the bench.

I decided to press on. "Your honor, it cannot be said that an officer can come into a private home and just search that home without having a suspicion that a crime had been committed, and then use the fruits of that search to charge somebody with a crime. They must first have probable cause that a crime had been committed before they can search."

"And they did have probable cause that a crime had been committed because the defendant's UA showed that the defendant was high on opiates," Kevin interjected. "Since she was high, it followed she possessed drugs. That gave the officers a reason to search for those drugs."

"But your honor, I submit that the officers had no reason to even give my client a UA in the first place. They didn't know Tracy had died of a drug overdose, and there was nothing in the arrest record that would indicate that my client was showing physical signs that would be consistent with somebody high on opiates or any other drug. They didn't have even a reasonable suspicion that my client was high, let alone probable cause."

"Your client consented to the UA," Judge Watkins said.

"Yes, again, because she didn't believe the officers were going to place her under arrest. She wasn't driving. She was sitting in her home. They didn't have probable cause for that UA, either."

Judge Watkins finally sighed and shook his head. "Here's what I'm going to do, counselor. You have a good argument that both the UA and the search of the premises were illegally obtained, even though your client consented to both of them. She wasn't under arrest during this period of time, and it was true that the officers who were on the scene could not have known during that time that Dr. Dunham died of an overdose."

Sounded good so far, but I heard a "but" coming. Which it was.

"That said," the judge continued, "if the officers had a reasonable belief that Dr. Dunham died of an overdose, and there were exigent circumstances, which there were in this case if your client was high at the time Dr. Dunham died, that gave them a reason to give her a UA. So, I will let the results of the urinalysis stand."

I sighed. I knew this would be the ruling, but I had to try. At any rate, I had issues to take up on appeal if it came to that.

"Furthermore," the judge went on, "once the UA was given and it showed your client did indeed have opiates in her system, that gave the officers probable cause to place her under arrest, and it gave them probable cause to search her premises for the source of the opium found in her system that night. The fact they did not put her under arrest that night is non-dispositive to my analysis."

I had a feeling the judge would make this kind of a roundabout argument, so I was prepared for it.

Kevin was looking at me with a smirk on his face. He really thought he had me on the ropes. He had to have known I was counting on that heroin being suppressed.

I walked out of the courtroom feeling defeated and knowing that there was only one way this case would be resolved.

In a trial. A trial I could very well lose if I didn't figure out what the hell was going on.

Thirteen

The next day, I was greeted with a very hostile scene. I walked into the suite, and Pearl, our office manager, stood up. "Damien, what the hell were you thinking?"

I was confused at first, but then I saw a guy sitting in the office suite, looking about ready to kill me. He was tall, and dark headed, and he looked like somebody who was an MMA fighter. When I came in the door, he stood up, his fists clenched.

I nodded my head at Pearl. Nobody had to tell me who this man was. It was clearly Michael Reynolds.

"Where is Harper?" was the first thing that came out of my mouth. I suddenly realized that my little plan to file a lawsuit against Michael was probably backfiring on me in a spectacular way.

"She's in her office," Pearl said. "She came in the door, saw this guy sitting there, and the first thing she did was run into her office. I wouldn't be surprised if she called the cops on him. In fact, I clearly would've called the cops on him by now. I don't know why he's in this office, but he said he was looking for you."

I turned to the man who was standing there with his fists clenched. "Michael Reynolds, I presume?" I said, looking at him.

"You're damned right, I'm Michael Reynolds," he said, standing up.

He was intimidating in size, but I knew I could take him if it came to that. I had beat up guys bigger than him in prison.

I nodded. "If you'll excuse me, I'll be right with you."

I went down the hall and knocked on Harper's door. I would have to come clean on what I was doing. I was prepared for her to read me the riot act and I probably had it coming.

Harper answered the door and she peeked her head out the doorway, looking one way and then the other, and then grabbed me by my lapel and pulled me into the office. "Get in here."

She sat down behind her desk, and I sat down in the chair in front of it. "Harper, I'm so sorry."

"What are you sorry about?" Her hands were shaking. "That guy out there, did you see him? Is he still out there?"

I took a deep breath. How would I explain it to her? "Yes, Harper I saw him. And I know who he is. And he's here because of me, not because of you."

Her face got really white, and she stood up, and sat back down. "What do you mean he's here because of you? How do you even know him?"

How could I tell her this? "Harper, I don't know if you read in the paper about a woman by the name of Carrie Blackwood. She was a minor pop star back in the early two thousands, I think she had a song on the radio. Anyhow, she committed suicide recently because of a viral video of her and Michael Reynolds that was posted. She was a pediatrician, and she lost her practice because of it."

Harper's face started to regain its color, but her hands were still shaking. "Okay, go on. Tell me more about this Carrie Blackwood, and how are you involved in the middle of it?"

I took a deep breath. I had no idea how Harper would react to my confession, but I had to hope that maybe she would surprise me. "I might have gone to Carrie's mother and talked her into her filing a lawsuit against Michael for wrongful death. Not to mention invasion of privacy."

Her eyes got big. And then she did something that was totally unexpected. She got up, walked over to me, stood behind me, and wrapped her arms around me from the back. She squeezed me tightly, and I could feel her head in my shoulders. She was sobbing.

I gently stood up, turned around and wrapped my arms around her. "I don't know how to interpret this reaction."

"Damien, I've never had somebody do something like this for me," she said. "I just wish you would've told me what you were doing, because then I wouldn't have had this really bad surprise for me when I walked in the door this morning. But I love you for doing this. And I really do hope you can get this bastard and make him pay out the nose. I did read about Carrie Blackwood in the papers and online. It's kind of a big story, because of the viral video, and the fact that she killed herself. Also because she was a minor pop star. When I found out about that, I was enraged, but I didn't want to do anything about it. I felt like that was a third rail for me after what happened with my criminal case with him. I knew I couldn't be objective, and, besides, I felt like I would be setting myself up for another bar complaint if I would've pursued him on this. I'm just happy that somebody's trying to bring him to justice."

I felt relieved, to say the very least. I was hoping she would react like this, but I wasn't sure. "So, you're okay with me doing this?"

"Oh, I'm more than okay with this. You don't know how okay I am with this. But you need to get rid of him. He's not supposed to be here anyway, since you're suing him. You need to tell him he'll have to find a lawyer and you'll talk to his lawyer but not to him."

"If he's not yet represented by counsel, I can talk to him now," I said. "But I don't think that's a good idea. You're right, he needs to find a lawyer, and I'll talk to his lawyer. Unless, of course, he agrees to settle with me for millions of dollars right here and now. That's how much I'm asking for – $10 million. Most of that is in punitive damages. Now I know Michael Reynolds doesn't have that kind of money, but the woman he's still married to does."

Harper shook her head. "Unfortunately, he's not married to her anymore. I knew they were separated and not living together. His wife got smart and filed for divorce, and the divorce just came through, just a couple of days ago. I accessed his divorce judgment online, and he presently doesn't have a pot to piss in, as your mother might say. His wife showed the court that it was more likely than not that he killed her father, so she convinced the judge that he wasn't entitled to a thin dime of her fortune. Not even the amount of money the two of them earned during the marriage. So if you get a judgment against him, unfortunately, he won't be able to pay."

That was unfortunate. But, then again, it would be worth it if we could drive this guy into the poor house. The punitive damages would be something he could never get out from under. I knew something about bankruptcy law, and you could not discharge punitive damages in any kind of bankruptcy. In fact, there was a good chance that none of the debt would be dischargeable in bankruptcy, as you generally cannot discharge damages that result from a willful and malicious injury on the part of the defendant.

That would mean he couldn't rely on his wealthy wife to pay the judgment and the judgment would follow him around for the rest of his life. I would attach anything he presently owned and anything he might own in the future, garnish his paychecks, freeze his bank accounts, do whatever it took to collect as much money as I could for my client. And that would be a substantial hardship on him.

"Is it selfish of me that I'm happy he's divorced from his wealthy wife and received no money out of the divorce? I mean, it would obviously would've been better for my client if he would've gotten money from his divorce, and then we could've taken all of it, but, this way, he can be haunted by any judgment we're going to get against him. He'll never get out from under it. He'll never own a house and future employment opportunities will be limited because he'll have a large judgment on his record and employers don't look kindly on that. I know the last position he had was fairly high up in an advertising agency, and if he wants to get a similar position, he'll have a hard time doing that. I'll freeze his bank accounts. He can't run away from this. If he was still married to his ex-wife, the judgment would be paid, no matter how big the judgment is, but what fun is that? The only person who would've been paying out the nose would've been his wife."

Harper grinned. "Yeah, in a way it is selfish of you to be thinking that way. Of course, you want him to have the ability to pay any judgment to your client, but I know what you're saying. It's much more fun to know he'll be twisting in the wind, completely on his own, with this one." She rubbed her hands together. "Twisting in the wind. I love it."

I nodded and left Harper's office. Michael Reynolds was still waiting for me, his fists clenched.

I went over to him. "Mr. Reynolds, I'm so sorry, but I can't speak with you. I filed a lawsuit against you and you need to find a lawyer."

He looked like he was about to deck me. "I'm sorry, but this lawsuit you filed against me is bullcrap. Listen, you think you know what's going on with this, but you don't. She tried to tell people she wasn't with me consensually, but that's crazy. Why would I post a video online if it was something not consensual? That would open me up to all kinds of criminal liability."

I wanted to tell him that revenge porn, in general, also opened him up to criminal liability, but he didn't have a lawyer, so I didn't want to speak with him.

I shook my head. "Again, I can't talk to you about this. Go ahead and hire a lawyer. I'll call your lawyer, and we can maybe settle this. But I won't talk to you. Now please leave the premises or I'll have to call the police."

He pointed his finger at me. "You're making a mistake. A mistake. She wanted me to post that video online. That was the kind of person she was. She wanted me to."

I didn't say anything to him, but in my head I was thinking about what kind of line he was trying to give me. Why would a pediatrician, whose practice relies upon parents of young children coming to her and trusting her, want something like that to be posted online? That made no sense to me.

"Again, I don't want to go through this with you. You need to hire an attorney and then we'll get the ball rolling."

His face got really red. "I can't afford an attorney. I was calling attorneys today and everybody's charging out the nose. $300 an hour and up. I'm broke. I can't afford an attorney."

"Not my problem."

"What I'm saying is that if I can't afford an attorney, then I won't get one. I'll have to represent myself. Which means that you'll have to deal with me and only me."

I shrugged my shoulders. "Suit yourself. You'll have a fool for a client, that's for sure."

At that, he stormed out of the office suite, and I felt a sense of relief. I knew that if he didn't get an attorney, the case against him would be easier to win than I thought. If he had the money for some hired gun, who would bury me with discovery requests, as much as I would bury him with discovery requests, then this case would've been a lot of work. But if he couldn't afford an attorney, then I would bury him with discovery requests, but the discovery requests wouldn't be coming my way. Such a unilateral case would be easy to win.

Then again, I didn't want to jump the gun.

That always got me in trouble.

FOURTEEN

In the afternoon, Harper and I went to see the office manager for Dr. Dunham. Her name was Sally Wallace. She was a petite blonde, with blue eyeshadow and heavy lipstick. She was probably in her late 40s but was trying to look younger.

Her eyes lit up when we came in, and Harper nudged me and smiled. Harper was always teasing me about how women reacted to me, not that I ever noticed it.

"Hello," she said to us when we came in. "You must be Damien and Harper. I'm Sally, the office manager for Dr. Dunham and Dr. Gregory. Dr. Gregory is now the only doctor in this office."

"Dr. Gregory. And what kind of a doctor is Dr. Gregory?" I asked her.

"Same as Dr. Dunham. Dr. Gregory is a pain management doctor. He's a little bit different from Dr. Dunham was, however. He's more conventional. People come to him for management of their pain, and he doesn't try to recommend they go through acupuncture or acupressure or yoga or any of that. He doesn't recommend dietary changes or meditation, and he certainly doesn't use that specialized technique Dr. Dunham was using with his patients."

We followed her into the conference room, which was in the back of the office suite. The office suite itself was a typical medical suite, but was a bit more high-end than some. The lobby had marble floors, a large fish tank with saltwater fish in it, and huge jugs filled with cucumber and strawberry waters. The conference room was large, with a distressed wood table in the middle, wood paneled walls, and a wall of windows. It was on the 50th floor of a high-rise building downtown, and the view of the city was quite remarkable.

Harper and I sat down, and Sally poured us both a glass of cucumber water. "Now, what do you need to ask me?" she asked us.

I didn't want to beat around the bush. There was no reason to. "Your boss, Dr. Dunham, died of a heroin overdose. Does that surprise you?"

Sally hesitated. She bit her lower lip. "Does it surprise me? Well, no, in the sense that nothing surprises me anymore. But if you're asking me if I saw any signs that Dr. Dunham had a problem with drugs, the answer is no. I had no idea he had a problem. However, if he had a problem with drugs, I wouldn't have necessarily known it. People get pretty good about hiding such things."

"You must see a lot of addicts here in your practice, between Dr. Dunham and Dr. Gregory. Is that safe to say?" I took a sip of my water, which was quite tasty. I'd always liked cucumber water. Cool, refreshing and so incongruent with the weather that was starting to get bitterly cold.

"Yes, yes," Sally said. "Of course we see addicts. But, you have to understand one thing. A lot of addicts were coming to Dr. Dunham because they wanted to kick that addiction. Word got around to people all over the country that Dr. Dunham was doing something pretty special for pain management. He had a really thriving practice, much moreso than Dr. Gregory. I mean, Dr. Gregory has a very good practice, but Dr. Gregory is doing what too many other pain management doctors are doing. He just gives out prescriptions for opiates and sends them on their way. Dr. Dunham, on the other hand, could charge top dollar for his services. He was getting ready to export his technique to doctors everywhere around the country. He had a lot of doctors interested in that."

This was interesting to me, but I couldn't quite put the puzzle pieces together. "I understand he was seeking a patent for his technique. By the way, what is his technique?"

"He used a combination of radio and sonar waves to pinpoint the overactive nerves that cause of a lot of pain in patients. That gave a lot of relief to patients having chronic pain. In fact, I had quite a few people coming in here telling me, for hours, how much they got pain relief from Dr. Dunham. How grateful they were. They would tell me they had gone to one doctor after another and could never get any kind of relief, but they came to Dr. Dunham and he cured their pain. And that was any kind of pain, too. Not just the kind of pain that comes from overactive nerves, like fibromyalgia, but also people who had been in car accidents, who had chronic migraines, anybody, really, who had a lot of pain. He helped almost everybody, without drugs."

I made notes as she spoke. "He helped everybody without the use of painkilling drugs. Is that what you're telling me?"

"Yes. That's the reason why he had such a loyal following. People knew they could get relief from their pain without opioids."

"So are you saying he didn't get visits from pharmaceutical reps trying to get him to push their drugs on his patients?" I asked her.

"That's exactly what I'm saying," Sally said. "I mean, I got inquiries constantly on his behalf from this pharmaceutical company or that pharmaceutical company. And, Dr. Gregory got a lot of visits from pharmaceutical reps. They were here like every other week, giving him samples of drugs and taking him out to eat and to go golfing and different things like that. He got to stay in some really nice hotels, sometimes in the penthouse suite, all on the dime of the pharmaceutical companies. I didn't think that was ethical, but who am I to say what's ethical and what's not? Who am I to really say anything to him? So I didn't say anything to him or the reps. But I really thought Dr. Dunham was running a good, clean practice. He wasn't tarnished by those pharmaceutical reps like Dr. Gregory was."

"So, are you saying there was not an opportunity for Dr. Dunham to be exposed to opiates? At least, there wasn't an opportunity for him to take samples from reps and maybe take them himself?"

Sally shook her head. "No, I'm not saying that at all. In fact, what happened a lot in this office was that the patients would surrender their drugs to him, but he had a protocol for disposing of those drugs. Dr. Dunham knew he was breaking the law when he accepted these drugs from his patients, but, at the same time, he thought it was the right thing. These patients were trying to get off drugs, and if he had to rely on them to go through the rigmarole of disposing of these drugs on their own, they probably wouldn't do it."

"How are you supposed to dispose of drugs here in Kansas City?" Harper asked her.

"It's kind of a pain in the tuchus, to be honest with you. You're supposed to take it to some kind of drop off spot, but there's only 12 of them around the city. If a patient came in and told Dr. Dunham they want to be off the drugs and didn't want them around the house anymore, then Dr. Dunham took the drugs from them. Once a week, he would go in and drop them off at the drop-off spot."

My ears perked up, as Sally was admitting that Dr. Dunham didn't do things exactly the way the law required him to. I understood why he chose to dispose of the drugs for his patients, but I also wondered if that would have been a way for him to have taken drugs. He simply could take the pills surrendered to him to consume for himself.

"Now do you keep separate calendars for the patients and for other events that might come up? So, one calendar for patient visits and another calendar for non-patient visits?" I asked her.

"I know Dr. Dunham had a personal calendar. He kept it on his computer. It was a calendar that scheduled different things, like social events and continuing education courses he might be taking. He didn't put any of his patients on that calendar. I kept the calendar that scheduled the patients."

I nodded my head. "Would you be willing to give me a copy of that other calendar?"

"I don't see why not," Sally said with a smile. "Hang on, I'll go into his computer and get a copy of that for you. Sit tight."

When she left, Harper looked at me. "Just curious, what do you think we'll see on this calendar?" she asked me.

"I don't know. I just have a hunch. I mean, Sally said that pharmaceutical reps didn't visit Dr. Dunham, but they visit Dr. Gregory. I just wonder if maybe there's something on his calendar that would contradict that."

"Why would Dr. Dunham try to hide something like that?" Harper asked.

"I don't really know. I don't know if that's even the case. He obviously had an interest in making Sally believe that he wasn't prescribing drugs to his patients. And if he wasn't prescribing drugs to his patients, then why would he have a need for pharmaceutical reps to come in here? I have to admit, it's very unusual for a pain management doctor to not prescribe opiates. I mean, a lot of doctors also have alternative ways of managing pain, but they still prescribe drugs as a last resort."

Sally must've overheard us talking, because she jumped into the conversation as she walked through the conference door with a calendar in her hand. "I know, Dr. Dunham was very unusual. He used to prescribe opiates as a last resort. But within the last few months, he decided to deal with his patient's pain exclusively without drugs. He really felt he was on the cutting edge and that his method of pain management would become the protocol for doctors everywhere in the future. Clearly he had hope to do his part in making sure the opioid crisis came under control. I mean, there will always be people taking drugs for reasons other than pain, to get high or whatever, and Dr. Dunham couldn't do anything about that. But he really thought his new technique would be something used nationwide by every pain management doctor, and the opioid crisis caused by chronic pain would be wiped out. That was his ultimate ambition."

I looked at the calendar, seeing that it was mainly a social calendar, but there was a weekly visit by an individual by the name of Sharita Vance. Her visits to Dr. Dunham were once a week in the evenings.

"What are your hours here, Sally?" I asked her.

"8 to 5, Monday through Friday. I also come in from 8-noon every other Saturday."

"You don't work evenings?"

She shook her head. "No. I work enough hours as it is. I have a kid at home and I'm a single parent. Dr. Dunham never had me work late."

I decided to change tactics with my questioning. "Now, the accused in this case, Olivia Ward, she told me that Dr. Dunham was getting a lot of attention for his pioneering pain technique. Can you tell me a little bit about that?"

Sally's face brightened up. "Yes. That was most exciting thing about what he was doing. I mean, he was perfecting something. What he was already doing for his patients was amazing, but he was working hard, most nights, on perfecting something even more special and unique. He was looking to conduct a clinical trial on it, because he did a clinical trial on the last technique that was so amazing and he had already gotten inquiries from doctors around the country. He was going to be interviewed by some national magazines. *Self, Prevention,* even *Time* magazine. He was even getting invitations to appear on *The View.* He was about ready to blow up huge when he died. It's such a shame."

I showed her a copy of the calendar she had printed out. "There's a name I see coming in here every Wednesday evening. Her name is Sharita Vance. Does that name ring a bell to you?"

Sally looked perplexed. "Can I see that? That calendar I just gave you? I'll admit, I didn't really take a look at it before I gave it to you."

I handed her a copy of the calendar, and she put on a pair of reading glasses. She handed it back to me after looking at it for a minute or two, the confused look still on her face.

"Yes,"she finally said. "Ms. Vance is a pharmaceutical rep. I know who she is, because she sees Dr. Gregory all the time. I'm so sorry, I guess I was telling you the wrong thing when I said Dr. Dunham didn't see pharmaceutical reps. I guess he did." She continued to stare at the calendar while shaking her head.

I was getting ready to ask another question, when I saw she was still looking extremely confused. Her eyebrows were scrunched up, and she was staring at the table. She looked like she was lost in thought. Her lips were moving, as if she was talking to herself.

"So, you had no clue Dr. Donovan was seeing a pharmaceutical rep, right?" I asked her.

She sighed. "I guess he was. I don't know, I thought I knew him. I thought I knew what kind of practice he was keeping here. I really thought he was different from all the other pain management doctors. But maybe he wasn't. Maybe he was prescribing medicine and he just told me he wasn't."

"And this bothers you?" I knew the answer to that question. It clearly did bother her. If it didn't bother her, then she wouldn't be looking as if someone had killed her dog.

She didn't answer for a few minutes, but then she just shrugged. "I mean, he was a pain management doctor. All the other pain management doctors prescribe opioids, so I guess he was entitled to prescribe them, too. I guess I'm just disappointed. I thought he wasn't like the other doctors." She lowered her voice, and looked around, as if she was afraid somebody would hear her. "I thought I was working on behalf of a cause, not just working on behalf of a doctor. I don't want to raise my voice about it, because I think Dr. Gregory is sensitive to this sort of thing. I don't want him thinking I'm judging him or anything. But maybe I am."

Sally's reaction to finding out that Dr. Dunham had been seeing a pharmaceutical rep was interesting to me, to say the very least. "You just said you're judging him? Dr. Gregory? What do you mean by that?"

Her face got red. "Well, I think that one of the biggest crises in America today is the opioid crisis. I keep reading about how many overdose deaths are occurring every year and it's scary. I think most pain management doctors are part of the problem, not the solution. I mean, I don't want to have to look for another job, and I would have to if Dr. Gregory knew how I felt about this, but I think doctors like Dr. Gregory are the root cause of the opioid epidemic. Patients come in here with pain, he sees them for like five minutes, and they leave with a prescription for Oxycodone or Fentanyl or something else that's really addictive. He gets them hooked."

She paused for a moment and then looked around again to make sure nobody was around to hear her.

"I don't know, I guess I just don't approve of doctors who don't at least try to look for an alternative solution to drugs," she said. "I know it's easier just to give a prescription for pills, but it's really not doing anything for people. Especially people who have chronic pain. And what happens is they start to get addicted and Dr. Gregory has to cut them off. You know, he finds out they're going around to other hospitals and other doctors, trying to get prescriptions all over town, and Dr. Gregory has to say he can't give them pain meds anymore. And then they get cut off everywhere, so they have to find a street vendor to score heroin. So the opioid epidemic becomes a heroin epidemic. It just keeps going on and on, and doctors like Dr. Gregory are the reason why."

I was a bit stunned that she was so open about the role of pain management in the opioid epidemic this country was experiencing. It couldn't have been easy for her to be working for somebody who she found so abhorrent.

She shook her head. "God, I sure hope this room doesn't have a bug or anything like that. If it does, I'll lose my job. Dr. Gregory has no idea I feel this way and I can't afford to lose my job. I get paid pretty well here – $15 an hour. It pays the bills."

Sally had the demeanor and expression of somebody who had held somebody up on a pedestal and that person came crashing down before her very eyes. That probably was the case here. She thought Dr. Dunham was one thing and apparently he was somebody else. Of course, being an attorney, I didn't want to necessarily judge him without further evidence. I did, however, want to find out who this Sharita Vance was.

"So, Sharita Vance. You're familiar with who she is?" I asked Sally.

She nodded. "She's one of the usual suspects. She's pretty high-level over at Osiris pharmaceuticals. I don't know much about her, but I talked to other office managers around town, and she's everywhere. She goes to just about every pain management doctor in town and sells them on all the latest drugs that Osiris is coming out with. That's all I really know about her." She steepled her hands. "I'm just so disappointed in Dr. Dunham. I mean, he lied to me when he told me he wasn't prescribing those medicines to patients."

I had a few more questions for her. "I want to ask you about whether or not other people might have noticed that Dr. Dunham had an addiction to drugs. To your knowledge, has anybody filed a complaint against him? And that would mean not just patients, but professional organizations, like the AMA? Has anybody ever suggested he needed to be supervised?"

She appeared to think about that question for a minute or two, but then she shook her head. "No. And I would know about it. I mean, I'm the person who would field questions like that from somebody. Or a complaint like that from somebody. He trusted me and if something like that came down the pike, I would handle it. So I don't think it did. I don't think there was any need for supervision or any complaints or anything like that."

That didn't really tell me anything, except that maybe he was just very good at hiding what he was doing, assuming he was taking drugs. That was a fair assumption, considering how he died. However, it would've been helpful if there was some kind of evidence that people were concerned about him taking drugs.

I bounced my pen up and down upon the yellow pad, and I looked over at Harper. "Do you have anything you want to ask her?" I asked Harper.

She shook her head. "No," Harper said. "Thank you very much, Ms. Wallace, for seeing us. For taking the time to speak with us."

"Not a problem," she said. "If you need any more help, I'll be glad to assist you in any way I can. Don't hesitate to call."

She showed us out and I was anxious to talk to Harper. I was working on a theory in my head, but I wasn't quite sure exactly where the theory would go. There were several puzzle pieces missing, even in my head. I wanted to bounce some stuff off Harper and see what she was thinking.

We got out of the car, and Harper turned to me. "I think we need to get this Sharita Vance in for a deposition. Or, at the very least, interview her."

"I'm thinking the same thing," I said, "but I don't really know how she fits into this."

Harper looked out the window. "I don't really know how she fits into it either, but I think she somehow does." Harper looked like she was contemplating something. "You know I was reading about Tracy Dunham online and his family. One of the things that stands out to me is that his family has diversified its wealth over the years. They started out, way back when, with the old man who made his money in the railroad back in the day. But, since then, they've gone into shipping, tech, and pharmaceuticals. Pharmaceuticals."

Harper kept saying the words pharmaceuticals over and over under her breath. That was her way of brainstorming, saying something out loud, and then, sometimes, she would hit on what the right answer was. Just by saying a single word.

"Pharmaceuticals," I said. "I guess we're going to have to look and see what pharmaceutical investments his family is involved with. However, I'm not really positive exactly why it would be that his family being in pharmaceuticals would be behind what happened to Dr. Dunham."

Harper clenched her fist and unclenched it. She did that several times. "He hasn't come into his inheritance yet, remember?"

"Yeah," I said. "That does seem rather unusual. I guess we'll have to find out exactly what kind of family feud caused him to be cut out of his inheritance. I mean, not cut out exactly, but from what I can see, he hadn't gotten it at the time he died."

Harper tapped her fingers on the dashboard of the car. "How do we know he wasn't cut out completely from his inheritance? I know the records show that he hadn't yet received his inheritance at the time he died, but what if the will of his grandfather, the man responsible for the Dunham heirs getting their money, actually cut him out? What then?"

"I don't know. What are you getting at?"

She narrowed her eyes. "I don't really know. I'm just thinking out loud. Don't mind me."

We got to our office, and Harper got into her car to go home. It was getting late, and I knew I had to get home to Nate and Amelia and spend some time with them. I was just going to have to compartmental-ize, which meant that when I went home, I would have to leave my work behind. As much as I wanted to sit and stew and pick apart my inter-view with Sally Wallace, it wouldn't do Nate any favors if I did that.

As I drove home, I was apprehensive. I was getting further and further away from the answer to the question about what exactly was going on.

And I wondered if I would ever get closer to it.

FIFTEEN

Later on that day, I made an appointment to see Sharita Vance. I
called her and she told me she was busy all day on sales calls but
would fit me in that evening. As much as I hated to do that,
because I was trying to get home every evening early to see Nate and
Amelia, I also thought that maybe Sharita would be a good witness for
me. I didn't know why I was thinking that, but I did.

Harper decided to come along with me too. She still didn't have a
whole lot going on, as far as large cases. I knew why she didn't have
anything major on her plate. She didn't have the mental energy to really
take on a large case, except for second-chairing this one with me. She was
very much in demand because she had tried so many high-profile cases
and everybody knew about her. But I really got the impression that her
dance card was not so full only because she wanted it that way.

It was burnout, but it was also what was going on with Axel and
Michael Reynolds. I had great sympathy for her.

We met Sharita at Messenger, a coffee shop located downtown. It
was a large coffee shop, three stories, with overhead pipes exposed and
super high ceilings. It was definitely a very trendy place.

I went towards the back, where Sharita was sitting at a table, sipping
out of a cup. I recognized her because she told me she was wearing a

light blue cotton dress and a dark overcoat. She was an attractive black woman with short braids. She was long and lean, and when she stood up, she was a towering figure.

I shook her hand and so did Harper.

"I'm Sharita and you must be Damien and Harper. I know you talked to me over the phone about what you wanted, but I don't really understand what you're getting at. I know you want to talk to me about my visits with Dr. Dunham. But I'm confused as to how I'm going to be helping you."

I was working through a theory but I wasn't quite sold on it. "Thanks for meeting us. I know I gave you short notice and you had to squeeze us in, so I appreciate it."

She looked at her watch. "Yes, I squeezed you in. I have two more sales calls to make this evening. I make sales calls in the evening all the time. In fact, I kind of work all the time." She shrugged. "The money is good, though. If it weren't, there's no way I would be busting my tail the way I am. I want to have a life, but it's hard to do. So I'm glad you wanted to meet me here at a coffee shop because I really need to take a little break and have a croissant and a cup of coffee. So, two birds one stone, as they say."

I sent Harper over to get two cups of coffee and she walked over and placed our order. "As I was telling you over the phone, I wanted to talk to you about Dr. Dunham," I said to Sharita. "Now, I understand that you were going to his place of business once a week on Wednesday. I looked at his calendar for this year, and it seemed scheduled you into his office every Wednesday evening at 7 o'clock. Can I ask you what was the nature of your business relationship with him?"

"I was his sex slave." Then she rolled her eyes. "I was selling him on drugs, which is what I do. What other reason do you think I would be seeing him? Sorry, he wasn't my type." She sipped her coffee and didn't smile but her eyes crinkled slightly in evident mirth.

She was a bit sassy but I liked it. "Well, I figured that was probably the case. It's just that Dr. Dunham had held himself out as somebody who didn't prescribe drugs to people. That's why I was so surprised to see you had seen him once a week, every week, for a year."

"Did you ever consider that maybe, just maybe, the good Dr.

Dunham was lying to whoever thought he didn't prescribe drugs? I mean, come on, the guy was a medical doctor. An MD. He's not some farty doctor of naturopathy or something like that. Do you think a guy who's an MD and who completed a residency in pain management is never going to prescribe drugs? That's the fun part of his job."

I felt I had to correct the record just a little bit. "You do know that a doctor of naturopathy completes just as much schooling as an MD, and some are MDs, don't you?"

Sharita shrugged and sipped on her coffee. "If you say so. Hey, I'm not knocking naturopathic doctors. They have a place in the medical establishment, same as anybody else. I'm just saying that if he wanted to become a naturopathic doctor, he would've done his residency in that particular area of medicine. He didn't, so of course he's going to prescribe drugs. As I said, that's the fun part of his job."

"What new drugs did you introduce to him?" I asked her.

When I asked her that question, she shifted uncomfortably in her seat, sipped on her coffee and her eyes did not meet mine. "Why do you want to know that? What business is that of yours?"

"I was just wondering what drugs you introduced to him." She was suddenly was getting defensive and I didn't know why.

She raised an eyebrow. "If I don't answer the question, what are you going to do to me?"

I glanced over at Harper, and I saw Harper was thinking the same thing I was. I had unwittingly struck a nerve with Sharita. I had no idea why, but it was evident she did not want to answer this particular question.

"I can get you under oath, either in a deposition or at trial."

"At trial? Why will I be a relevant witness? Listen, my dad's a lawyer and I know all about fishing expeditions. Seems to me that you're trying a fishing expedition with me and I'm not having it. If you try to drag me into this case, I'll get my lawyer to quash any subpoena you try to give me. I know my rights."

I cocked my head and looked over at Harper. She was as curious as I was.

"With all due respect, Ms. Vance, you're acting like somebody who has something to hide. I'm going to find out what it is, just so you know.

And I have a feeling that once I find out what you're hiding, it'll be no problem at all trying to show a judge that you have relevant information. Which means that you *will* be a party to the case. I mean, not a party, but a witness. In trial. Now you can simply tell me what drugs you sold to Dr. Dunham, right here and now, or you can tell me in a deposition or trial. Either way. You choose."

Sharita shook her head. "You're not going to get me like that. If I tell you what you want to know, you'll drag me into the case anyway. But if I don't tell you, good luck trying to find out. And I mean that in the best possible way – good luck."

I tapped my fingers on the table. This conversation had taken a really odd turn, to say the very least. "Ms. Vance –"

She stood up and I saw she had her satchel in her hand. She threw down a $20 bill, took a sip of her coffee, and walked away without another word. I saw her go out the front door and I turned to Harper.

"Well, looks like we'll have to do some digging to find out what that was all about. I mean, all I asked her was what drugs she pitched to Dr. Dunham, and boy, did she get nasty. Very defensive. So there's something to that, obviously," I said to Harper.

"Yes, there is something to it. But how will we find out what she's hiding?"

"We're going to get a read out of Sharita's client list and the drugs she's pitched to her clients. That shouldn't be too hard to do for Anna. Assuming that the Osiris company keeps that kind of thing on the cloud. And I would imagine they probably keep it on the cloud, as the team leaders usually have to see what their team members are doing as far as what they're selling and to whom. If we can get a copy of Sharita's client lists, and what she sells to her clients, we can find out what she's been selling to Dr. Dunham."

Sixteen

20 minutes later, after Harper put in a phone call to Anna, Anna did her due diligence. Which meant she accessed Sharita Vance's client list from the cloud. In it, Harper and I found our answer.

Dr. Dunham wasn't one of her clients. We looked very carefully on the list. We even uploaded it to the computer, and did a search for the term "Dunham." But it didn't come up anywhere on her list.

"That's weird," I said to Harper. "To say the least. She was paying a visit to Dr. Dunham every week on Wednesday evening, he had her penciled in, but he wasn't one of her clients. Combine that with the fact that she got so defensive when we asked her about that, and I'm going to go out on a limb and state that something is very wrong here."

We were sitting in my office, me behind my desk, and Harper in the big leather chair in the corner of my office. She didn't seem relaxed, though - her feet were on the ottoman, but she was wiggling them to and fro.

She was playing with a Rubik's cube, mindlessly. That was something she did to focus her mind and was something I did to focus my mind as well. We had that in common.

"Maybe she was having an affair with him?" Harper said to nobody in particular.

Truth be told, that was the first thing I thought as well. But then again, it didn't make much sense to me. "No. I don't think so. Why would he put her on his calendar every week? Why would she try to play it off like she was paying him professional visits?"

"It's pretty obvious. The guy was married, so Sharita had to come up with a good answer on what she was doing in his office every week. Maybe she's just really weird about adultery. Maybe she's embarrassed. Ashamed. People do all kinds of things when they're embarrassed and ashamed, including lie."

I thought about that for a few minutes, but it just wasn't ringing true to me. "No. I think it's something else. I think it's something much more nefarious, but I just can't put a finger on what. She's got a game going and I don't know exactly what that game is."

Harper got up from the chair and went over to the window. She put her hands on the window ledge and stretched her legs. She looked a bit like a ballerina, and I thought that maybe she was doing it unconsciously. Harper wasn't acting like she was very comfortable, and I didn't really know why.

"Well, I'm not really sure how we're supposed to get a straight answer from her," Harper said. "We certainly can't tell her that we illegally obtained her client list. And she's right about one thing – it's going to be tough to show the judge her relevance in this case. Unless we think that maybe she killed him but that's a long shot. We're going to have to gather something else on her, something we can sink our teeth into, before we can drag her into this case. If we drag her into this case, then we can obviously get her to answer questions under oath, but we're going to have to come up with more."

"I can just depose her and hope she doesn't come up with a motion to quash the deposition subpoena. After all, Rule 25.12 says we can depose any person. It doesn't say, obviously, that the person has to be material. And who knows, she might end up becoming material by the end of this."

Harper turned around. "I suppose it's a good idea to get her to answer questions under oath. I just wonder if she'll be the kind to actually tell the truth. Somehow, I think she won't be."

Harper started to pace. She was making me a bit nervous, so I decided to try to talk her down.

"Harper," I began. "What's going on? You're as nervous as a pregnant nun."

She put her hand through her hair and pulled it. "You noticed. I don't know, I'm still rattled over seeing Michael Reynolds in here. I'm just afraid he's going to do something to me or my daughters. You have to remember, he hates me. He went to prison because of me. Well, no, that's not necessarily true. He went to prison because he killed somebody, but he would've gotten off the first time if I didn't do such a terrible job with his case. He blames me because that's just the kind of person he is. He'll never take responsibility for the things he's done. And I know he thinks I put you up to suing him. I just think he's dangerous."

"Harper, the guy killed somebody. And he has raped at least one person, you, and probably many more. I think it's a safe assumption that he's dangerous. And I'm sorry for bringing him back into your life. I didn't think would just show up here, although I probably should've figured that would happen."

"Damien, it's okay. Really, it's all right. I'm happy you're bringing a lawsuit against him. It's just that, I don't know, seeing him triggers me. All I want to do is find a gun and kill him myself. Put him out of his misery, along with the world. The world would be such a better place if he wasn't in it."

I started to think that maybe the whole bringing-a-lawsuit-against-Michael-Reynolds-thing was not such a good idea. Yet I also needed to see it through. I started to think Harper would need this as a kind of catharsis.

She sat back down. "Don't worry, Damien. I'll be okay. Now where were we?"

Harper and I sat and mapped out a strategy about how we would get Sharita to admit to why she visited Dr. Dunham's office so frequently. But first, I figured it was important to talk to my mother about it. I had a feeling that maybe she knew more about Tracy Dunham than what she was letting on.

I also had a feeling that maybe she had an answer about the mysterious Sharita Vance angle.

SEVENTEEN

"Sharita Vance," Mom was saying when I went to visit her at her trailer. It was just the two of us, as Harper had an emergency to attend to. Something about Rina's boyfriend breaking up with her, or something of the sort. All I knew was that Harper took the call and was trying to talk Rina down. She was apologetic, but said she had to get home because Rina was apparently hysterical.

"Yes, Sharita Vance. Did Tracy ever mention somebody by that name?"

Mom shook her head. "I don't know nobody named Sharita Vance, and I don't know that Tracy knew somebody named that, either. Unless..."

"Unless, what?"

Mom looked like she was lost in thought. "Oh, I don't really know. I do remember that one night, my car broke down, and I called him to see if he could give me a ride somewhere. I think I was feeling cooped up in here, and I had to get out of here or else I would run screaming into the night. So I go out and start my car, it's deader than a doornail, my neighbor Vicki, she's not around. So I called Tracy. He tells me he can't come and take me anywhere, because he was meeting some woman at his office."

"Is there anything else you can remember about this woman?"

Mom got up and went to her fridge, and brought back two bottles of beer, one for me and one for her. I opened it up, and took a sip. It was Milwaukee's Best, not my favorite - I preferred PBR when I was drinking cheap beers - but it would have to do.

"I'm thinking, I'm thinking." Mom took a sip of her beer, and shook her head. "I don't know. I'm thinking Sharita Vance might be the name of the woman trying to get him drugs to push on his patients, but that was all she gave him. You know, they got those people that go to doctors' offices and try to push different kinds of pills down the doctors' throat. Then the doctors are supposed to push those same pills down their patient's throats. Tracy, he told me he don't push pills down patient's throats, so I asked him why he would have a pill-pusher lady in his office. He just laughed."

This was getting interesting. From the look of Dr. Dunham's calendar, Sharita Vance was seen in his office every week for at least a year. If she wasn't selling him on drugs, what was she doing there?

"He never told you why he had a pharmaceutical rep in his office every week?"

Mom just shrugged and took a sip of her beer. "I don't know, I guess maybe she was pushing pill samples on him."

What did that mean? Maybe Sharita was dropping off pill samples of some sort to Dr. Dunham, but there was no way she could've been dropping off pill samples germane to Dr. Dunham's practice - opioids, being a controlled substance, weren't offered by pharm companies in sample form.

Curiouser and curiouser...

"Why are you so hot onto this Sharita Vance woman?" Mom asked me.

"I don't really know. I just have a feeling she's going to be the linchpin of this entire case. I don't really know how she fits into it, however."

Mom just laughed. "Damien, Tracy bit it because of heroin, not some namby-pamby prescription drug. That woman was pushing the hillbilly heroin, not the real stuff. Unless she had some business going on the side."

Maybe that was the case. Maybe Sharita was a pusher of illegal drugs. That would actually make some sense in my mind. I thought about what she said, about how she complained about working all those hours but was happy with the money. What if she was looking to get out of the pharmaceutical sales game, and all of its long hours, and into something much more lucrative with fewer hours?

I didn't want to jump the gun, but I wondered if Sharita was the illicit drug dealer I was trying to find.

If so, how would I prove it?

I decided to see Tracy Dunham's office manager again. I remembered she was very helpful the first time I went to see her, and very good about answering questions to the best of her knowledge. So I made an appointment for Harper and me to go back over to the office.

I also hoped that maybe she would let me into Tracy's actual office, so I could take a look around. I'd hoped to find any pills lying around the office, as I knew the police had not yet cordoned off Tracy's office for investigation. I didn't know if they were going to cordon off his office. I thought they probably would not since this was not a typical murder case. It was a drug overdose case treated as a murder. Because of this, the investigation had not yet extended to Tracy Dunham's place of business. Until I got notice his office was treated as a crime scene, it was fair game, as far as I was concerned.

When Harper and I went to see Sally Wallace, she was just as helpful as the first time. I was afraid that wouldn't be the case, like maybe somebody had gotten to her, but she seemed to be open to whatever we needed to do.

"Now, what do you need from me again?" she asked me.

I cleared my throat. "The last time I was here, I wanted to ask you if you would allow me into Dr. Dunham's actual office. And I was wondering if you would let me do that." I would be looking for any drugs left in the office by Sharita.

I think Sally read my mind, because she handed me a garbage sack filled with little boxes with pills in foil packs. "Maybe this is what you are looking for?" She lowered her voice and looked around. "I don't want anybody to know I found this. I don't know, I guess I was maybe wrong about what I told you about Dr. Dunham."

"What do you mean?"

"He might have been prescribing opioids to patients. Well, I mean, he didn't prescribe opioids to patients, but he was apparently prescribing opioids to one patient."

"Who?"

"Sharita Vance." She took a deep breath. "I went into his office and found his scrip pad. It has carbon copies, like a checkbook. And he apparently prescribed Oxycontin to Sharita Vance every single week. A seven day supply of Oxycontin every week."

Huh. That was weird. "Are you sure about this?"

"Yes. I mean, her name was the only name on his scrip pad. The only one. But I'll tell you what was weird."

"And what's that?"

"Well, I found this." She handed me a bottle of Oxycontin. I looked at the name on the prescription bottle, and the name was Sharita Vance.

I furrowed my brow. "I wonder why he would have a bottle of her prescription in his office?"

"I don't know," Sally said. "That's the question I had."

I opened up the bottle and saw one more pill. "Do you mind terribly if I took this bottle and this pill?" For some odd reason, I thought it was important to keep it.

"No, of course not. Go ahead and keep it. Maybe it will help you solve the mystery somehow."

"Yeah, maybe." I shook my head. "Weird. Well, thank you very much for being so cooperative."

Sally smiled. "Of course I'll be cooperative. I want you to get to the bottom of this, the same as anybody else. Probably more than anybody else. I just hate thinking that Dr. Dunham died not because he was addicted, but because somebody wanted him dead. And I don't think that somebody was your client."

It was odd that she would say that. "Now, why do you think somebody wanted him dead?"

"It's just a hunch I have. I can't really explain it. It's just something that makes the hair on the back of my arms stand up. Maybe it's just because I didn't know he was entertaining a pharmaceutical rep, and now I found out who it was. And now I see he was writing a scrip to Sharita Vance every week. Something's just not right. I hope you can find it."

I left her office after asking a few more questions, but my interrogation of her was just sticking with me. She was so sure that there was something more to Dr. Dunham's death than what I was seeing, and I would have to figure it out.

EIGHTEEN

I went back over to my mom's and she was lying on the couch.

"Come on in. Don't mind me, even though I'm feeling like death warmed over. Again."

"What? You're sick?"

"Yeah. I am. I had a bladder infection a couple of months ago, and now I'm feeling like an elephant's sitting on my chest. I still got some of those antibiotics I got from the bladder infection, so I'm going to take them for this, too."

I rolled my eyes. "Mom, you do know the first rule of antibiotic usage, don't you? The first rule is that you take every single pill prescribed, even if you start feeling better. If you don't, you'll get sicker the next time because you don't kill off every bad bug. You just kill off the weaker bugs, leaving the stronger ones behind. That means you get a super-bug the next time."

Mom just shrugged. "I don't need your lecture, Dr. Damien. I felt better in a day, so I just started drinking cranberry juice. I ain't gonna waste antibiotics because you never know when you're gonna need them again." She started hacking and then lay back down. "Like now. If I didn't have those leftover antibiotics, I'd just have to suffer. Ain't no way I could afford to see a doctor again and buy more antibiotics. That crap's expensive, especially if you don't have insurance. And I ain't got no insurance, so there you go. It's all expensive for me."

Missouri was a state that refused to expand Medicaid, so that meant people like my mom, who was making $10 an hour at Wal-Mart, weren't eligible. Nobody was eligible for Medicaid in Missouri except if you had minor children, which she didn't. Unfortunately, since my mom worked only part-time, sometimes 30 hours per week, sometimes less, she made too little to qualify for Obamacare subsidies. She was in that donut hole - didn't qualify for Medicaid, because she didn't have minor children, making too little to qualify for Obamacare subsidies, and her job didn't provide her health insurance.

That meant she had two choices - don't get sick or pay out the nose for care. I was always trying to help her out financially, but she would never take it. I quit trying after awhile.

"I'll just come back," I said. "When you're feeling better."

Mom rolled her eyes. "I ain't catching, son. You can stick around. You came here to ask me stuff, so ask me."

"Mom, I-" I stopped, because I remembered reading something about false positives on drug tests. She took the antibiotics a few months ago? "Wait, were you taking those antibiotics the night they took your drug test? Is that right?"

"Yeah, that's right. I was feeling like crap for days, not pissing like I should be, feeling like I always gotta pee but nothing would come out. Then I started pissing blood, so I went to a doctor and she set me up with an antibiotic prescription. Why?"

"Let me see that bottle," I said.

"Go and get it. I don't feel like getting up off this couch." She hacked some more and I went into her bathroom and opened her medicine cabinet.

The antibiotic prescribed to her was Cipro.

I went back into the living room, where mom was laying on the couch. "Mom, how do you take this antibiotic?" I already knew she didn't take it correctly, as she apparently quit taking the drug before she was done with the course of treatment.

"What do you mean, how do I take it?"

"I mean, do you take it as prescribed - twice a day?" I looked at the bottle and saw it directed her to take two a day, every day, for 10 days. I knew something about antibiotics and realized that mom must have had a serious infection by the time she saw her doctor. Usually the course is only 3 days.

Mom coughed some more. "Son, I was feeling like crap. So I took five pills one day and five the next. Cleared it right up, although it did make me feel sick. Now I got the other 10 pills left and I'm gonna take them for the crap I got right now."

I closed my eyes. "Mom, did you take these pills before they gave you the urine test the night Tracy died?"

"Yeah I did. I took those ten pills in two days and they gave me a drug test that night, right after I took all ten of those pills. Why do you ask?"

I shook my head. "Nothing, let me check something real quick."

I got on the Internet and Googled "False positives for opioids." I looked at the chart that showed all the drugs that would cause false positives for various narcotics and saw that Fluoroquinolones was implicated in causing false positives for opioids. A quick check on Fluoroquinolones showed that Cipro was a type of Fluoroquinolone.

I nodded my head. "I think I know why you tested positive for opioids." I pounded my fist on the desk. "Dammit. No way I can ask for a re-test now. I'm just going to have to attack the test in court." I looked again at the drug test done on my mom, and saw the threshold for a positive test was 2000 ng/ml, which stood for nanograms per milliliter. That was a high threshold, but some quick reviews of the medical journals on the topic of false positives for opiates showed that false positives happened in opioid testing even when the threshold was as high as 2000 ng/ml. Sometimes a poppy seed bagel would be enough to cause a false-positive, but at lower ng levels.

And my mom was taking more of the Cipro than prescribed. Much more. That would have set off the drug test for sure.

Mom finally got off the couch, hacking away. "Damien, what's going on?"

"Mom, I think can show the jury that you weren't taking heroin or any kind of opioids. I'm probably going to have to get your medical records entered into evidence under the Business Records Exception to the Hearsay rule. Then I'll have to hire an expert who can come in and testify that Cipro can cause a false positive on a drug test. But that's all I can really do. It'll be up to the jury to believe it or not. I don't know Mom, it might be a long-shot, as false positives happen rarely, even when you take antibiotics."

Mom shook her head, coughed some more, and then lay back down on the couch. "Damien, I feel like crap. Give me some of that Cipro."

"Mom, no. I'm not going to let you do that. You probably have a respiratory infection, which means it's a different thing from your bladder infection. You probably need to take different antibiotics for it. I'm going to take you into Urgent Care and see if you can get a whole new prescription for what you have. In the meantime, I have to figure out what expert can come into court to testify about the possibility that you had a false positive on your drug test."

Mom looked confused. "Damien, does that mean those bastards are gonna have to drop the charges against me? You show them I ain't taking no drugs when Tracy was here and the prosecutors will say 'never mind?' Because that's what I'm looking for."

I sighed. "I can try that, but I don't think it'll work. For one, it's a long-shot that your drug test was a false positive. For another, there's the issue of your BP drugs actually being heroin, but I can challenge the chain of custody on that one." Then again..."Well, considering you were taking, what, five times the dose you were supposed to, it was probably a pretty high probability that the drug test you took would go off on opioids. What were you thinking?"

Because she was only supposed to take one pill every twelve hours and she apparently took 10 pills in two days, I figured her blood had five times the amount of the drug than normal, at least if the test was done right after she took the last five pills. An expert could speak to that a bit better, however.

"Don't lecture me, Damien. I felt like crap. I needed to get better quick because I had to work. If I don't work, I don't get paid. I figured that if I took a bunch of the pills at once, it would knock the crap out my body that much faster. It worked. I always put more spices into my food than recipe books ask for, and it's the same principle. A recipe calls for 1/4 tsp of rosemary, I put a tablespoon in. Always makes it better. The more the merrier."

"Mom, these are not spices we're talking about. We're talking about a drug. If a doctor tells you how to take a drug, you take it just like they say. Now, we're going into Urgent Care to get you some new antibiotics for your apparent respiratory infection, which might just be a cold. If it is a cold, no antibiotics will work for you."

Mom coughed and then shook her head. "What do you mean, antibiotics don't work for a cold? I always take antibiotics whenever I get a cold."

"Colds are caused by viruses. So are viral flus and viral pneumonia. Any kind of virus. And how can you afford to keep getting antibiotics whenever you get a cold, anyhow?"

She shrugged. "I used to get them from Nicolle, my across-the-street neighbor. She had some kind of sickly kid and had a bunch of leftover antibiotics. I'd get them from her. She moved away a few months ago, though, so I had to get my own prescription for antibiotics."

I groaned. I was tempted to go off on her on how dangerous it was to take antibiotics, pell-mell, willy-nilly, but I figured it would fall on deaf ears. Most of the things I said to my mother usually fell on deaf ears. My mother wasn't one to be reasoned with, I had discovered over the years.

Mom stood up and pointed to me while hacking. "You ain't taking me nowhere, son. Listen, I gotta work in a couple of hours. I get into one of those Urgent Care circles of hell and I'll never get out of there anytime today. You ever been to one of those places? Nothing but hacking kids and old people sleeping in the chairs. It's November, there's going to be lots of those snot-nosed brats, too, screaming and crying. No, thank you. I'll just take the rest of this Cipro and I'll be fine."

Ordinarily, I would throw up my hands in frustration when my mother stonewalled me on something like this. But I had leverage this time and I would use it.

"Mom, either you come with me to the Urgent Care or I'll withdraw from your case and you'll have no attorney at all." I crossed my arms in front of me. She wasn't eligible for the Public Defender's Office, as she was out on bail, and it was the policy of the PD's office to not take clients on if they had the money to put up for bail. I had faith in the Kansas City Public Defender's office, but Mom wasn't eligible, and that was that.

"Go right ahead," Mom said. "I'll just go down and get me one of those public defenders. I hear those lawyers are pretty damned good."

I shook my head. "You don't qualify. You made bond, so you theoretically have enough money to hire your own attorney. They won't take you. Now you can try to defend yourself in court, but boy, if you do that, you'll have a huge fool for a client. You won't even know how to defend yourself, so don't even try."

Mom waved her hand at me dismissively. "You won't leave me high and dry. I'm your momma. You're too high-falutin. If you admit to your muckety-muck friends that you got a momma in the joint, you won't get invited to your fancy parties no more."

I sighed. "Mom, I don't go to fancy parties. And my friends, the only ones I care about, anyhow, were all in prison themselves until just recently, or did you forget about that? I hardly think they'll care if you're sent up the river yourself. You're making excuses and it's time to stop. You need to come with me and get some antibiotics geared towards a respiratory infection, if that's what you got."

Mom shook her head, but then she made a fist and looked like she would haul off and hit me. "Damien, do you ever get tired of trying to run my life? From where I sit, you've made a pretty good mess of your own life, so where do you get off trying to tell me what to do?"

Mom was really good at throwing my past in my face, I gave her that.

"Mom, you're right. I've made a mess of things in my personal life. No doubt about it. But that has nothing to do with this. You need to see a doctor and try to get well. Personally, I suspect you probably have a regular cold, so you can't get antibiotics, but if that's the case, then that's the case. You'll just have to rest and wait it out, just like the rest of the world. But what you cannot do is take the rest of your Cipro and call it good. Now, either you come with me to the Urgent Care or you can represent yourself in your murder trial. Your choice."

I had her there and she knew it. She could try to call my bluff, and, truth be told, I had no idea what I would do if she did.

To my relief, she got up and went to her coat closet and put on a coat. "I'll be waiting in the car."

I smiled. "I knew you would be."

NINETEEN

After I took Mom to the Urgent Care - it was just like she said it would be, with a waiting room filled with sniffling kids and old people falling asleep - and the doctor informed her that she tested positive for the common cold, therefore she couldn't get antibiotics, after which my mom apparently threw such a fit that she came away with a prescription for Amoxicillin, I went home to see my kids.

I resented my mom because getting her to do anything was always like pulling teeth. It took forever to convince her to go to the clinic, and the only reason I had to go with her in the first place was because of her stubborn insistence on treating herself with leftover antibiotics. I really should have been home with the kids instead of dealing with my mom's nonsense.

I had dinner with the kids, and Nate was seeming more upbeat than I had seem him in a long time. I still hadn't gotten the anti-depressants I was supposed to pick up, and I felt that maybe I wouldn't need to after all. Nate seemed to thrive on the basketball team and he managed to get to practice and back by getting a ride with a new friend, Austin McCray. I was happy Nate was hanging out with Austin. I worried he was too much of a loner and maybe he wasn't fitting in at school. I was even more encouraged to find out that Austin was one of the more popular kids at Nate's school.

After dinner, Amelia broke the news to me. "Dad, Nate's gay. Austin is his boyfriend." She said that so matter-of-factly that I thought she was joking. She was like that a lot of times. She had a wry sense of humor that was remarkably well-developed for a 9-year-old.

"What are you talking about? He's 11."

Amelia shrugged. "So what? I have a gay kid in my fourth grade class. You don't think kids are gay at Nate's age?" She snorted. "Welcome to the twenty-first century, Dad."

I nodded. It was all making sense. I wondered how long Nate had been struggling with this. Maybe his being gay was the reason he had been so depressed for so long? I thought, all along, that it was some kind of chemical imbalance and he had clinical depression. That wouldn't have been out of the realm of probability, as Sarah always showed signs of mental illness, including depression, throughout our marriage. I just figured Nate got Sarah's bad genes.

But if he was gay and was struggling with it...

"How do you know Nate's gay?"

Amelia got up from the dinner table, took her plate into the kitchen, and then sat back down at the dining room table. "I heard Nate talking to Austin on the phone. I can tell."

"What do you mean, you can tell?" I asked her. She was being too vague for my taste.

"I can just tell, that's all, Dad," Amelia said. "Can I be excused? I got homework to do."

"Yeah, sure," I said. "Where's Nate right now?"

Amelia rolled her eyes. "Zooming with Austin. Like, they see each other at school all the time, you'd think they wouldn't have anything to talk about, right? But they gossip worse than any girl I know at school. It's weird. I mean, I guess Nate's more of a girl than a boy, so maybe that's why he never runs out of things to talk about with Austin. Can I be excused?"

"Yeah, I said you could," I said, maybe in a snappish tone I didn't really mean. "And listen, I don't want you saying rude things about your brother behind his back."

She rolled her eyes. "What did I say?"

"You said he was more of a girl than a boy. I don't want to hear those demeaning things out of your mouth. Not to his face and not behind his back."

Amelia gave me a look. "Sorry," she said in a bratty tone-of-voice, so that it came out drawn out like sorrryyy. Then she ran upstairs and slammed her door.

I sat at the dining room table, staring at the leftover chicken and sad mashed potatoes, wondering how to talk with Nate about his sexuality. When a kid at school, James Royal, teased Nate and bullied him about being gay, which ostensibly was the reason why Nate brought a gun into his school that one day, I didn't think anything of it. I just figured James didn't know what he was talking about.

Now, if Amelia was right, Nate really was gay. There was just no way I could bring it up to him, though. I figured that if he wanted to tell me, he would. He didn't talk to me about it, so I had to think he wasn't ready to go into it.

I cleared the table, and made myself a glass of scotch on the rocks. I took it into my den and put the television on. Some program was on, but I wasn't really tuned into it so much. All I could think about was that my son was possibly gay and I wasn't quite sure how to handle it.

I wanted to talk to somebody about it but I thought I would be betraying Nate if I called Harper to ask her about it. He hadn't told me, so who was I to turn around and tell somebody else his secret?

I shook my head and drank some more. I was just going to have to forget about this Nate thing until he was ready to talk, and just focus my energies on the two cases occupying my mind.

I called Harper and tell her about the antibiotics thing. I wanted to pick her brain on what expert we could hire to explain the concept of false positives on a drug test. If I could just show the jury that my mom maybe didn't have opiates in her system at the time of Dr. Dunham's death, then maybe, just maybe, I could win the case - at least assuming I could challenge the heroin found at the scene.

I would try to challenge the finding of the drugs on two different grounds - one, I would have to show it was an illegal seizure. My mother wasn't under arrest at that time, nor was there probable cause to arrest her. She gave them permission to search her medicine cabinet, that was true, but that didn't negate the fact that they didn't have probable cause for the search in the first place. If the probable cause thing didn't work, and the judge allowed testimony on the drug, then I would challenge it on the grounds that a very poor chain-of-custody record was kept. If the cops couldn't show the drug tested in their lab was the same drug they took from my mom's house, and they couldn't in this case, because they didn't keep a decent record, I could get it thrown out that way.

Once I got that heroin thrown out, it would be a matter of me working on the dirty UA. The prosecutors were relying on the fact that my mother was high and had evidently supplied drugs to Dr. Dunham that night in order to show my mom was liable for his death. If Mom wasn't high, and the heroin gets thrown out, their case would fall apart. They could still try to show my mother supplied him with drugs but that would be really hard to do. If she wasn't high, why would she give him drugs? That didn't make much sense - if somebody comes over to your house, you wouldn't give that person drugs if you weren't also going to take them.

At any rate, if I was able to successfully challenge the drug test, the prosecutor suddenly had a very shaky case. Even more shaky than it already was.

Harper picked up on the third ring. "Hey, Damien," she said. "How are things?"

"Fine," I said, then the words just tumbled out of my mouth. "Nate's gay and I don't really know how to talk to him about it." I shook my head and silently kicked myself. That wasn't supposed to happen. I wasn't supposed to be calling Nate out like that. "And also, my mom was taking Cipro at the time of the drug test. Taking it badly, I might add. She took five pills the night she was arrested and five pills the night before. I think I can challenge the drug test and I was wondering if you knew a good expert who could testify about false positives."

"Well, yeah, I have a good hired gun for something like that. That's interesting that your mom was taking a drug known to cause false positives for opiates. I guess we'll just have to get her medical records into evidence and get a hired gun and approach the trial that way. I think we can show Dr. Dunham's overdose was an unfortunate accident."

I felt embarrassed about blurting out about Nate, so I wanted to get off the phone before she could ask me any questions about my son. "Well, good talking to you. I'll be seeing you tomorrow. We can brainstorm this a little bit more, huh?"

"Yeah." She hesitated. "So, Nate. Are you sure?"

"No, I'm not sure. I shouldn't have said anything. Forget I said a word. Please, Harper, forget I said anything."

"I will," she said. "But if you need to talk to me about it, don't hesitate. I know something about it. My dad turned out to be gay, after all."

"Yeah, thanks," I said. "I'll see you tomorrow."

At that, I hung up the phone, forgetting to even say goodbye.

After I got off the phone, I put my head in my hands.

Just one more thing I would have to deal with.

Another day in the life of Damien Harrington.

No big deal.

TWENTY

Things were going along pretty well on the Michael Reynolds front. I got him scheduled in for a deposition and I had bombarded him with discovery requests. True to what he was saying, he didn't hire an attorney. I had a feeling that, before everything was said and done, I would get a default judgment against him. That was because the guy didn't have an attorney and I was intentionally burying him in discovery requests. If he didn't have an attorney to guide him on the proper procedure to make motions to the court about my discovery requests, because even I had to admit they were unduly burdensome, then I thought he couldn't comply. I thought he probably couldn't come up with all the documents I'd asked for and probably couldn't answer all the interrogatory questions I sent to him.

Not only that, but I anticipated that he would miss some filing deadlines. I would make it as hard as possible for him in hopes of wearing him down, make him miss a filing deadline or not come to a deposition, and then I would ask the court to enter judgment on my client's behalf.

On the day of the deposition, Audrey Blackwood appeared. She was dressed in a new suit, her hair in a bun. She looked very anxious and nervous. As she sat in my office, she had a handkerchief in her hand that she was wringing, over and over and over.

I felt a great amount of compassion for her. This was a woman who was broken, grieving intensely. Her pain was palpable – I could feel it on my skin.

"Now tell me again why I'm here?" she asked me. "I guess I don't really understand what a deposition is. I mean, why can't we just go to trial and make him testify on the stand?"

I explained to her my strategy for this case. Ordinarily, I scheduled depositions as a discovery device. They were usually useful to find out information and other avenues I needed to pursue, and maybe the names of other people who might be useful to the case. Also, depositions were helpful to lock-in testimony. That way, if the person tries to get up on the stand and lie, I'd have their answers in the deposition to show the jury they were lying.

In this case, however, the deposition served those purposes, but it was also designed specifically to be another burdensome exercise that Michael Reynolds wouldn't participate in. If he didn't show for the deposition, I could ask for a contempt order and probably receive it, and it would be one more building block in my eventual motion for a default judgment.

"The deposition is important as a pretrial discovery device," I explained to Audrey. "It locks in testimony so that if he tries to lie on the stand, I can hit him with a prior inconsistent statement. Also, the questions I ask him will be designed to lead me to other avenues I might explore. I'll also ask him about witnesses and questions of that nature. Also, taking a deposition will help me see what the weaknesses are of the case."

"What if he doesn't show?" Audrey asked, her hands still wringing the handkerchief tightly.

I smiled. "If he doesn't show, then I can ask a judge to hold him in contempt. That would mean he would have to pay attorney's fees and the cost of having the court reporter here. If he doesn't show repeatedly, or if he's ordered to pay fees and doesn't do it, I can ask for him to be thrown in jail. He wouldn't be able to get out of jail until the fees are paid, or he is no longer in breach of the order, whatever that order may be."

Audrey nodded. She bit her lower lip. "I have to say, I'm a little bit nervous about all of this. I've never done anything like this before. I've never been in a lawsuit or anything like that before. And I'm scared. I'm scared about what he's going to say about my daughter. I'm afraid he's going to say things about her that maybe I don't want to hear."

I had to admit, that was concerning me. It seemed that maybe Audrey Blackwood might have known something about her daughter that she wasn't telling me.

"Why are you nervous about that? Was Carrie a different kind of person than what you told me?"

Audrey was silent for a few minutes, but then she shook her head. "No. No. Carrie was a good girl. She would never willingly participate in something vile like a sex tape. I believed her when she said she was raped by that man, and I believed her when she said she had nothing to do with that video going online. I believed her. There's no reason I wouldn't have believed her."

Audrey was not exactly convincing me, but there was nothing I could really do about it. I would just have to get into the particulars of this case and hope everything worked out in the end.

Harper poked her head into the office. "I was going to get some lunch and I was wondering if you wanted anything? I'm going to that Mixx place to get a salad."

The Mixx was a little salad and sandwich joint by the Plaza library. Harper loved that place because she could get any kind of salad she wanted and the place just mixed it up. You could get any kind of vegetable, meat, seed, cheese and salad dressing, in any combination. It was a very popular joint and Harper went there all the time. Especially since our office was right off the Country Club Plaza, that place was very convenient.

"Uh, Harper, this is Audrey Blackwood. She's a plaintiff in the case against Michael Reynolds." I had told Harper ahead of time that Michael was scheduled in for a deposition, and Harper told me she wanted to meet Audrey. That was probably the reason why Harper chose this time to ask about whether or not I wanted lunch at The Mixx.

Harper came into the office and sat down next to Audrey. "I'm very glad to meet you." Harper took Audrey's hand and clasped it with her own. "I wanted you to know that I think it's incredibly brave what you're doing. It can't be easy for you to have to relive your daughter's situation."

Audrey smiled. "It's not easy. It's never easy. You know the old cliché, you're not supposed to bury your child. You're not supposed to be the one who lives on. It's not the natural order of things. I never dreamed I would die after my daughter. I think about her every day. Every minute of every day. I wonder what I missed. How could I have missed the signs that she was so depressed? I don't know how I couldn't see how humiliated and degraded she felt when that video went viral. I don't think I can ever get over it."

Harper nodded. I knew she was feeling this woman. Harper was too professional to tell this woman what Michael had done to her, but I knew that it was on the forefront of her mind.

Harper looked at me. "When is Michael supposed to be here?"

I looked at the clock. "A half-hour ago. The court reporter has been sitting in the conference room waiting for him to show. He doesn't have an attorney. He told me he wouldn't hire counsel, so I wouldn't be surprised if he missed this. I wouldn't be surprised at all."

Harper still sat in the office. It looked like she was just going to hang out with us, and not get lunch after all. I thought Harper was just as anxious as Audrey, maybe moreso. Harper knew, as well as I did, that if Michael Reynolds didn't appear for a deposition, and didn't respond to discovery requests, and didn't file an answer to my petition, I could get a default judgment against him, which would be the best thing for everybody except for Michael himself. I knew Audrey wanted her day in court, and I didn't want to deny her that, but I also thought that it would be mentally and emotionally better for her if she didn't have to sit through a protracted trial.

. . .

An hour later, Michael still hadn't shown, so I sent the court reporter away. I then sat down at my desk and immediately prepared a motion for sanctions, and a motion to hold Michael in contempt of court. As far as I was concerned, I was one step closer to getting a default judgment against the guy. One step closer to ruining his life without him even being aware of it.

I felt a certain sense of satisfaction with my strategy. If it worked out, it would be maximum punishment for him and minimal work for me.

This would be the easiest judgment I would ever get.

TWENTY-ONE

When Harper got into the office the next day, I asked if she could meet me in the conference room. I wanted to brainstorm my mom's case with her, and I knew she had court in the afternoon, as did I. Mine was just a DUI plea, but I nevertheless had to show up for my client.

"Sure," Harper said, a cup of coffee in one hand and a donut in the other. "I'll be in in just a second."

I went down the hall into the conference room and spread out the information I had on the conference table. Harper came down and joined me in a matter of minutes.

"Okay," I said to Harper when she came into the conference room. "I wanted to brainstorm this whole thing with you. I got to thinking last night that I maybe knew where this was going, but I had a weird dream last night about Sally Wallace. In my dream, she kept saying that somebody wanted Dr. Dunham dead. Also, if we could convince the jury that mom's drug test was a false positive, we might conclude that Dr. Dunham's death was an unfortunate accidental overdose and call it a day. We might be able to show the jury that, too. But I have a feeling there's something more. We need to dig deeper on this."

Harper sat down, took a bite of her donut and a sip of her coffee and nodded. "I agree, actually. I was just thinking it would be easiest to convince the jury it was an accidental overdose that your mother had nothing to do with. That would be easiest, but you're right. I think there's something more and I keep circling back to Sharita Vance and her weird reaction when you asked her what drugs she pitched to Dr. Dunham. I think we need to figure out what was going on."

She pointed to the bottle of Oxycontin on the conference table, the bottle we got from Sally Wallace. "I think that we need to send that pill in for testing. Find out what was in it. I mean, I know it says Oxycontin on the bottle but I still think we should have it tested. I just have my own gut feeling about this case, and I think the key to the case is showing Dr. Dunham might have ingested a drug he wasn't prepared to ingest."

I had to admit, I didn't think about that angle. "Tell me your thinking," I said.

"Well, here's what I started to put together last night after I put the kids to bed. I was up until 4 in the morning, trying to put the puzzle pieces together. And you and I kept talking about why a pain management doctor would take a street drug like heroin. I started to really think about it, rolling that question around in my mind, over and over."

"Go on..."

"Well, Sally genuinely thought Dr. Dunham didn't prescribe pain meds, right? Yet he prescribed them - once a week, every week, to Sharita Vance. She was the only person he prescribed drugs to."

"Right...." I had no idea where she was going with this, but she did.

"Well, okay. He's prescribing drugs to Sharita Vance once a week, and she sees him once a week. Now, don't you think that's a little bit odd? I mean, yeah, when you're on opioids, you have to come in for follow-up visits, but every week? And why wasn't she on his patient list?"

"That's right, she was on his social calendar, not his patient calendar." I had to really think about this.

"Right." Harper was nodding excitedly. "So, we have four weird things about this. One, Sharita was seeing him every single week for something. It wasn't follow-up visits, because you don't have to see your doctor every time you get a prescription refilled, not even with opioids."

"And two..."

"Two, Sharita wasn't on his patient calendar. Three, she was the only person he was prescribing drugs to. And four, the bottle of Oxycontin with Sharita's name was found in Dr. Dunham's office. Why would he have a prescription with her name on it in his office?"

"So, what's your theory?"

"Here's what I came up with. What if Dr. Dunham was prescribing drugs to Sharita and she was selling them back to him?"

I thought about what Harper was saying. "Huh...let me think about this."

"It makes sense," Harper said. "It's the only thing that makes sense to me. I mean, it would work beautifully, if you think about it. If Dr. Dunham was a drug addict, how would he get his hands on drugs? Pharmaceutical reps can't send him samples. Opioids are Schedule II, which means they're controlled. He can't write scrips to himself. So, he gets a confederate, he gives her a bogus diagnosis of some kind of chronic pain, he writes her a scrip, she sells it back to him."

"I've never heard of that kind of thing."

"Neither have I, but can you poke a hole in that theory?"

I shook my head. "No, actually. I think it would work. But Dr. Dunham died of a heroin overdose, not an Oxycontin overdose."

"Right," Harper said. "That's why I want to send that pill in for testing. I'm thinking that if we do that, we'll find the pill isn't Oxycontin at all, but pure heroin."

"Come again?" I asked her. I still wasn't quite on her level of thinking. I knew she had a flash of insight and had worked it all out in her head, so she was way ahead of me.

"I think there's a good possibility that Dr. Dunham thought he was ingesting Oxycontin, but it was actually heroin."

It was starting to make sense. "That's how he was murdered."

"Right."

"What brought you to this insight?"

"Well, it makes sense on two levels. One, why would he ingest heroin? He was a doctor. He had to know the dangers of heroin. He knows heroin is often cut with rat poison and the purity level is always varying. You never know what you're going to get with heroin, because it's not regulated. Why would Dr. Dunham take a chance like that? Especially if he had a game going with Sharita to where he was getting Oxycontin every week."

I looked out the window and steepled my hands. "Yes, and the other level?"

"Sally seemed convinced that somebody did Dr. Dunham in. The perfect way of doing that would be to tamper with the Oxycontin he got every week and put heroin into the pill instead. Dr. Dunham ingests it, thinking it's his usual Oxycontin, it's actually heroin, and he dies. That's my theory, anyhow."

"Yeah, yeah," I said, thinking she might be onto something yet. "Well, it wouldn't hurt to have the drug tested. Then, it's just a matter of finding out who was behind tampering with the Oxycontin and why. I guess that we can implicate Sharita, considering how weird she got when I asked her a simple question on what she was pitching to Dr. Dunham, but we're going to have to find a motive for her. I think we need to look closer at the drug company supplying the Oxycontin itself. Osiris."

"Here's the thing, though," Harper said. "There was only one pill left in that Oxycontin pill bottle. It was a seven-day supply. It's possible that only one of the pills was tainted, because it appears he took the other pills in the bottle without any ill-effects. So, the pill left over might or might not have also been tainted. I guess it's possible that two pills were tainted and the rest were not." She nodded. "I'm just trying to temper expectations."

"Noted," I said. "Maybe we'll get lucky and the one pill left over was also tainted. If it was, it would certainly make our job much easier. It would be much easier to show he was murdered by somebody other than my mother."

I went to find Pearl to ask her to call a chemist who worked for a pharmaceutical research company, Dr. David Dudley, so we could have the pill tested. I came back and sat down. "Okay. Now. Let's see. Dr. Dunham has been denied his inheritance thus far. His brother, Robert Dunham, is a major shareholder in Osiris." I picked up the documentation we had on Robert Dunham. "Looks like he has 75% of the stock, plus he sits on the Board of Directors for that company."

"Do you have any information on that company, as far as financials go?" Harper asked.

I looked through my file and pulled out the information I had gathered on Osiris. "Yeah. Looks like the company does about $500 million in sales a year." I looked through the portfolio more closely. "Also looks like the main thrust of this company, which is relatively small in comparison with the biggies that do literally billions of sales a year, is opioids." I read a bit further. "Looks like their researchers are hard at work at bringing a new opioid to the market early next year. That's just one of the drugs they're working on."

Harper nodded her head. "It's all fitting together. But we're going to have to find out what was going on with Dr. Dunham and his brother. I have a feeling the brother might have been behind Dr. Dunham not getting his inheritance just yet. Or maybe he would have never gotten his inheritance. At any rate, we're going to have to get to the bottom of that."

I suddenly knew we had a firm direction to go into.

And I owed it all to Harper.

A few days later, our theory got stronger. Harper had Anna download Sharita's bank account information, and we saw a direct deposit from Dr. Dunham to Sharita made once a week. The deposit was for $500.

"Okay, so now we know," Harper said. "Dr. Dunham was paying Sharita for something. It makes sense that he was paying her for delivering Oxycontin to him. He writes her the prescription, she gets it filled, and she sells it back to him."

"Sounds about right," I said.

Now, to prove it.

Twenty-Two

In the meantime, I had to deal with the Michael Reynolds situation. Thus far, he had not done anything to defend our petition. My discovery requests went unanswered and he hadn't even filed an answer.

It was time to apply for a default judgment.

I prepared a motion for a judgment in default, and gave it to Pearl to file.

Then I went into Harper's office to tell her what I did.

When I went into her office, she was sitting at her desk, looking very pale. At first, I thought maybe she was feeling sick. She was wearing a shawl she kept pulling tighter and tighter around her and she was shaking a tiny bit.

I cocked my head. "Harper? What's going on?"

She pushed a thumb drive towards me. "Here," she said. "This is what's wrong."

I didn't know what the thumb drive was, but, from Harper's expression, I could tell that whatever was on there was freaking her out.

I went over to Harper's computer. "Do you mind if I play this?"

"That's why I gave it to you." She started to bite her nails. "Oh, God, if anybody finds out about this…"

I took a deep breath, not liking the look of this at all.

I stuck the thumb drive into Harper's computer and immediately saw it was a video diary for one Carrie Blackwood. It started two years ago, and it was segmented out so I could jump to any diary entry wanted to.

"Go ahead," Harper said. "I've watched the entire video diary. Most of it is pretty irrelevant. She documents her day-to-day struggles with her job and her relationships. She also talks a lot about recovering from anorexia. I think that stuff is interesting and it kinda explains why she committed suicide. It wasn't just the fallout from the video. She's apparently been suffering from depression and anxiety for quite awhile."

"Well, that's okay," I said. "Her having pre-existing depression isn't fatal to our case. The point is, the viral video pushed her over the edge. I think we could win this case even if the guy wasn't in default, which he is."

"Oh, you haven't gotten to the good stuff yet. Look at her October 13 entry. Go to that one. You'll see what's going to sink us like a torpedoed submarine."

I got to that diary entry, and I watched.

Carrie was sitting in front of the camera, smiling. "I've decided I'm going to do it. It's something I've always wanted to do, and I'm going to. I'm going to make a sex tape and put it on-line." She laughed. "I've even found the guy willing to do it. His name is Michael Reynolds and he's really game for it. I met him last night at a bar and we hit it off. We had sex last night and I asked him this morning if he would make a sex tape with me and he's totally down. So I'll be making that tape and it'll be live in the next few days. I don't know, it feels right to do something so kinky and out of character. I'm tired of being the depressed pediatrician. I want to do something wild and this is it!"

I sighed. "Michael posted the video," I said. Dammit. "But it was apparently at her request."

Harper nodded her head. "The next entry explains why Michael posted it and not her."

I went to the next entry, which was dated October 15. "We did it. Michael recorded us, but I don't know how to get it on-line. I'm pretty illiterate when it comes to technology. He knows how to do it, though so he'll load it up and put it on-line."

This was bad. Very bad.

The last video entry was Carrie talking about how her life had been destroyed by the video. "This video was a mistake, a horrible mistake. I didn't think that it would go viral. I thought that..." She shook her head. "I don't know what I was thinking. But all I know is I can't function anymore. I don't want to wake up in the morning. I've been zoning out at work, making mistakes. I don't feel like I can face the parents of my children. I've been so paranoid that they've seen the video and just are too polite to say anything. So, I've told each one of my patients to find a new doctor. I just can't face them. They're going to find out about me, sooner or later, and they're going to think their child's doctor is a pervert and that would be humiliating."

And...it was getting worse and worse. She lost her practice not because the parents of her child patients fired her for being in a sex video, but because she got rid of them.

There was no rape. No invasion of privacy. And no loss of business. Her suicide was because she had struggled with depression and anxiety for years. Apparently, she also was slightly paranoid, so there must have been some other kind of mental illness lurking about.

I looked over at Harper. I had no idea how she would react to what I was about to say.

"Do you remember us talking about *The Postman Always Rings Twice?*" I said to her.

She nodded her head. "I do. I love that movie." She nodded. "Tell me what you're thinking."

"I saw it after you talked about it, and it's fitting for this situation. As you remember, in that movie, a man, Frank, commits a murder, but he escapes detection. He isn't tried for the murder so he was never brought to justice. Then, later on in the movie, he accidentally kills his former lover. It was a pure accident, but he's charged and convicted for her murder. He's on death row for that accident. He's not that upset about being on death row for a murder he didn't commit, though, because he knows he was guilty of another murder for which he was never brought to justice. He knows his punishment is well-deserved, so he accepts it."

Harper looked like she was only half-listening. "Okay," she finally said, looking miserable. "Go on."

"Well, you and I know Michael Reynolds is a bad guy who has done bad things in his life. Many bad things. He killed his father-in-law in cold blood. He raped you. Those are just two despicable things he's done in his life, and, so far, he's not been brought to justice. He was in prison for awhile after you threw him under the bus by throwing his murder case, but he got out, and he's now free as a bird. He was never charged with raping you, because you were afraid to go to the authorities. He's probably done a lot of other bad things we don't even know about, but a rape and a murder are pretty bad just by themselves."

Harper's face was starting to color again. She nodded, but it looked like she was still lost in thought. "And..."

"And, well, we now know Michael wasn't guilty of raping Carrie Blackwood. He wasn't guilty of invading her privacy. He didn't cause her suicide. But the guy was guilty of so much else. Maybe we need to keep pursuing this case and pretend we never saw that video. We have him on the ropes because he didn't respond to our petition and discovery requests. A judge will sign this default judgment and we'll have him on the hook for millions. A judgment like this will ruin him. It'll follow him around for his entire life. He won't be able to rent an apartment, let alone buy a house. He'll have problems finding employment because most employers do background and credit checks. His bank accounts will be frozen."

"I-" Harper began but then stopped.

I wouldn't go forward unless Harper gave me the go-ahead, so I found myself literally holding my breath.

"Harper?"

She swiveled in her chair and bit her nails. "I don't know. It goes against everything I've learned in the practice of law. I mean, I know I threw his case, but that was different. He was guilty as sin in that case. His girlfriend told me the plot and admitted Michael pulled the trigger on that judge. I threw it but he was good for that murder. Otherwise, I wouldn't have thrown it." She took a deep breath.

"I won't take my cut of the judgment," I said. "If that helps."

"We'll get a judgment and then what? He appeals it and-"

"He won't appeal it. He doesn't have the money to hire an attorney to defend himself. He certainly won't have the money for an appellate attorney."

"He appealed his murder conviction and won," Harper said.

"He had the money then. He was still married to his sugar momma. He doesn't have the money now."

She looked down at her hands. "Somebody knows about this video diary. I don't know who, because it was sent to me anonymously. If he can hire an appellate attorney, he'll be sure to win on his re-trial."

"Whoever sent it didn't send it to help him. Otherwise, Michael would have a copy of it and he would have given it to us in person. That's what I would do if I were him and I knew about this video diary."

"But who would send this to us? Why?"

"I don't know," I said. "Honestly. But I say we go ahead and file for a default judgment and just hope this video doesn't surface anywhere near Michael Reynolds. If it does, it does. But I think it won't."

Harper nodded her head. "Give me a copy of the judgment. Let me read it."

She read it through, seeing that the judgment was for $10 million, which included $8 million in punitive damages.

"Okay," she finally said. "File it."

I took the judgment back but I didn't leave her office.

"Harper..."

"I'm okay," she said. "I'm good. I agree, after all he's done in his life, he needs to pay. I just wish I felt better about this."

"Harper, if you don't want me to file this, I won't. I'll dismiss the case."

She swiveled some more in her chair. "No, file it. File it. Let him twist in the wind. Let his life be ruined, like he ruined mine." Then she smiled, but it was a rueful expression, not one of joy or mirth. "I think I'm just having a hard time finding the joy in anything these days. Axel is gone and this victory is Pyrrhic now. My life is still ruined by what Michael did all those years ago, and nothing will change that. We can get

1,000 judgments against him for things he didn't do, but that won't change how I feel about myself. I don't know. It all just seems empty."

I shook my head. I was hoping Harper would be happier about finally bringing this guy to justice. I wasn't ready for this reaction.

I put my hand on her shoulder and she put her hand on mine. She squeezed it, and then she stood up and threw her arms around me.

"Thank you, Damien, for doing this for me. You don't know how much I appreciate it. You're willing to go above and beyond to help me get justice. I love you for it, because I know you're only doing this for me. But-"

I nodded. "I'll dismiss the case."

She smiled. "I think it's best." Then she took a deep breath. "I think it's best. You better call Audrey Blackwood and tell her."

Audrey. She would be devastated to know her daughter wasn't the person she thought she was.

Then again, maybe she sent the video to Harper. Maybe it was on her conscience and she couldn't stand it, so she sent the thumb drive to us.

Maybe we would never know.

Later on that day, before I got a chance to file the dismissal, justice was well and truly done.

Michael Reynolds was hit head-on by a drunk driver and killed instantly. It was front-page news. The irony was, he was on his way to hire an attorney to defend his case at the time of the accident. I got in touch with his girlfriend after I found out about the accident, and she told me he was on his way to see an attorney to defend him in the wrongful death case when he was killed.

If we didn't file the case against him, he wouldn't have died, in other words. I drew a strange sense of satisfaction in knowing that I, along with a willing universe, helped in making this guy meet his fate.

I went to see Harper to tell her and she evidently already knew.

She was smiling and looked like a million pounds of stress had been lifted off of her.

"The postman always rings twice," she said with a smile. "The postman always rings twice."

TWENTY-THREE

After Michael Reynolds bit it on the highway, Harper seemed as if she had turned a corner. She was back in AA and was talking to a brand-new sponsor, Amber Wittig. She told me every day when she came into work that she had called Amber the night before instead of taking a drink. And that's what she was supposed to do. She was even starting to accept the fact that Axel was no longer in her life. He had moved back to Australia and the two of them agreed it best they didn't keep in contact. They both wanted to move on with their lives without stringing the other along.

She still seemed to be sad but not quite as devastated as she was. I think she realized the universe had finally taken care of her problem. The man who tormented her for her entire adult life was now no more and he got his just desserts.

I felt the same way.

So Harper was sitting in my office when I got the phone call from Dr. David Dudley. Dr. Dudley was the chemist to whom I sent the Oxycontin packaged in the box given to me by Sally Wallace, Dr. Dunham's office manager.

Dr. Dudley was a friend of mine for I had used him on other cases. Never for something like this, but he had testified as an expert witness on a few medical malpractice cases I had in the past. He was an excellent chemist and his reputation was beyond reproach. He would make a very good expert witness on the stand if it came to that.

"Hey, David, good to hear from you. What did you find?" I asked him.

"You better come into my office. I don't really want to talk over the phone."

That was weird. "What time do you want me there? What time is good for you?" I asked.

"I have an opening today at 2 PM. You can bring Harper if you like. I know she's your second chair on this and I need to talk to both of you."

I thought about it, realizing I didn't have court in the afternoon nor did I have any depositions or client meetings that afternoon. I looked over at Harper and nodded at her. "Do you have an opening today at 2 PM to go to the lab?" I asked her.

She took a glance at her online calendar. "I have a new client intake at 1:30, but I'm sure Pearl can move it around for me. I'm sure it won't be a problem, it's just a new domestic case I might be getting into." Harper had decided to take a limited amount of divorce cases, against her better judgment. She felt it was time to diversify her practice a bit more and get out of having so many criminal cases sapping her mental energy. Or at least, that was how she had explained it to me. Personally, I thought it was out of the frying pan and into the fire, but if it made her happy to not have so many criminal cases, more power to her.

"We'll be seeing you at 2 PM, David," I said to him.

"I'll be seeing you then."

I got off the phone and looked over at Harper. "It's odd, don't you think, that David couldn't just tell me over the phone what was going on?"

Harper shrugged. "I suppose, but maybe he just wanted to meet with us face-to-face. Sometimes people are uncomfortable talking over the phone about something like this."

Maybe. But I just had a feeling there was something else behind David's request to meet in person behind closed doors.

TWENTY-FOUR

At 2 o'clock that day, Harper and I found out exactly why David had requested a face-to-face meeting. To my surprise, when I went to the pharmaceutical headquarters where David worked as a drug chemist, he was standing in the parking lot, scanning it and obviously looking for us. When I parked my car, he was right there, looking in the window.

I put down the window, and he peered in.

"Can I get into the car and we can go somewhere? I'm so sorry, I should not have invited you to my office. Not for this. I don't know what I was thinking, but I really need to not be in this office and we need to go someplace else to talk."

I unlocked the door and he got into the backseat.

As I drove off, he was looking anxiously out the back window.

The name of the pharmaceutical company David worked for was named Anastas. Like Osiris, the pharmaceutical company Dr. Dunham's brother worked for, Anastas was a relatively small player in the pharmaceutical business. It did a hundred million dollars in annual sales. Also like Osiris, Anastas' major line of products were opioids.

I looked into the rearview mirror at the very nervous-looking David. He still was looking out the back window, an anxious look on his face.

"Where do you want to go?" I asked. "You want to go to a restaurant?"

He shook his head. "No. Listen, I just want to maybe just drive around and you can bring me back. I'm so sorry, I just really don't want to be in a public place seen with the two of you. Just drive out of the parking lot and I'll explain everything."

I drove out of the parking lot and into the street, feeling apprehensive. After a few miles, David seemed to relax. "So, what's going on?" I asked him.

"Listen, Damien, I know you want me to help you out here. And I will. But only if I can find a different job before the trial. I'll be looking for one very soon. I really didn't anticipate I would be looking for a new job, but here we are. If I don't have a new job by the time you go to trial, I can't promise to be your expert witness on this. And you are going to need an expert witness to testify on the stand. That much is clear."

I felt a sense of excitement building as he spoke. "I'm assuming you tested that pill and you found out it was not Oxycontin?"

"No, it wasn't. It definitely was not Oxycontin. I tested it and I found it was heroin. Extremely pure - so pure it would undoubtedly cause an overdose in almost anybody. Anybody but a regular junkie who was used to that sort of thing. I'm not at all surprised Dr. Dunham overdosed. I'm not at all surprised about that."

I looked over at Harper. She looked surprised, but not really.

"Tell me more. And, while you're at it, tell me why the cloak and dagger? Why are you so afraid to be seen with us?"

He looked out the back window again as if he was afraid something would out of the shadows. "Because of who you are. Because of who you represent. You have to understand, there are some major forces who want to make sure they stay hidden on this. It's not just my company but other companies too. Anyhow, I'm not even positive about anything but I just have seen too many internal memos to ignore this as just a coincidence."

"Internal memos? What are you talking about?"

David just shook his head. "I've said too much. Too much. I need to find a new job before I can talk. I know now that I need to find a new job. And when I do, you'll be the first to know. But I can't tell you anything more than what I've already told you. I'm sorry it had to be so cloak and dagger. But it can't be helped. If anybody ever saw me with the two of you, well, let's just say I would be forced out by the end of the day. And I can't afford that. Christmas is coming and my wife is expecting me to take her to Barbados. I can't very well do that if I lose my job right now. I told you all I can tell you and hopefully you can just put the puzzle pieces together from there."

Internal memos? I wanted to have access to those internal memos, but there was just no way I legally could. No judge would sign off on a discovery request for internal memos of a random pharmaceutical company not involved in the case. Osiris, the pharmaceutical company that manufactured the tainted pill, probably also had internal memos on whatever David was talking about. Which was not clear. But even getting a hold of those internal memos legally would be an uphill battle.

But perhaps it wouldn't be, once I showed the drug was tainted.

"Okay. Well listen, I appreciate you doing this for me. Does anybody know about the work you did on my behalf?"

"No. When your assistant called and told me what she wanted, I decided to keep it a secret. I'm sorry, I just feel so uncomfortable letting anybody know what I was doing on your behalf. You don't know what kind of crazy atmosphere has been going on in my company and other companies. I wish I could tell you more, but, as I said, I have to find a new job first. Then I can talk."

As I looked in the rearview mirror, I just had a chill. He was looking so scared. I wondered if he was frightened about not just losing his job.

Maybe he was afraid of much worse.

TWENTY-FIVE

That night, I got the answer to that question. The headlines in my Yahoo! News said that Dr. David Dudley was found dead in his office of an overdose.

I closed my eyes. Then I opened them, and read about how it was a mystery why a chemist would be using drugs in his workplace. The article quoted employees of Anastas, who told the reporter that Dr. Dudley been depressed and had openly spoken of suicide.

And that was that. I just knew nothing more would come of the investigation into why Dr. Dudley died.

Dr. Dudley knew the truth about that Oxycontin pill. He was the only one who knew the truth about it. The problem, of course, was that the one and only Oxycontin pill we managed to get out of Dr. Dunham's office was presently in Dr. Dudley's possession.

Which meant that, of course, it had been destroyed.

I called Harper to tell her the news.

"Oh my God," she said. "Is a man dead because of us?"

"Yes. That's my short answer, yes. A man is dead because of us. We were apparently not supposed to get this far. One thing is for sure, somebody will go to great lengths to cover all this up."

Harper was quiet on the other end of the line. "I feel so bad. I really liked that guy. Not to mention, he's been a very good expert witness for us over the years. Now what are we going to do? How can we prove the truth?"

"The same way we always do. With the rest of our evidence. We issue some subpoenas to key people in the Osiris company and break them down on the stand. Methodically. I'm also going to at least try to show the judge that internal memos from the Osiris company would be relevant, although that's a long shot. Without showing that drug was tainted, I just don't see how we can possibly subpoena any kind of documents from Osiris. We're going to be lucky if we can get top officials from Osiris to testify in court. I expect lots of stonewalling on this. After all, if the company is willing to kill somebody to protect their secret, whatever that secret happens to be, they'll go to great lengths to make sure they don't have to appear in court to answer questions. But I'm going to make them. I'll fight, tooth and nail, any motion they make to quash a subpoena. And I know the main person I want to get into court is that damn Robert Dunham. Dr. Dunham's brother. I just have a feeling he's the key to this, but it's more than him. I just have a feeling this whole thing goes to the highest levels. And I'm eager to show just how high up it goes."

The good thing was, I now had a clear path on how to defend my mother. And, if it worked, I could not only get her off scot free, but I would hopefully see an entire industry put on trial.

The pharmaceutical industry.

It would be one of the more important cases of my entire career.

TWENTY-SIX
MARCH 15, FIRST DAY OF TRIAL

It was the first day of trial, and I wasn't really all that nervous because I figured out exactly what happened in this case. Whether or not I could prove it was another story. However, I knew how this case would go and that was important.

The prosecutor in this case was Kevin Williams. He was a thirtysomething black man, known for sharp dressing and even sharper cross-examination skills. One thing was for sure, he would be a formidable foe. He wouldn't give me any quarter, which was made clear when I tried to get him to drop the case once I got my mother's records that showed she had been sick when she took the first drug tests and taking an antibiotic that was well-known for causing false positives on such tests.

"Sorry, Damien, no can do. I can't drop the charges against your mother because the chances of a false positive on the drug test are infinitesimal. I think you know that. Besides, I'm under orders from people higher up that I can't do anything with your mama's case. Don't ask me anything more than that." Kevin leaned back in his chair and raised his eyebrows. I got the message. The prosecutor's office, for some reason, would prosecute my mom to the extent of the law. I had no idea why.

But, over the months, I figured it out. I had uncovered a vast conspiracy. There was something rotten in the state of Denmark, for sure, on this case. I would have to prove that it went into the very top of the food chain in the prosecutor's office. That would be fun.

I waited for my mom in front of the courthouse. She was running late and I was getting annoyed. Harper was standing right next to me on the sidewalk, clutching her briefcase. As for me, I had boxes and boxes of documents on a wheeled cart. I managed to get documents for just about everything in this case, along with depositions from all the key players.

I felt as ready as I could be but I was still slightly apprehensive. After all, this was my mother's life on the line. Granted, she wasn't much of a mother and she never was. She was still blood. She was still beloved by my two kids, so I knew Nate and Amelia would be devastated beyond measure if she went to prison for any length of time.

I had to think about them.

I had to give this case my all.

This was especially true because I was at a point with Nate where things could get better, or get much, much worse. Because Dr. Jordan, my appointed therapist, made it clear that I would have to get a prescription for antidepressants for Nate, I did that. I got a prescription for Prozac but I never gave him any. I would just wait and see if he could pull out of his depression without them.

He was doing just that. He was getting better and better, happier and happier. He was playing basketball on a weekly basis and he was hanging out with his friend, Austin. The boy who Amelia informed me was Nate's boyfriend.

The thing of that was, Nate never told me in his own words that he was gay. And I never brought the subject up to him because I figured that if he wanted to tell me, he would tell me. In my eyes, it was simple as that. As for Harper, she knew about Nate, because of my blurting it out to her over the phone that one night. She had never brought up the subject, either. I would imagine her reasoning for not bringing it up to me was the same reason why I didn't bring it up to Nate – she figured that if I wanted to talk about it, I would talk about it.

The upshot was that nobody was talking about anything. I thought the whole thing with Nate was fragile and dependent upon external forces over which I had zero control. His mental health seemed to be dependent upon his continued success on the basketball court and his continued relationship with Austin. I felt like I was constantly holding my breath, waiting for the next shoe to drop. Waiting for Nate to go back into his depressed, sullen state, which was likely to happen if there was a falling out with him and Austin or if he got benched on the basketball court.

I didn't like that Nate was not relying on his inner fortitude for his happiness. If there was one thing I had learned over my life, it's that if you rely on external forces for your happiness, you're on a very fragile platform.

Nate was right there, on the precipice, ready to fall off.

So it was more important than ever that my mom did not serve a prison sentence. Yet, the prosecutor's office was determined to make her do just that. They were determined to make her pay for what was not an accidental overdose, but, as Sally Wallace had intuited, was a deliberate act of sabotage. That was made clear when the test results of the Oxycontin we'd sent to Dr. Dudley came back showing the Oxycontin pill had indeed contained pure heroin.

Of course, I was never able to prove the pill had contained pure heroin. That secret died with Dr. Dudley. I also was not able to subpoena the internal memos of the Osiris pharmaceutical company, let alone the pharmaceutical company that Dr. Dudley worked for, Anastas. I tried to subpoena both companies, but the judge did not allow either subpoena. The companies were able to successfully show that their internal memos on the topic of Dr. Dunham's pioneering pain management system were private and confidential, and, since I didn't have enough relevant information to make either company a party to the case, the memos were beyond the scope of evidence that the judge was willing to allow.

It was frustrating because I was hitting walls at every turn. I subpoenaed several people from the Osiris pharmaceutical company to come and testify in court, however. I presented to the judge the theory that I was working on that the Oxycontin sample consumed by Dr. Dunham was tainted. I told the judge that was my theory of the case and he allowed subpoenas of individuals from the company to come in. He would not allow the memos to be subpoenaed from them, because that was privileged information, but he did allow subpoenas for testimony.

I at least had that.

And I knew exactly where I would hit them. What questions I would ask them. Yes, I would put them on trial, but not just them. I would also put the pharmaceutical companies in general on trial in a very deft way. As long as the judge allowed me enough rope, and allowed my leash to go as far as it could, I felt confident I could overcome the long odds in this case.

My mom was still nervous. "Damien, I don't know why you don't look more scared crapless. I'm about ready to pee my pants. Yet, there you are, standing there just like an oak tree. How do you do it?"

I had to admit that, for her, she was looking pretty good. Her hair was back to its usual dark color, with gray roots, and she had put on a few pounds in the last few months. She told me that was from stress eating, but, quite frankly, I thought she looked better with a few extra pounds. She was just too skinny before.

"Mom, I'm not as confident as I look. Not at all. I mean, I'm reasonably sure about what happened in this case and who is responsible for the death of Dr. Dunham. But one thing is for sure, the prosecutor won't go easy on you. Again, I don't really know why. I mean, I understand exactly why Dr. Dunham overdosed. But I don't really know why the prosecutor is choosing to go so hard on you. Except to say that putting the heat on you takes the heat off the real person behind all of this. And that person happens to be somebody of means, a lot of means, and I highly suspect that some money changed hands in the prosecutor's office. I certainly cannot say for sure, but that's my suspicion."

"Well, Damien, if those prosecutors have such a hard-on for me, what makes you think the judge won't too? What makes you think I'll get a fair trial no matter what? Tell me that and I'll calm down just a little bit. But if you can't tell me that, I'm going to continue to crap my pants. I'm scared, Damien. I'm scared of spending the rest of my life in the joint for something I had nothing to do with."

Harper put her arm around my mom. "Olivia, we can't assure you that you'll be acquitted. But we can do the best job possible. Damien subpoenaed key witnesses in this case and they'll lie on the stand. But if Damien can get the story out there, even if the witnesses lie on the stand, he will have done his job. And that's important. It's important to show reasonable doubt. He doesn't have to prove anything on that stand, just put reasonable doubt in the jury's mind."

Mom was shaking. I had never seen her so scared.

"Tell me again about reasonable doubt?" she asked me. I had gone over her testimony, and all my trial preparation, for hours on end. Most of the time she was distracted, so a lot of what I said to her probably did not sink in.

"Reasonable doubt is just that," I said. "Any kind of doubt in a person's mind that you did it. The jury doesn't have to be convinced either way. It's not up to me to prove something one hundred percent. The burden of proof is on the prosecutor, not me. The prosecutor has to prove the case beyond a reasonable doubt. I don't think I can. So, please relax. I got this."

"If you got this, why am I still going to trial? Why has this case not been thrown out like yesterday's garbage? I don't understand why I'm still going to trial on this."

I shook my head. There was no getting through to her. I talk to her until I was blue in the face and it wouldn't do a bit of good. I had tried to tell her, over and over, that I suspected corruption in the prosecutor's office. Corruption I would have to show on the stand.

"Mom, please, just trust me. For once in your life, can you just do that? Trust me? And trust Harper?"

Mom looked skeptical. "I'll trust Harper. I think she's a good lawyer."

I wanted to slap her. Here I was, her son, and she was openly saying she didn't trust me but trusted my partner.

I should not have been offended, but I was.

"Come on, Mom. Let's go into the courtroom."

We went into the doors of the large Art Deco 1920s era courthouse. One thing about this courthouse, it was as grand as the art museum off The Country Club Plaza. Well, not quite as grand as that art museum, but I always liked the interior of the lobby of this courthouse. The ceilings were about 30 feet tall, the floor was marble, and the ceilings were pure art. It was an old-school courthouse, in every sense of the word. At least when it came to the lobby, that was a good thing.

The actual courtrooms, they were another story. They were cramped, too hot in the wintertime and too cold in the summertime. The spectators sat on hard wooden benches. They needed to be renovated, and I would not have been surprised to find out they had not been updated since they were built in the 1920s.

We made our way to the elevators and into the courtroom. It was time to make any kind of pretrial motions we needed to do, pick a jury, and get the show on the road. I was kind of anxious to do all that.

The judge in this case was named Judge Watkins. He was a relatively new judge, having come out of the public defender's office, so I was happy I drew him. Because he was a public defender, prosecutors didn't like him because of the perception that he was a defendant's judge. Personally, I didn't think he was. I thought he was fair. But then again, maybe I was just biased.

Kevin was already there, standing in front of the judge. The second chair was Shelley Jenkins. Both Kevin and Shelley were known to be top-drawer prosecutors and I knew they would be going for the jugular. I would have to be on my toes, prepared for anything.

"Hello, counselor," Judge Watkins said in a friendly manner as I walked through the door. "I was just talking with Mr. Williams and he says he doesn't really have any major pretrial motions to bring up, however he reserves the right to bring in motions *in limines* at any point in time in the case. I was wondering if you had any pretrial motions of your own?"

I had more than one trick up my sleeve.

"No, your honor," I said.

"Okay, then, let's bring in the jury panel and get this show on the road," he said. "Let the circus begin."

Let the circus begin was Judge Watkins trademark phrase. It always made me smile, as I thought of clowns, elephants and tigers dancing on platforms. Fire-breathers, and, back in the day, bearded ladies, giants, dwarfs and others deemed by society to be misfits and "freaks."

It was usually a fitting metaphor for a trial, really. Because they usually turned into some kind of a semblance of a three-ring circus, with feats of strength and sleights of hand dazzling the audience, AKA the jury.

Four hours later, we had our jury.

And the circus was truly going to begin.

I just hoped I didn't fall off the high-wire.

TWENTY-SEVEN

Opening statements were afoot and Kevin came out with his.

Kevin's greatest strength, in my estimation, was his charm and his disarming smile. He had a way with the ladies, because he could talk an Eskimo into buying an electric fan for his igloo and he had a droll wit and effervescent way of talking. He could sell anything to a jury. Plus, he spoke on their level, never trying to talk above them. He really made a person feel that he was one of them, no matter if that person was homeless or a multi-millionaire. It was a rare talent, one to be admired.

"Ladies and gentlemen of the jury," Kevin said, his smile engaging and huge, "the facts of this case are really pretty simple. A man, Dr. Dunham, is dead. The reason why he is dead is because the defendant supplied him with drugs the night he died and he overdosed on these drugs.

Now, I know when I went through *voir dire* that several of you were skeptical that the facts of this case would warrant a murder charge, but let me remind you of the concept of felony murder. This means that if a person dies during the commission of a felony, the person who committed that felony can be found liable for that person's death. And let me remind you that distribution of drugs is a felony in the State of

Missouri. The statute is called Delivery of a Controlled Substance, and to be guilty of this felony, a person must knowingly deliver a controlled substance. That would mean that, when the defendant gave the deceased heroin, she was delivering a controlled substance, which, in turn, made her guilty of a Class C felony. The evidence will show that this is what happened the night of October 21 - Olivia Ward gave Dr. Tracy Dunham heroin. When Dr. Dunham died, therefore, he died during the commission of a felony. That would fulfill the elements of a felony murder case here in the State of Missouri.

And that's really all there is to it in this case. The defendant supplied the deceased with drugs, and the deceased died from ingesting these drugs. You will hear a toxicologist testify that Dr. Dunham died of an overdose of pure heroin. You will hear a chemist who works for the Kansas City Police Department testify that a vial of blood pressure medicine seized from the defendant's home was tested and was found to be pure heroin, the same type of heroin found in the bloodstream of the deceased. Both the heroin found in the bloodstream of the deceased and the pills in the bottle was diamorphine hydrochloride, the very purest form of the drug known to man. The street name for this particular strain of heroin is China White, and it is an often lethal strain responsible for many deaths across the country. Also, it was determined in the toxicology examination of the deceased that Dr. Dunham took this heroin in pill form. The heroin found in the defendant's home was in pill form as well. This establishes that the defendant gave the deceased a pill that was pure heroin and the deceased died from the ingestion of this heroin pill. This deadly heroin pill.

Now I know a few of you are skeptical that a murder charge was the appropriate charge in this case, but, after you hear the evidence, you will agree with me that a murder charge is the only charge appropriate in this case. The defendant gave pure heroin to a man and this man is dead. Pure heroin is lethal, much more lethal than other strains mixed with other substances. The defendant might as well have given the deceased poison that night. Think of it that way - think of the pure heroin as being a poison, because that's the way it operates in the bodies of those not used to the drug. It's poison.

Thank you very much for your attention to this case. I know that all of you have responsibilities that don't make coming to jury duty easy to do. It's your civic responsibility, and I know that all of you will take that responsibility seriously. After hearing the evidence, I will respectfully ask for a verdict of guilty on all counts. Thank you again."

Kevin sat down and I stood up. He was good, very good. Succinct. Didn't waste his words or beat around the bush. Just told them straight up what he would prove, and, I had to admit, if he actually could prove the drug found in my mother's medicine cabinet was the same strain of pure heroin found in Tracy's bloodstream, I would have a hard time trying to convince the jury not to convict.

I suddenly realized my battle might be more uphill than I originally thought. But, I had faced long odds before and I would face them again. I simply had to do the best I could with the facts I had.

I went over to the jury box and looked all of them in the eye.

"Ladies and gentlemen of the jury, I'll admit one thing. Mr. William was good in his opening statement. Very good. Hell, if the facts were as he said they were, I'd convict my client."

The jury laughed lightly at my little joke, which was encouraging. I was getting them to warm up to me and that was important.

"But, unfortunately for Mr. Williams, the facts aren't as black and white as he says. First of all, I will present evidence that the drug taken out of my client's medicine cabinet was blood pressure medicine. Nifedipine. Nothing more and nothing less. It was tested at the lab, and the results came back that it was diamorphine hydrochloride, otherwise known as China White, otherwise known as pure heroin. The purest form of heroin. But here's the thing, ladies and gentlemen - I will show you just how easy it would be for a policeman on the scene to replace a normal prescription drug with a street drug. How easy it would be to frame somebody.

Secondly, the state will show my client was administered a urinalysis at her home that showed the presence of opiates in her system. However, you will hear evidence that my client was actually taking an antibiotic that night called Ciprofloxacin, commonly known as Cipro. You will hear testimony from an expert witness who will establish that this antibiotic is commonly the cause of false urinalysis positives, specifically that it tends to cause false positives for opioids. So, in other words, things are not as they seem.

Here is what my evidence will show. My evidence will show that the heroin ingested by Dr. Dunham was accidentally ingested by him. Dr. Dunham thought he was taking Oxycontin. Dr. Dunham was addicted to Oxycontin. Oxycontin was a drug of choice for him. However, there is no evidence Dr. Dunham had ever taken heroin willingly. So, if you're a user not used to heroin in any way, shape, or form, it stands to reason that if you are exposed to an extremely pure form of the drug, you probably will overdose. In fact, that's a common reason why heroin addicts overdose – they are exposed to a form of the drug more pure than what they're used to, therefore they are apt to overdose on just a small amount.

And how did he come to be exposed to heroin? How did he accidentally take it, thinking it was Oxycontin? That, ladies and gentlemen, is the result of a conspiracy. You see, Dr. Dunham was working on something extremely dangerous to the pharmaceutical industry. The pharmaceutical industry relies upon you getting sick. It relies on you getting hurt. Suffering is its *raison d'être*. And the opioid business is extremely lucrative for all pharmaceutical companies. According to a pharmaceutical analysis firm, *Citeline,* annual opioid sales will hit $14 billion. That's billion with a B. In other words, opioids are a cash cow for the pharmaceutical industry. Never mind that opioids are a cause of so much misery in this country. The opioid epidemic has led to the heroin epidemic, as opioid users go on the black market to get their fix when they're turned away from the medical establishment. This is after said medical establishment did all they could to get the people addicted in the first place.

So what would happen if a doctor pioneered an effective alternative to opioids? What if a doctor not only pioneered this effective opioid alternative, but that doctor was getting national attention for his technique, had plans to nationalize it, and had the goal of making his technique the standard of care for doctors around the country? Could you imagine anything more disruptive to the pharmaceutical industry? If that came to pass, and a doctor truly came up with a technique that effectively ended pain without drugs, the pharmaceutical industry would lose billions of dollars in sales every year. Imagine all the share-holders in these pharmaceutical companies losing their investments. Imagine the stocks for these companies plummeting, as they could no longer effectively push their opioids down patients' throats anymore. The country would benefit greatly if there could be a national technique that could resolve pain without drugs. The pharmaceutical industry, not so much. Remember, their raison d'être is your suffering. Without people suffering, they would not exist.

You might be sitting there wondering where I'm going with this. Well, I will tell you where I'm going with this. My evidence will show that Dr. Dunham was a major threat to the pharmaceutical industry. Specifically, he was a threat to Osiris Inc. Osiris Inc. is a relatively small pharmaceutical firm. It only does about $500 million in sales a year. That might seem like a lot, but when you understand that the big pharmaceutical companies do billions in sales a year, you understand that Osiris was a small player in the realm of the larger industry. And Osiris was not a diversified firm. It's main thrust was manufacturing opioids. It did $500 million in sales annually, and $400 million of those sales were opioids. Oxycodone, Hydrocodone, Fentanyl. Opioids.

So when you think about a small pharmaceutical company where 80% of their sales come from opioids, you realize this company is seriously at risk if anybody came along with a disruptive technique that would make their main product obsolete. Which is what Dr. Dunham did. That made him dangerous.

And consider this. Dr. Dunham's brother, Robert, was the main shareholder of Osiris. This is important, because the two brothers were estranged. The bad blood began when Dr. Dunham had an affair with his brother's wife, Naomi, while Naomi was still married to Robert Dunham. This was the cause of Robert and Naomi's divorce, which, in turn, caused Robert to become estranged from his five children with Naomi. Robert Dunham was an heir to the Dunham fortune and he came into his $100 million inheritance when he was 21 years old. With that $100 million, he helped found Osiris pharmaceuticals. Like Osiris, he was not diversified. Most of his wealth was tied up in Osiris. So, Robert Dunham, a man so manipulative and vengeful that he prevented Dr. Dunham from getting his inheritance from the Dunham fortune, saw that his brother, his hated brother, would go big with a technique that threatened his bottom line. If Dr. Dunham's procedure became nationalized, to the point where opioids eventually became obsolete, or, at the very least, sales dramatically lessened, Robert Dunham stood to lose a fortune.

So Robert Dunham came up with a plan to eliminate his brother. Robert Dunham knew his brother was addicted to Oxycontin. He knew Dr. Dunham saw a pharmaceutical rep by the name of Sharita Vance every week. Ms. Vance was involved in an agreement with Dr. Dunham to provide him with Oxycontin in exchange for money. Money under the table for her. Ms. Vance was a woman with issues. Specifically, she had gambling debts. She saw a chance to make some money and she took it. Specifically, her chance to make some money involved giving Dr. Dunham pure heroin, not the usual Oxycontin delivered to Dr. Dunham. Robert Dunham was the mastermind of this particular nefarious plot and Ms. Vance was the deliverer.

Also, Osiris was in talks to merge with a larger pharmaceutical company. Sisto, a pharmaceutical company that does 20 billion annually, was in talks with Osiris, because they were interested in acquiring them. Osiris knew that if they lost their main source of income, namely opioids, they would not have a very good position in this merger. You will hear evidence that Sisto was concerned that Osiris was not diversified and was concerned that Dr. Dunham would make opioids effectively obsolete. You will hear evidence that Robert Dunham reassured Sisto that he was taking care of the Dr. Dunham issue.

You may conclude that greed was behind this murder. And you would not be wrong. The fact of the matter is, Dr. Dunham was a big threat to Osiris and to the pharmaceutical industry in general. He was a threat, so he was eliminated. It's as simple as that.

My client had nothing to do with this person's death. She was sitting at home, minding her business, when Dr. Tracy Dunham came to her house. She was not doing drugs. In fact, she was sick with a urinary tract infection for which she took antibiotics. Remember, these are the antibiotics that caused a false-positive on the urinalysis given to her. She was minding her business, she let him sleep on her couch, she woke up, and he was dead. She did not give him any drugs. She did not have any drugs on her premises, nor did she have drugs on her person. She was completely innocent in this situation. She let him sleep on her couch because he'd been thrown out by his wife. And now she's up for murder, proving the old axiom that no good deed goes unpunished.

This, ladies and gentlemen, is the real story on what happened here. It's not as black-and-white, open and shut, as the prosecutor will lead you to believe. It's much more complex. My evidence will point to the real story and you will have no choice but to acquit my client on all charges. Thank you very much."

I sat down and looked over at Kevin. He knew where I was going with this and what my case would hinge on. He was sitting there smiling and shaking his head. I think he thought I was crazy. I thought the same about him.

The judge nodded. "Okay, both counselors have given their opening statements. I would like to take a five minute break and then the state will put on their side of the evidence."

TWENTY-EIGHT

Five minutes later, Kevin was ready with his first witness. I guess he wanted to get the entire chemist controversy out of the way, for he decided to call Dr. Wexler. Dr. Wexler was the chemist who worked in the crime lab for the Kansas City Police Department. He was the person tasked with testing the substance seized from my mother's medicine cabinet. I was anxious to tear this guy apart, but I realized he was probably the innocent party in all of it. He was given a substance that was heroin. However, he was not at the other end – he was not the person tasked with ensuring the sample taken from my mom's medicine cabinet was the same sample given to him. Nevertheless, I figured he might know something.

However, before that chemist took the stand, Kevin apparently changed his mind. He shook his head. "A rookie mistake. I'm sorry Your Honor, I need to call a different witness. I need to call Officer Conrad."

Officer Conrad was the first responder to my mother's home. Well, he was the first officer on the scene. The medical examiner was the first person at the house, after my mother called 911. Officer Conrad was the first officer.

He was sworn in, and Kevin asked him a series of questions. I was anxious to cross-examine him, because I knew from the report that he'd indicated there was no real reason to ask my mother to take a urinalysis. He did not indicate that she seemed high at all. I thought it very odd that a urinalysis was ordered when there was no physical manifestations of having taken drugs.

"Could you please state your name for the record," Kevin asked him.

The officer leaned closer into the microphone. "My name is Officer Leon Conrad," he said.

"And, Officer Conrad, were you the first responder to the home of Ms. Ward, the defendant?"

"Yes. I was. I was the first officer on the scene. However, the paramedics had arrived at the house before I got there."

"But you arrived on the scene at the request of the paramedics?" he asked him.

"Yes. That is correct. The paramedic, Truman Wilson, who was the true first responder, contacted dispatch, and Officer Black and I arrived at the scene."

"And when you arrived at the scene, what did you find?" Kevin asked him.

"The paramedics were still at the scene, having tried and failed to revive Dr. Dunham. My job was to speak with Ms. Ward, as the paramedic had indicated the possibility that Dr. Dunham might have passed away of a drug overdose. I knew the exigent circumstances of the scenario would dictate that it was imperative to administer urinalysis of Ms. Ward."

"So you administered urinalysis to Ms. Ward at the scene, correct?"

"Yes. That is correct."

"And what was the results of your urinalysis?"

"The preliminary results of the urinalysis were that Ms. Ward had opioids in her system."

"What did you do once you discovered she had opioids in her system?"

"I asked permission from Ms Ward to search the premises and she gave me this permission. Because her urinalysis was positive for opioids, this gave me probable cause to search her premises."

"And what was a result of your search?" Kevin asked the officer.

"In her medicine cabinet, I examined the pills in her prescription pill bottles. In one of the pill bottles, in the bottle that contained what was supposed to be the drug Nifedipine, I smelled a substance consistent with high-grade heroin. I therefore seized this drug from her medicine cabinet so I could have it tested in the crime lab."

"To your knowledge, did the drug you seized from Ms. Ward's medicine cabinet test positive for an illicit substance?"

The officer leaned closer to his microphone. "Yes it did."

"What substance did it test as?"

"Diamorphine Hydrochloride, commonly known as high-grade heroin."

"I have nothing more for this witness." At that, Kevin sat down, and I stood up.

I nodded. "Officer Black, you stated on direct that the exigent circumstances of this particular scenario would dictate you administer a urinalysis of Ms. Ward, my client. Is that right?"

"Yes," he said, leaning closer to the microphone.

"And what exigent circumstances existed that compelled you to give my client a urinalysis?"

He took a deep breath. "The paramedic on the scene, Truman Wilson, had indicated his suspicion that Dr. Dunham had passed away from a drug overdose."

I paced the floor and then stood right in front of him, crossing my arms in front of me. "Truman Wilson told you he suspected a drug overdose." I decided to solicit hearsay, as I knew the paramedic would be called by Kevin next. "What led to his suspicions? Did he tell you?"

"He told me the death was suspicious, as the deceased had no known medical conditions."

"And how did the paramedic know about the deceased's medical conditions or lack thereof?" I asked.

"He explained to me that, once he got there and tried and failed to resuscitate Dr. Dunham, he contacted his wife, Sherry Dunham, and his primary care physician, Dr. Littman, to ask about any medical conditions that Dr. Dunham might have suffered. Both told him that Dr. Dunham was not suffering from any known medical conditions. That led Mr. Wilson to contact the police department, as he suspected that Dr. Dunham might have passed away from a drug overdose."

I nodded. "But you didn't see any proof of this overdose, did you?" I asked the officer.

"What do you consider to be proof?" he asked me.

"Any drug paraphernalia, any drugs, residue, anything that would tell you, definitively, that drugs were involved in this man's death. Did you see anything like that around Dr. Dunham when you arrived on the scene?"

He shook his head. "No. I did not."

"And when you spoke with my client, did she tell you she suspected that Dr. Dunham might have died of a drug overdose?" I asked.

"No."

"What did my client tell you about Dr. Dunham's condition before he died?"

"She told me she had no idea how he died. She said he came over to her house the night before, having been told to leave by his wife, and asked if he could sleep on her couch. She said he could and then woke up the next day to find he had passed away."

"I see. She said nothing about suspecting Dr. Dunham was high, then?" I asked.

"No. She said nothing about that."

"And when you spoke with Sherry Dunham, did she say anything about suspecting Dr. Dunham might have taken drugs the night before?" I waited for Kevin to object to the hearsay, but he did not, so I looked at the officer for an answer.

The officer must have also been waiting for a hearsay objection, for he didn't answer right away. He looked over at Kevin, who eventually just shook his head. Sherry Dunham was on his witness list, so he probably would call her anyhow, which would negate the hearsay objection, as I would have the opportunity to cross her.

"No, sir," the officer eventually said. "She did not say anything about Dr. Dunham having taken drugs the night before his death."

"And Dr. Littman, did he indicate he suspected that Dr. Dunham was taking drugs?"

"Objection, hearsay," Kevin finally said.

"Dr. Littman is on my witness list," I said, "and I plan to call him."

The judge nodded his head. "So, he is. I'll allow it."

I looked over at the officer. "Please answer the question."

He looked over at the judge and then moved closer to the microphone. "He did not suspect that Dr. Dunham was taking drugs."

I nodded my head. "In fact, there was no clear-cut sign that Dr. Dunham had died of an overdose at the time you demanded my client take a urinalysis, isn't that right?"

"Mr. Wilson told me he suspected Dr. Dunham had died of a drug overdose," he said.

"I know, you've established that. But do you agree that there were no clear-cut signs that Dr. Dunham had died of a drug overdose when you demanded a urinalysis from my client?"

His eyes looked over at Kevin, then looked at the judge. "No, I guess there wasn't."

"In fact, there was no probable cause to ask my client for something as intrusive as an urinalysis, isn't that right?"

"Well, I asked if she would take one and she told me she would," he said. "I got her consent to a UA."

"Yes, but there wasn't probable cause to ask for one, was there? There wasn't even reasonable suspicion, was there?"

"No, sir."

"And, in fact, you didn't arrest her that night, did you?"

"No, sir."

"And you didn't arrest her because there was no probable cause to arrest her, was there? Even if her urinalysis showed the presence of opioids in her system, it's not against the law to be high, isn't that right?"

He took a deep breath. "It is against the law to possess illegal drugs," he said.

"You aren't answering my question. My question is, is it against the law to be under the influence of drugs?"

"It's against the law to drive while under the influence," he said. He obviously would deflect by answering every question but the one asked.

"Again, not my question. My question is, if somebody is sitting at home under the influence of drugs, and there are no actual drugs in the house, and no drug paraphernalia, would there be probable cause to arrest that person?" I asked.

He hesitated, evidently trying to figure out how to deflect my question some more. "No," he finally said. "There would be no reason to arrest somebody if they do not possess an illegal substance and they are not on the road."

I paced back and forth. "So, you admit there wasn't probable cause to arrest my client that day, was there?"

"No," he said. "There was not."

"Because her dirty UA, without more, would not be a reason to arrest her, isn't that right?"

"Yes. That is right."

"So, it follows that there was not a reason to have seized the drugs in her medicine cabinet, isn't that right?"

"It was exigent circumstances," he said. "I had reason to believe that Dr. Dunham died of a drug overdose, and if I did not seize those drugs at once, they were in danger of being disposed of."

I sighed and hung my head. "But there wasn't any kind of concrete evidence that Dr. Dunham died of a drug overdose. By your own admission, there wasn't any kind of concrete evidence. So, isn't it true that you did not have probable cause to test my client for drugs, let alone search her property and seize anything from her premises?"

He swallowed hard. "No," he finally said. "There was not. But she consented to both."

"I understand that. She consented to both because she literally had nothing to hide. But there was no reason to ask her in the first place, was there?"

"I had a hunch," he said.

"But a hunch isn't a legally permissible ground for a search and seizure, is it?"

"No, I guess it isn't."

"I have nothing further for this witness."

The judge nodded at Officer Conrad. "You may step down."

I felt satisfied that I had drawn blood from that officer, but the fact remained that the UA and the seizure of the drugs were still going to be in evidence, no matter what that officer admitted to about the lack of evidence when he was on the scene.

One thing was for sure, however. If I lost this trial, I would have excellent grounds for appeal. No way the UA and the drug seizure would still be a part of this case.

The paramedic on the scene, Lincoln Wilson, was next. He admitted he had no real reason to suspect that Dr. Dunham had died of a drug overdose, either. He talked about how he called Dr. Dunham's doctor and wife and confirmed that Dr. Dunham was not suffering from any health problems and wasn't suspected of having a drug addiction.

Since that testimony was essentially duplicative of Officer Conrad's testimony, I didn't hammer too hard on the paramedic.

The next person, however, was somebody I was very interested in.

Dr. Thomas Smith, the chemist in the Kansas City Police Department Crime Lab, was about to take the stand.

TWENTY-NINE

D r. Smith was a renowned chemist who had been working for the Kansas City Crime Lab for the past 20 years. He was distinguished and had earned a PhD in chemistry from the University of Chicago. I had deposed him earlier, so I knew what he would say, and I knew that it would be damning, to say the very least.

He was a tall man, long and lean, with ascetic features – a long, pointed nose, a thin face with a powerful jawline, and green eyes that were slightly too close together. He walked with a slight stoop of his shoulders and it looked like he hadn't combed his wild curly hair in several days. He dressed in a brown tweed jacket with patches on the elbows and dark blue pants that didn't match his jacket in the least. His pants were high-water and he wore no socks.

He took the stand, raised his hand and took the oath, stated his name, and Kevin got to work.

"Now, Dr. Smith, could you please tell the court what your role is with the Kansas City Police Department?"

"I'm the lead forensic chemist."

"So, what are your duties as the lead forensic chemist?" Kevin asked.

"I test samples brought to me after a seizure."

"And what are your credentials that would qualify you to become a forensic chemist?" Kevin asked.

"I received my BA in chemistry at the University of Missouri, where I also received my master's. I received my PhD at the University of Chicago. I was hired by the Kansas City Police Department to work in the crime lab 20 years ago, and I have been the lead forensic chemist for the KCPD for the past 15 years."

"And did you test the sample brought to you that was seized from the defendant's home in this case?"

"Yes, I did."

"And what was the drug that was brought into you labeled?"

"Nifedipine, which is a common blood pressure medicine."

"And when you tested it, what was actually in this medicine container?"

"Hydrochloride diamorphine, commonly known as high-grade heroin."

"Could you tell the court how you came to the conclusion that the drug that you tested was high-grade heroin?" Kevin asked.

"I first put the chemical through a presumptive test, which means looked at it under a microscope to analyze the structure of the material brought to me. I then put it through an ultraviolet spectroscopy, which exposed the substance to a UV light, which allowed me to measure how the material absorbed the light. I then subjected the substance to confirmatory testing, which is a two-step process. I first separated the compound using gas chromatography, and I then used a mass spectrometer to identify each component by comparing the chemical signature against reference materials."

"And could you tell the court a bit more about this gas chromatography procedure?" Kevin asked.

"This is a procedure where substances are separated into individual components by dissolving the material into a liquid solvent. The liquid is then put into a superheated oven and pushed through a capillary tube using helium."

I was interested in this, but more interested in the protocol.

"So, you examined the drug brought into you, which was ostensibly a prescription blood pressure medicine known as Nifedipine, and it turned out to be high-grade heroin, correct?" Kevin asked.

"Correct."

"I have nothing further for this witness."

I sighed and stood up. "Dr. Smith, isn't it true that the standard protocols for lab testing are strictly followed in every case?"

"Yes, that is true."

"And the standard protocol is that the sample is individually labeled and sealed at the scene into a tamper-resistant seal placed on the container?"

He looked at the judge furtively. "Yes, that is correct."

"And that the package, once it is individually labeled and sealed, is supposed to be forwarded by a certified service?"

"Yes. That is part of the protocol as well."

"And that the sample is assigned a unique laboratory case number, and that the individual who signs the drug into the lab, the forensic technician, matches this unique case number with the sample you are assigned to test, correct?"

"Yes, that is correct."

"And this submission is logged into your database by the technician, isn't that right?"

"That is correct."

"But this protocol isn't fool-proof, is it?" I asked him.

"In what way?"

"I mean, if, say, the officer who collected the sample switched the Nifedipine with high-grade heroin before he bagged it and tagged it, this would not necessarily be something you would have knowledge of, would it?"

"No, that is true. If an officer wanted to surreptitiously replace one substance with another substance, that would not be something I could detect."

"And is this something that has been known to happen – the officer who gathered the evidence tampers with this evidence before labeling it and placing the substance into a tamper-proof container?"

"Yes, that has been known to happen," he said.

"So your lab has no protections from that kind of thing, isn't that right? There's no way to protect against tampering if the seizing officer decides to tamper with the substance before labeling it and placing it in a container?"

"Yes, that is correct," he said.

"I have nothing further."

My plan was to re-call Officer Conrad to grill him about the procedures he used to collect the evidence. I knew he planted the heroin in my mother's pill bottle, and I knew why he did it. How I would prove it, I didn't really know, but I would have to break him down. It was shown in my cross examination that he was sloppy in his procedures, as he didn't have a reason to ask for a UA from my mother, so hopefully the jury would conclude that he was the kind to cut corners all the way around.

The state called several more witnesses before the judge called it a day.

"Be back here tomorrow at 9," he said, banging his gavel.

The jury left, and I hung back in the courtroom. I would have to answer my mom's questions, because I knew she had quite a few.

"Mom, what are you thinking?" I asked her. She was sitting in her chair, shaking her head.

"I'm thinking I'm gonna puke," she said. "And that's no lie."

"Then please, Mom, go to the bathroom if you're serious about that. I don't really want you to puke in the trash can."

"Harper, why didn't you question nobody today?" she asked Harper. "You've been as quiet as a church mouse over there. What gives?"

"Olivia, I'll be taking the lead during our part of the trial," she said. "On certain witnesses, anyhow."

"Damien, I don't understand," she said to me. "That pig Conrad was lying. He had that junk in his pocket and put it into my BP bottle. How you gonna show that to those jurors?"

"I'm going to re-call Officer Conrad during my case in chief and ask him about that," I said. "After I establish what happened with our other witnesses."

"I'm really gonna puke," she said. And then she got up and ran out of courtroom, presumably to go to the ladies' room to throw up.

I turned to Harper. "How do you think things went?" I asked her.

"Fine," she said. "I think you did a good job establishing that Officer Conrad had no probable cause to get a UA, let alone probable cause to seize those BP meds. It's just hard to show there was tampering. He obviously did it in secret, without anybody seeing what he did."

Mom came back in several minutes later, looking paler than she did before. "I had the dry heaves," she said. "My head is pounding like a snare drum. Boom, boom, boom."

"Come on," I said. "Let's get out of here."

The three of us left the courtroom. I knew the state had several more witnesses they would call the next day, and then I would put my evidence on.

And I was looking forward to bringing my witnesses on.

Very much.

THIRTY

The next day, the prosecutors brought the primary care physician for Dr. Dunham, whose name was Dr. Littman, along with Sherry Dunham, Dr. Dunham's wife. The two witnesses were important for establishing that Dr. Dunham did not have a known heroin problem. My closing argument would include the logic that Dr. Dunham could have very well brought his own stash of heroin over to my mother's house or have gotten high before he got there. They were brought on to establish that this probably wasn't the case.

Their testimonies did not add anything to anybody's understanding, except they both said they did not notice that Dr. Dunham had any signs that he was addicted to drugs, let alone heroin. I cross-examined them gamely, but it was like trying to prove a negative, I thought. Yeah, his wife never knew him to take heroin, and his doctor didn't suspect anything. So what? It's not like drug addicts weren't the masters of hiding their addictions. Dr. Dunham was apparently a drug addict, just not a heroin addict, and his wife and his doctor apparently had no idea. No clue.

That's okay, I thought. I would have my own witness who would confirm that Dr. Dunham was, indeed, a drug addict. That witness was

Sharita Vance, who would testify that she gave Dr. Dunham drugs every week, up until April of last year. He didn't dispense them to patients, and she knew it. She knew he was probably consuming them, in other words.

Her testimony would make it much more likely that he brought the heroin to my mother's home, although that wasn't necessarily what I was trying to prove, either. I just wanted to refute the "Dr. Dunham was pure as the driven snow and was corrupted by that evil Olivia Ward" narrative.

Several more witnesses, including that of Dr. Warren, who performed the autopsy, and several of whom were essentially duplicative of the Dr. Littman and Sherry Dunham testimonies, and it was, once again, time to call it a day.

I felt, by the third day of the trial, that things weren't going in the wrong direction. They weren't necessarily going in the right direction, either, but at least things weren't looking completely bleak.

I was looking forward to putting on my evidence, though.

Because then things were really going to get good.

THIRTY-ONE

Several days later, it was time to put my witnesses on. I would grill some of the witnesses, but I would have Harper grill Robert Dunham, because I had worked out that Robert Dunham was the perpetrator of this entire conspiracy.

I, however, would be the person to grill Sharita Vance. She was the person who delivered the fatal heroin pill to Dr. Dunham, and I knew she had her own reasons for this.

That morning, I announced that Sharita would be my first witness. She was not happy about being called to account for what she did. Nevertheless, I knew she was under a subpoena, so she had no choice but to testify on the stand.

Sharita was called to the stand, and she had a look on her face like she wanted to cut a bitch. Her hair was tightly wound in tiny braids that framed her beautiful face, and she was dressed to the nines – high-dollar suit, shoes buffed to a sheen, with a diamond necklace and matching earrings. She was carrying a high-dollar bag that was designer – Hermès.

She didn't look at me as she walked to the front of the courtroom and was sworn in. Then she sat down, in a petulant manner, crossed her legs, glared at me and dared me, with her eyes, to come forth and question her.

Bring it on, I thought she was thinking. *Bring it on.*

Okay, I will.

I approached her. "Please state your name for the record."

"Sharita Vance," she said with a roll of her eyes. She looked directly at the judge. "I have no idea why I'm here."

"Just answer the questions, Ms. Vance," Judge Watkins said. "Without commentary, please."

She crossed her arms in front of her and smirked. Her eyes said she wouldn't make things easy for me.

Challenge accepted.

"Ms. Vance, did you know the deceased in this case, Dr. Tracy Dunham?"

"Yes, I did." She shifted uncomfortably in her seat.

"And what was the nature of your relationship with Dr. Dunham?"

"I pitched him pharmaceuticals. I'm a pharmaceutical rep. That's what I do. I go to doctor's offices, pay them visits and introduce them to the latest and greatest in our repertoire."

"And you work for Osiris Pharmaceuticals, isn't that correct?"

"Yes, that is correct."

"And you gave Dr. Dunham pharmaceutical samples, is that your testimony?" I asked.

"Yes, that's what I said. I give samples to doctors in hopes they prescribe them to their patients. That's what I do."

"Yet, Dr. Dunham didn't actually prescribe pharmaceuticals," I said.

She shrugged. "Listen, I just introduce the drugs to the doctors. If those doctors prescribe them to their patients, it's none of my concern."

"Permission to treat this witness as hostile," I said.

"Permission granted," Judge Watkins said. "Please proceed."

"Isn't it true that you didn't actually sell Dr. Dunham on any drugs at all?" I asked her.

"What's that supposed to mean? I told you, I pitched him on our drugs, the same as any other doctor."

"You didn't. Dr. Dunham didn't prescribe drugs, so he had no use for your visits to him. Yet, you visited him every single week, didn't you?"

"Yes, I visited him every week, and I sold him on drugs." She narrowed her eyes and looked like she wanted to cut me. "Dr. Dunham was a medical doctor and he prescribed medicine to his patients. It was my job to inform him on all the different cutting-edge medicines our company was producing and give him samples of these meds so he could prescribe them. And that's that."

"No, that isn't that. I'm going to bring in a witness who can testify that Dr. Dunham did not prescribe medicine to his patients. No kind of medicine. He preferred to treat them naturally. Yet you visited him every single week."

"Yeah, so?"

"Isn't it true that the real reason why you were visiting Dr. Dunham was because you were delivering him Oxycontin?"

"What's that supposed to mean?"

"I mean that you and Dr. Dunham had an agreement wherein he wrote prescriptions to you for Oxycontin, you got the prescription filled, and then you sold those drugs back to him for $500?" I asked her.

She glared at me. "Why would I do something like that?"

I walked over to the defense table and then whirled back to face her. "Ms. Vance, do you have a gambling issue?"

She looked over at the judge and then over to Kevin, looking for either man to save her.

Kevin, who was distracted at his table briefly, was on his feet with an objection.

"Objection, relevance," he barked.

"She's a piece of my puzzle," I said to Judge Watkins.

"Meaning?" Judge Watkins asked me.

"Could I please approach?" I asked him.

Judge Watkins nodded and motioned us up to the bench.

In a low voice, I explained why I needed to go into Sharita's background and, in particular, why I needed to inquire on her financial situation.

"My theory of the case is that Sharita Vance was working with Robert Dunham in this case, and the reason why she was working with him was because she was hard-up financially."

Judge Watkins looked at me quizzically and then nodded. "I would like to call a short recess," he said. "So I can confer with counsel in my chambers. Ms. Vance, I apologize for this, but I need you to just sit tight. Ladies and gentlemen of the jury, I also need you to sit tight. We will be back on the bench within ten minutes."

At that, me, Harper, Kevin and his second-chair, Tim Byrd, followed Judge Watkins into his chambers.

"Have a seat," Judge Watkins said, motioning to the four chairs right in front of his enormous desk. "Now, counselor, could you please expound on your theory about Ms. Vance further? I need to hear what you plan on proving with her before I can make a decision on whether or not I'm going to allow you to inquire about her financial issues."

I cleared my throat. "Your honor, here is what I plan on proving to the jury. Robert Dunham is the deceased's estranged brother. He's also the main shareholder for Osiris Pharmaceuticals, the drug company that employs Ms. Vance. Specifically, he owns 75% of that company's stock."

Kevin started to get impatient. "Where is this going?" he asked me.

I rolled my eyes. "I'm getting there. Anyhow, your honor, Mr. Robert Dunham and Dr. Dunham were estranged for several reasons. Specifically, Dr. Dunham had an affair with Robert Dunham's wife, and she actually left Robert for that reason. Which caused Robert Dunham to go to the Dunham patriarch, Earl Dunham, who died last year, and influence him to cut Dr. Dunham out of his will. Earl Dunham was in the late stages of Alzheimer's disease at the time Robert Dunham convinced him to cut Dr. Dunham out of the will. Well, of course Dr. Dunham decided to sue about this. Suffice to say that the two brothers were not close and, in fact, they hated one another."

"Your honor, so far, I'm not hearing one thing that would warrant Mr. Harrington asking Ms. Vance about her financial situation," Kevin said to Judge Watkins.

Judge Watkins looked at me. "I suppose that this long and winding story will eventually get to where we are going, but I would ask you, counselor, to get to the point."

"Well, here's the thing. Dr. Dunham was on the verge of getting a patent on a technique that would revolutionize the treatment of pain management. His technique would have made pain-killers eventually obsolete. Well, that might be a slight exaggeration, but this technique definitely would have decimated the opioid industry. Osiris Inc. does

$500 million in annual sales, and 80% of that is in opioids. Robert Dunham decided to kill two birds with one stone, and murder his own brother. That accomplished two things for him – one, his company, the company for which he owned 75% of the stock, would not have to deal with a revolutionary technique that would kill their opioid sales. And, two, he could get rid of the brother he hated."

Kevin rolled his eyes. "And Ms. Vance fits into this wild scenario how?"

"She delivered the lethal dose of heroin. She did it knowingly, and for money. A lot of money. Specifically, she received a payment of $50,000 right before Dr. Dunham died."

Judge Watkins appeared to consider my scenario. "I'll allow your line of questioning about her financial issues," he said. "Within reason. If you get too far afield, though, I will shut you down. *Sua sponte.*" *Sua sponte* meant that the judge would go ahead and shut me down, even if there wasn't an objection from Kevin.

I took a deep breath and looked over at Harper. She nodded. We knew how vital Sharita would be in this whole scenario. I figured I could break her down easier than I could break down Robert. I was counting on her rolling on Robert if the chips were down, and they would be if I did my job. If I got my mother off, which I knew I could, Sharita would be vital in making sure Robert got his.

We all went back into the courtroom, where Sharita was sitting in the witness stand, still looking like she wanted to cut a bitch. I walked over to her and got right to work.

"Ms. Vance, isn't it true that you have significant gambling debts?" I asked her.

She looked over at Kevin, as if to say *you're really going to allow this tool to throw me under the bus?* She crossed her arms in front of her, glared at me, and said nothing. She apparently was waiting for another objection.

"Please answer the question," Judge Watkins admonished her.

"Yes," she finally said, hatred burning in her eyes.

"And your gambling debts totaled $50,000, isn't that true?" I asked her.

"Yes." She looked away. She didn't have the option of declaring bankruptcy on her gambling debts because she had too many assets. She also was facing the real prospect that she would be banned from that casino if she didn't pay her debts. Not only that, but, because her particular gambling debts were from a casino in Las Vegas, she faced the prospect of being charged criminally. Nevada law considered stiffing a gambling mark to be a Class D felony.

I thought the prospect of her not being able to gamble in that casino was personally more of a deterrent than the fact that she could've been prosecuted in criminal court for what she did.

"And your gambling debt was in the form of a marker owed to the Las Vegas Hilton, isn't that correct?"

"Yes, that is correct."

"And if you didn't pay that marker, you would be banned from gambling in that casino, isn't that right?"

"Yes."

"And bankruptcy wasn't an option, was it?"

"No. I own my downtown condo. I would have lost it in a bankruptcy."

"And if you didn't pay the marker, you could have been charged with a Class D felony in Nevada?"

"Yes."

I paced around. "So you owed $50,000 to the Las Vegas Hilton and had no way of paying it. Is that your testimony?"

"Yes, but I don't know what that has to do with the price of tea in China," she said.

I ignored her interjecting. "Now isn't it true that you entered into an agreement with Robert Dunham to supply Dr. Dunham with drugs?"

She rolled her eyes. "No."

I decided to try a different tact with her - circle back to her agreement with Dr. Dunham.

"I want to get back to why you visited Dr. Dunham in the first place. You knew he didn't prescribe drugs, didn't you?"

"Yes, but I hoped to change his mind."

"So you saw him every week for two years, and you never actually gave him samples of drugs, did you?"

"No."

"You're a tenacious one, aren't you? You go to the man's office every week for two years and you don't sell him on any kind of drug. Didn't you think you were wasting your time?"

"Hope springs eternal," she said.

I went over to the pill bottle I had found in Dr. Dunham's office. "Ms. Vance, I would like you to identify what I've marked as Exhibit A. Could you please tell the jury what this is?"

She looked at it. "Looks like it's one of my bottles of Oxycontin. So what?"

"This bottle was found in Dr. Dunham's medical office after he died. What was it doing there?"

She examined it closely, as if she was seeing it for the first time. More likely, she was trying to come up with a story on why her pill bottle was found in Dr. Dunham's office. "I don't know, I guess he stole it from me when I was last in his office."

"Oh? Did you report this theft to the DEA?"

"No."

"As a pharmaceutical rep, you do know the rules for a theft of a Schedule II drug, don't you?"

"Of course."

"So you know that you are required by law to report a theft of a Schedule II drug, such as Oxycontin, to the Bureau of Narcotics and Dangerous Drugs, or BNDD, as soon as you discover the theft, and that you're required to report the loss formally to the BNDD within 7 days of the theft?"

"Yes, I'm aware of this."

"And you also know that you are required to file a report with the DEA on Form 106?"

"Of course."

"And you know that you must take these steps when any kind of a Schedule II drug is stolen or lost, no matter how small the amount?"

"Yes." She crossed her arms and glared. "I know all this, of course. I'm in the drug business, I have to know things like this."

"So, did you do anything you are required to do by law?"

"No."

"No, you didn't, obviously. I checked the records for the DEA and the BNDD and no loss reports have been reported. Now why didn't you follow the law in reporting this theft?"

"I didn't know the drugs were stolen." She looked smug, like that was an answer I would accept without question.

I felt like howling with laughter at that answer. "You didn't know your painkilling drugs were stolen? Really?"

"Yes, really."

"Wait, didn't you need those drugs for your pain?"

She looked at Kevin, hoping he might save her, but he couldn't object to any of my questions, so he remained seated and busily making notes.

"My pain got better and I just didn't think about it that week."

"Well then, how, pray tell, could Dr. Dunham have even stolen them off you?"

"What do you mean?"

"Well, you're a pharmaceutical rep. I would imagine you know how to safeguard drugs."

"I do."

"And are you known to be a careless person?"

"I'm not, but-"

"So, what happened, then? Did you see Dr. Dunham for your refill visit, with a full bottle of pills, and then, what, put that bottle of pills on his desk and walk off? I mean, how could he have possibly gotten ahold of those pills without your knowledge?"

"I don't remember."

"But you were ostensibly there to see Dr. Dunham because you needed a refill, right?"

"Right."

"You already had a full bottle of pills, so why did you need a refill right then?"

She had no good answer for that one. I could tell. "I wanted to get ahead on my pills," she said.

"Getting ahead on your pills?" I shook my head. "You wanted to get ahead on a Schedule II drug?"

"Yes, that's right. I wanted to get ahead."

I shook my head. "Ms. Vance, with all due respect, your stories are getting more and more outlandish. Now, isn't it true that the reason that bottle of pills with your name on it was in Dr. Dunham's office was because you sold him those pills?"

"What's that supposed to mean?"

"I mean that you had an agreement with Dr. Dunham whereby he wrote prescriptions for Oxycontin for you, you got the prescription filled and then sold them back to Dr. Dunham?"

I saw her fidget in her chair. She hesitated in answering the question, which spoke volumes. It looked like the wheels were turning in her mind and she was trying to decide if she could get away with lying about this arrangement.

"Why would I do something like that?" she finally asked in a weak voice. Gone was the swaggering *I'll cut you* attitude, and, in its place was a woman who was increasingly realizing she was screwed, blued and tattooed.

"Because you needed money. Admit it, Dr. Dunham paid you $500 every week, and all you had to do was present a prescription to your local Walgreens, fulfill the prescription and then go back to Dr. Dunham's office to deliver the pills to him. Admit that was what was going on."

She finally lifted her chin and attempted to get her swagger back. "I wouldn't do something like that. I don't need money that bad."

"Well, let's see. The doctor listed on your Oxycontin bottle is Dr. Dunham. A man who doesn't prescribe drugs of any kind to his patients, yet he prescribed drugs to you. You saw him every single week in his office. Why were you going to his office?"

"I had to go to his office every week to get my prescription filled."

"Actually, you were going to his office every week to deliver the drugs prescribed for you, for a fee of $500, isn't that right?"

"No, that's not right."

"There was really no stopping this program the two of you cooked up, was there?"

"We didn't have a program," she said.

"Yes you did. Dr. Dunham didn't steal those drugs from you. There was no way he stole those drugs from you. There was no way you would just not notice that he stole them from you. You would have noticed that, and if you didn't report the drugs stolen, you would have been breaking the law. So, as I see it, the only way that bottle of pills with your name on it got into Dr. Dunham's office was if you gave them to him. Admit it."

She cocked her head. "I plead the Fifth," she finally said.

I smiled, knowing that particular answer was as good as her admitting that what I was pressing her on was right.

I nodded. "You take the Fifth," I said. "So, isn't it true that you would do anything for money? Including, but not limited to, delivering a tainted pill to somebody."

She didn't say anything, just crossed her arms in front of her and gave me her patented glare.

"Okay, then, I think it's well established that you were hard-up for money on July 13, the day Dr. Dunham died. You were drowning in gambling debts, you were facing criminal prosecution in the state of Nevada, and, perhaps worst of all, you were going to be banned from the Las Vegas Hilton. All because you owed that casino $50,000. Isn't that right?"

"Yes, I said that was right earlier." She was back to being her defensive self.

"Isn't it true that Robert Dunham paid you $50,000 to deliver some tainted Oxycontin to Dr. Dunham right before he died?"

She looked at the ceiling, knowing she probably would lie about it, but not knowing what Robert Dunham would say about this.

She could make a calculated risk and tell the truth. She probably figured it would come out, sooner or later, so why risk a perjury charge?

Yet, she lied. Of course. "No." That was all she said.

"Oh? I would like to admit into evidence what I've marked as Exhibit B. Could you please look this over and tell me what this is?"

She looked at it and I could see the wheels turning. "These are my bank records," she said. "How did you get ahold of these?"

"The power of the subpoena," I said. "Now, I'm going to show the jury this, too, but on July 10 of last year, there was a large deposit made - $50,000. Could you tell me the name of the entity or person who made that deposit?"

She took a deep breath. "Robert Dunham."

"Oh, yes, Robert Dunham. While we're at it, I've also highlighted weekly transactions for $500, could you tell me who transferred those to you?"

"Dr. Dunham, but I told you I plead the Fifth on that."

"I understand," I said. "So, Dr. Dunham paid you $500 a week, every week, and then Robert Dunham paid you $50,000 on October 10. Now, why did Robert Dunham pay you $50,000 just three days before Dr. Dunham's death?"

"I needed money and he gave it to me."

"He did? Out of the goodness of his heart?"

"I don't know if he gave it out of the goodness of his heart, but he knew my situation, so he gave me the money to get out of it."

"Wow," I said. "That's very generous. I guess that means you and Mr. Dunham were close, then?"

"Well, no."

"No? What was the nature of your relationship with Robert Dunham?"

I had her there. If she tried to lie, it would come out, unless she and Robert Dunham practiced their theories beforehand so they could get their stories straight.

Somehow, though, I figured this was not the case. I had a feeling Sharita and Robert didn't try to get their stories straight, because they probably figured they wouldn't get nailed on the stand.

Sharita certainly didn't figure on my having her bank account information, that was for sure.

"He was on the Board of Directors for my company, Osiris," she said.

"Oh. I see. Ms. Vance, isn't it true that, prior to July of last year, you wouldn't have been able to have picked Robert Dunham out of a line-up?"

"I knew who he was," Sharita said.

"You knew who he was. So, you weren't close, then?"

"I knew who he was."

"I see. So, you weren't close, yet he just gave you $50,000?"

"Yes."

"I guess you paid him back, then, or you're making payments?" I said.

"No." She wasn't going to try to lie, because she was probably afraid I would bust out a document that showed she wasn't paying him back.

"No. So, it wasn't a loan, then?"

"No, not a loan."

I nodded. "Not a loan. Well, then, he certainly was generous, then, wasn't he?"

"Yes, I guess he was."

"Ms. Vance, let me remind you about the penalties for perjury. In the state of Missouri, when you lie on the stand during the trial for a murder case, it's a Class A felony. That's a minimum of 10 years in prison. Now why did Robert Dunham pay you $50,000 on July 10, three days before Dr. Dunham died of a drug overdose?"

I thought she would take the Fifth again, but she surprised me. I guess my admonishing her about perjury being a Class A felony in Missouri when it's committed during a murder trial scared her.

"He paid me to deliver some Oxycontin to Dr. Dunham," Sharita said.

The jury gasped, and I heard them start to chatter a little bit.

I smiled, knowing she was changing her game. I could almost see in her mind that she would roll on Robert Dunham the second she could. It probably would work, too - Robert Dunham instigated this whole thing, after all. She was just the messenger.

She crossed her arms and pursed her lips.

"He paid you to deliver Oxycontin to Dr. Dunham. $50,000. Now, isn't true that he specifically paid you to deliver those drugs to him because these drugs were tainted?"

"Listen, I don't know anything about the drugs being tainted. I only know he was concerned about his brother. He knew his brother was dry and was in serious withdrawal, so he wanted me to deliver him drugs."

"Oh, I see. He paid you that much money just to deliver regular Oxycontin?"

"That's right."

"And you didn't know the drugs were tainted?" I asked.

She rolled her eyes. "I told you, I have no clue what was in the pills delivered that night."

"But Ms. Vance, you know somebody isn't going to pay you $50,000 to deliver a drug for no reason, don't you? Common sense. If somebody is paying you a lot of money to deliver a drug, there's a reason behind it."

"I don't know."

"Ms. Vance, have you ever heard of the term willful blindness?"

"Yes, I've heard of that."

"Define it for me, as you understand it."

"It's when you don't know something because you don't want to know," she said.

I nodded. "Like when you're paid $50,000 to deliver a drug to a person and don't ask why you're delivering it and what that drug really is. That's willful blindness."

Kevin stood up. "I don't hear a question," he said.

I turned my head towards Kevin. "Okay, here's my question." I turned to face Sharita. "Ms. Vance, are you aware that willful blindness, under the law, is the same as knowledge?"

Her eyes got wide. She had walked into a series of traps and she was just now realizing it. "What does that mean?"

"That means that, in this case, if you delivered a tainted drug to Dr. Dunham, and you didn't ask why you were delivering it because you didn't want to know, you can still be charged with a crime as if you had actual knowledge of the event. Do you understand that?"

The implications of that were clear to her. I just let her know that if she delivered tainted drugs to Dr. Dunham, she was guilty of murder, whether or not she actually *knew* the drugs were tainted.

She took a deep breath. "I take the Fifth on that, too, then."

"So, you aren't going to go through anymore testimony about delivering drugs to Dr. Dunham on behalf of Robert Dunham, then?"

"That's right. I won't. I know my rights and I don't have to answer anymore questions about that topic."

I nodded. I just hoped the jury knew the implications of her taking the Fifth on this topic. "I have nothing further for this witness."

She rapidly stood up, but the judge asked her to remain seated.

"Ms. Vance, you need to remain seated in case Mr. Williams has any cross-examination questions." He looked over at Kevin, who apparently was busy scribbling notes during my exchange with Sharita. "Mr. Williams, any questions?"

I looked over at Kevin, who just shook his head. "No, your honor." He knew he was screwed and he wasn't about to make the damage worse. There was no rehabilitating Sharita at this point.

Judge Watkins looked at Sharita. "You're excused. However, I would like to advise you not to go too far. I have a feeling the authorities will want to ask you some questions."

Sharita started to shake, and she stood up and rapidly walked out of the courtroom.

I sat down, feeling pretty satisfied with my exchange with Sharita. I drew blood, a lot of blood, from Sharita.

But the best was yet to come.

"Counselor," Judge Watkins said, addressing me. "Call your next witness."

"The defense calls Robert Dunham."

THIRTY-TWO

I decided Harper would question Mr. Robert Dunham as he was apparently a misogynist in the highest order. He had many sexual harassment claims against him over the years, along with many sexual discrimination claims that he'd settled for millions of dollars.

When I found out he had so many claims against him and had to personally pay millions over the years, I discovered the true reason why Robert Dunham was so desperate to have his own brother killed – he had burned through his inheritance with the multiple sexual harassment and discrimination claims. His inheritance was $100 million, and all of the claims, put together, totaled about that much.

In other words, he needed money from his stake in Osiris. Desperately. If he didn't continue to receive his monthly dividends from that company, he would have to – gasp! give up his yacht on the Caribbean and might have to sell off a house or two.

For shame!

Harper called Robert and he appeared in the courtroom. He was around 50, tall and thin and walked with a stoop of his shoulders. He was dressed down, in a pair of jeans and a long-sleeve t-shirt. He looked like he intentionally playing down his wealth. I had a feeling this was the case – he seemed like somebody who would be manipulative in that way. Just from what I read about him, I knew the guy was devious.

Robert took one look at Harper, who was stunning, as usual, in her grey pantsuit and heels that boosted her from 5'8" to just under 6', and I knew she would throw him off his game. He seemed to have a weakness for beautiful women.

Harper was certainly that.

Robert took the stand, raised his hand and was sworn in. Then Harper approached him.

He appeared to almost drool when she stood right in front of him. Her scent was intoxicating, even to me, and her graceful walk, with her head held high, attracted the attention of every male within striking distance.

She would play this guy like a bass violin. And I would relish it.

"Mr. Dunham," Harper said. "You're the brother of the deceased in this case, correct?"

"Yes," he said, talking into the microphone. He looked Harper in the eye and bit his lower lip. "That is correct."

Harper cocked her head ever-so-slightly, and then walked closer to Robert. "Did you have a good relationship with Dr. Dunham?" she asked.

He nodded his head. "I did. He was my brother and we were close."

She smiled slightly. "Permission to treat as hostile," she sweetly asked the judge.

"Permission granted. Please proceed."

Robert looked at Harper when the judge gave her permission to treat him as hostile. "What does that mean, treat me as hostile? I'm not hostile. I'm the friendliest guy you'll ever meet." He raised an eyebrow and smiled at Harper. "The friendliest guy."

Harper looked back at me and raised her eyebrows. I smiled, knowing what her look was telling me. It was a *can you believe this guy?* type of look, and my silent answer was, *I know, right?*

Harper chose to ignore Robert's subtle come-on. "Mr. Dunham, isn't it true that Dr. Dunham had an affair with your wife, Naomi, 10 years ago?"

"Yes," he said.

"And that affair actually caused a divorce, isn't that right?"

He rolled his eyes, seeing that Harper would take no prisoners and wouldn't fall for his non-existent charm. "Yes."

"And you and Naomi had five children, isn't that right?" she asked.

"Yes." His posture was becoming more and more defensive. Like Sharita before him, he glared at Harper and crossed his arms in front of him.

"And those kids were all under the age of 10 when you divorced Naomi, isn't that right?"

"Yes."

"And Naomi got full custody of your five children?"

"Yes." He sighed. "Where is this going?"

Harper ignored his question and kept on going. "You don't have a good relationship with your children now, do you?"

He looked over at the judge, as if he expected Judge Watkins to save him. "I don't, no."

"And isn't it true that you feel you lost your relationship with your children because you divorced their mother and only got to see them on a part-time basis?"

"I don't know why I don't have a good relationship with my children," he said. "I just know they don't like me very much."

Harper nodded. "But you divorcing their mother when they were young children, and her getting full custody of them, with only weekend visits for you, certainly didn't help your relationship with your kids. Is that safe to say?"

"I guess," he said.

"And isn't it true that you blame Dr. Dunham for all of that – the divorce, the estrangement from your kids. All of it?"

"I don't know. I guess." He wouldn't give Harper a straight answer on that, but I knew the truth. I got ahold of the file and the depositions given in the lawsuit that Dr. Dunham had filed against Robert when he found out Robert had influenced Earl Dunham, the Dunham family patriarch, to cut Dr. Dunham out of the will. The depositions clearly indicated that Robert Dunham hated Dr. Dunham because he blamed Dr. Dunham for the disintegration of his family and his relationship with his kids.

That was just one of the reasons why Robert Dunham had Dr. Dunham killed. My research came across an even more compelling reason for this, and Harper would examine Robert Dunham about all of it.

"You guess." Harper nodded. "Mr. Dunham, isn't it true that Dr. Dunham filed a lawsuit against you just last year when he found out that you were the reason he was cheated out of his inheritance?"

His face got red. "Yes. He did."

"And isn't it true that the reason Dr. Dunham filed a lawsuit against you was because you were instrumental in making sure that Mr. Earl Dunham, your grandfather, cut Dr. Dunham out of his will?"

"I guess."

"You don't know? Mr. Dunham, were you or were you not the defendant in the case of Dr. Tracy Dunham v. Robert Dunham, a case filed in this circuit just last year?"

"I was the defendant in that case, yes."

"And isn't it true that case was filed against you because you influenced Earl Dunham while in the late stages of Alzheimer's Disease to cut Tracy Dunham out of Earl's will by telling Earl that Dr. Dunham was disloyal to Earl? In fact, you told Earl that Tracy was plotting to kill him, isn't that true?"

"That's what Tracy claimed I did, yes. But, as you know, that case was never settled or resolved, so nothing was ever proved."

Harper nodded. "No, that case was never resolved, but only because Dr. Dunham died before it could be resolved, isn't that true?"

"What are you getting at?" Robert asked.

"Nothing. I'm just pointing out that the case was never resolved because Tracy died before it could be resolved. That's all." She looked back at me and raised an eyebrow.

"Yes. That's true. Tracy died before that case could be resolved. That's true."

"Mr. Dunham, isn't it true that you received an inheritance of $100 million from Earl Dunham?"

"Yes, that's true."

"And isn't it true that quite a bit of that inheritance has gone to settle a series of lawsuits filed against you by 25 different women?"

He shifted uncomfortably in his chair. "Yes, I had to settle some extremely baseless claims from a bunch of women out to get me. Yes, that's true. Not one of those claims had any basis in fact, not one."

"Yet, you settled all of them, one by one, and you paid a great deal of your wealth to these women? You paid some $50 million to these women altogether, isn't that right?"

"Yes, that's true," he said. "But that wasn't all my wealth."

"No, it wasn't, was it? Actually, your main source of wealth over the years has come from your shares in a pharmaceutical company called Osiris, isn't that correct?"

"That's right."

"And you actually own 75% of this business, isn't that right?"

"Right."

"And this company annually has sales of $500 million, isn't that right?"

"Give or take," Robert said.

"And isn't it true that some 80% of Osiris' annual pharmaceutical sales are in the realm of opioids?"

"Yes, that's true," Robert said. "Around that."

"80% of Osiris sales are in opioids. That's what, $400 million a year in opioid sales?"

"Yes, that sounds about right," Robert said.

"A lot of money, wouldn't you say?"

"I guess."

"And if somebody, say, was to come up with a way of treating pain that does not involve opioids, it would seriously cut into Osiris' profits, wouldn't that be right?"

"I guess. But nobody is doing that type of thing, so that point is moot, isn't it?"

Harper nodded. "Oh, but somebody was doing that type of thing, wasn't he? Dr. Dunham was developing a method of pain management that did not involve opioids, and he was getting a lot of attention for this method, wasn't he?"

Robert shrugged, trying hard to look nonchalant. "I really don't know. He was my brother, but we weren't close, so I really don't know what he was doing in his practice."

"You didn't know? Is that your testimony?" Harper asked him.

"Yes, that's my testimony."

"Really." Harper nodded her head. "You didn't know. You own 75% of a pharmaceutical company and you really weren't hearing about your brother's advancement in the treatment of pain management?"

"That's what I said," Robert said defensively.

"Your brother was approached by national magazines such as *Time* and was approached by national television shows like *The View* and you, a man who has a large stake in a pharmaceutical company that focuses on opioids, never heard that Dr. Dunham was on the verge of nationalizing a new technique that would cut considerably into the opioid business?"

"That's right, I didn't know."

Harper nodded. "So, then, is it fair to say that you are not up on the new advancements in pain management?"

"Of course I'm in the loop on pain management advances, but only on the pharmaceutical side."

"So, you only focus on pharmaceuticals, then, not on other types of pain management?"

"That's right, I don't focus on advancements that do not focus on pharmaceuticals."

Harper knew he looked foolish as he was giving his testimony. It was common sense that somebody with a large stake in a pharmaceutical company would obviously stay current on all advances in the field, not just the advancements that had to do directly with new drugs.

She decided to pivot to a different topic.

"Mr. Dunham, isn't it true that your company, Osiris, was entertaining an offer to merge with another pharmaceutical company, Aestus?"

"Yes, that is true."

"And Aestus is a multi-billion dollar company, is it not?"

"Yes, that's true. It is."

"In fact, Aestus does $3 billion sales annually, according to the most recent company reports, isn't that true?"

"Yes, that's true."

"And if Osiris was to merge with this company, that would mean that you, as the 75% stockholder of Osiris, would have stood to make millions?" Harper asked.

"Right. I would have made millions."

"And the merger is still in the works, isn't it?" Harper asked.

"It still is, yes."

"But isn't it true that Aestus was going to back out of the merger deal with Osiris because it was concerned that Osiris was too focused on opioids in its portfolio?"

"Well, there was a concern about that, but we were able to show Aestus that our opioid lines were robust and would continue to be so into the future, so we addressed their concerns about that."

"But isn't it true that Dr. Dunham's pain management procedure seriously threatened your company's bottom line?"

"Again, I didn't know my brother was working on a pain management procedure that didn't deal with drugs, so I have no idea how I'm going to answer that question."

At that, Harper decided to bring out the smoking gun. It was a document in the merger file that was a matter of public record. It was a letter that Robert Dunham had written to Eugene McConnell, the point man of the merger between Osiris and Aestus. It was something that would definitively prove Robert knew damned well that Tracy was a threat.

"I would like you to read a letter you wrote to Eugene McConnell," Harper said. "I have marked this as Exhibit A. Would you please read the highlighted portion of this letter?"

Robert took the letter and looked at it, and I saw his face get whiter and whiter as he read every word. "I don't know this letter, I've never seen it before," he said.

"Oh?" Harper said. "You mean, this isn't your signature at the bottom of this letter?"

"Well-" He looked doubtful. He knew he had signed this letter and he no-doubt was afraid that Harper had the goods to prove it. She already told me that if she needed to call a handwriting expert to authenticate his signature, she would do it. In fact, a handwriting expert was on our list of potential witnesses.

Robert didn't know Harper had a handwriting expert on tap, but he had to know this was a distinct possibility.

"Yes, or no? Is this or this not your signature at the bottom of this letter?" Harper asked.

He stared at the letter some more, shaking his head the entire time. "Yes," he finally said. "Yes. This is my signature at the bottom."

"So, are you in the habit of signing letters of which you don't know the content and had not reviewed?"

He was faced with the prospect of either looking like a sloppy person if he answered Harper's question in the affirmative and like a liar if he answered it in the negative. Neither of these prospects would look good for him, but to admit he signed this letter without reviewing it or okaying its contents looked like the only prospect for him at that moment.

"Yes," he finally said. "I guess I didn't review this letter before I signed it. I guess I didn't know what the contents of this letter were when I signed it."

"Oh? Is that what you want the jury to believe?"

"Yes, that's what I want the jury to know. I'm not proud of this, but sometimes I get so many papers crossing my desk, I'll just sign my name without even knowing what I'm signing. It happens sometimes. I'm a very busy guy."

"In this case, there was a lot at stake, wasn't there? Specifically, what was at stake was a merger that would net you millions and would make your company potentially billions a year. So you're telling the court that, with all those millions and billions on the line, you're going to sign a letter to the merger point man, Eugene McConnell, without reviewing said letter. That's what you're letting the court believe?" Harper asked.

"I'm a busy guy," Robert said, in a rather pathetic voice.

"I get that." Harper nodded. "So you've said. Anyhow, I would like you to read the highlighted portion of this letter to the court."

At that, Kevin got to his feet. "Objection, hearsay," he said.

"Your honor, this is a letter this man wrote," Harper said. "It's his own words. Therefore, it falls under the prior inconsistent statement exclusion to the hearsay rule."

"But the witness just spent a lot of time stating this wasn't actually his statement," Kevin said. "He was adamant that he never read this letter."

"Counselor," Judge Watkins said, addressing Harper. "What say you about that? The witness did deny reading this letter before signing it."

"This was a signed letter and he admitted signed it. Your honor, Mr. Williams' objection is frivolous and I think he knows it. The witness can claim all he wants that he has no idea about the contents of this letter and didn't read it before he signed it, but his signature is proof of the letter's authenticity and veracity."

Judge Watkins nodded his head. "Objection overruled. Mr. Dunham, you must answer the question."

Harper nodded and pointed to the phrase in the letter she wanted Robert to read. "Please read the highlighted portion of this letter," she said.

Robert took a deep breath and pretended he was seeing the letter for the first time ever. He read slowly and painfully, his face scrunched up in a *what the hell is this letter?* way.

"Mr. McConnell," he said with a clear of his throat as he read the letter. "While I understand your concern that my brother, Dr. Dunham, is working on a procedure that will greatly lessen the value of Osiris, Inc., in that Dr. Dunham is working on a pain management technique that has the potential to reduce the usage of opioids in this country, I can assure you this will not be a problem in the future."

He handed the letter back to Harper. "I don't know who wrote those words," he said. "I really don't."

Harper nodded, ignoring his protestations. "This letter indicates that you did, in fact, know your brother was working on a procedure that had the potential to kill your company's bottom line, isn't that right?"

"That's what that letter seems to indicate, but I don't know who wrote these words. It looks like somebody is trying to frame me for something." He shook his head. "I'm going to find out who wrote this letter and fire that person immediately."

"What did you mean when you said Dr. Dunham wouldn't be a problem in the future? What did that mean?"

"I don't know. I told you, I didn't write those words. I don't know."

"Isn't it true that you wrote Aestus with those words, that Dr. Dunham and his technique wouldn't be a problem in the future because you knew you were going to kill Dr. Dunham, thus eliminating the problem?"

"No. I didn't write those words, but I don't read them in that way."

"What way do you read them, then?"

He took a deep breath. "The person who wrote this letter was probably thinking my brother's technique would fail, that's all."

Harper nodded. The guy was a terrible liar and a terrible actor. His face was red and he was visibly shaking. I knew Harper got him by making him read that part of the letter. She would keep him squirming, like a worm on a fishing hook, writhing around.

"So, you knew Dr. Dunham was a threat to your bottom line," Harper announced, not allowing him to interject. "Mr. Dunham, isn't it true that you gave Sharita Vance $50,000 to deliver Oxycontin to Dr. Dunham?"

He shifted uncomfortably. He wasn't in the courtroom when Sharita gave her testimony, so he didn't know what her answer were to this particular question. He had to have known the proof of this transaction was out there, though. He had to know that if he answered "no," Harper could trap him in a lie.

He apparently decided that lying about this transaction was too risky. "Yes, that's true," he finally said. "I paid her money to deliver Oxycontin to my brother."

"Not just money, but $50,000," Harper said dramatically. "That's a pretty penny, isn't it?"

He sighed. "Yes, I guess it is."

"And why did you pay her that kind of money to give drugs to your brother?"

He apparently came up with a wild story right on the spot. "Well, my brother, he called me up that night, desperate. I knew he was getting heroin on the street, and I was so worried about it. So worried about it. I did my research, and I knew these street drugs are dangerous. Very dangerous. Those heroin dealers, they cut their heroin with rat poison and Fentanyl and all kinds of dangerous things. Well, I was scared he was getting his drugs on the street and I knew Ms. Vance used to give him

Oxycontin on a weekly basis. I wanted her to give him Oxycontin again, because I didn't want him using heroin. But she didn't want to deliver him Oxycontin. She refused. She said she had a falling-out with my brother and didn't want to go. Well, I was desperate for her to deliver those drugs to him, so I paid her that money so she could do that."

He was admitting to a crime, just as Sharita had admitted to a crime – delivering drugs to somebody was a crime. At least it was in a case like this, where the person delivering the drugs knew they would be used for an illegal purpose, which is what was happening here.

Yet, it seemed that admitting to their role in distributing illicit substances to Dr. Dunham was a lesser issue than admitting they delivered a lethal dose of heroin to the man. They both seemed to take that calculated risk.

"Really," Harper said to Robert. "And you couldn't just deliver the Oxycontin to him?" She knew the answer to this. She knew Robert could have never delivered Oxycontin to Dr. Dunham at any time, simply because the two men were not speaking. Harper would trap him into admitting that Dr. Dunham never desperately called Robert that night, let alone that Robert was terrified Dr. Dunham was getting his drugs from a dangerous place.

"No," he said. "I couldn't."

"And the reason why you couldn't was because you and Dr. Dunham weren't speaking, isn't it?"

"No, I told you he called me that evening, desperate and needing a fix. That's why I sent Sharita over there."

Harper shook her head. "That makes zero sense. Zero sense. If he called you in a desperate way, and you then personally delivered the Oxycontin to him, he would have welcomed you with open arms. That is, if the story was the way you testified it was – he called you desperately that evening. You certainly wouldn't have to pay Ms. Vance $50,000 to deliver those drugs, isn't that right?"

He sighed, obviously thinking of a different excuse. "Okay, okay," he finally said. "I paid her all that money because I knew she owed the Las Vegas Hilton $50,000 and she came to me, crying. She told me the Las Vegas Hilton was threatening her with legal action and maybe charging her criminally. So, I felt sorry for her and gave her that money. That was the real reason why I gave it to her." He smiled at the jury, thinking he came up with a good story. He was being altruistic, you see. She needed him and he came through for her.

"Okay," Harper said, turning to the jury with an amused look on her face. "So, you did that for her from the goodness of your heart. Can you tell the court what your relationship was with Ms. Vance?"

"What do you mean?"

"I mean, how close are you with Ms. Vance?"

He took a deep breath. He didn't know what Sharita had said on the stand about the nature of his relationship with her. "I-"

"Isn't it true that you barely know Ms. Vance?"

"No, that's not true. She's one of our pharmaceutical reps. Of course I know her."

Harper nodded. "Oh, I see. So, if any one of your pharmaceutical reps came to you, crying, because he or she needed thousands of dollars to get out of a jam, you'll just cut a check to that person, right?"

"No, of course not. If I did that, I would go broke in no time," he said.

"Yes, that's right, isn't it? Yet, here comes Ms. Vance, just one of your pharmaceutical reps, with a sob story about gambling debts, and you just cut her a check for altruistic reasons. Is that what your testimony is?"

He was a cornered animal and he knew it. Harper was doing a masterful job of boxing him into a room with no doors. "Yes," he said in a small voice. "I guess she caught me at a generous time."

"A generous time?" Harper said in a wondrous voice. "You just got a desperate phone call from your brother, or so you say, and you were feeling generous at that moment?"

He nodded his head. "And I have a weakness for beautiful women," he said with a smile. He suddenly decided to use his sexual harassment claims to his benefit. "That's why all those women sued me."

"Oh? I thought you said earlier those women who sued you were out to get you."

"Well, I guess I said that because I was embarrassed, but the truth is, if a beautiful woman comes to me and asks me for something, I'm a sucker every time. Ms. Vance knew my weakness and took advantage of it, I'm afraid."

Oh, he was good. He was really making lemonade out of lemons, that one was. He was taking his sexual harassment suits to show he really might have given Sharita $50,000 out of the goodness of his heart.

But Harper was better. "So, if any random beautiful woman asks for thousands of dollars to help her out of a jam, you'll open up your check-book?" She looked over at the jury. "Take note of this, ladies of the jury. If you're attractive, this guy will automatically give you money."

At that, the men and women of the jury laughed nervously.

Kevin stood up. "Objection, mischaracterization of testimony."

"Sustained," Judge Watkins said, glaring at Harper. "You know better, counselor."

"I'm sorry, your honor, I couldn't resist." She made her point, though, and she knew it.

She turned back to Robert. "Sorry for the commentary, but the question was valid. If any random beautiful woman came to you, asking for tens of thousands of dollars, you'll open your wallet and say 'have at it?'" she asked.

"Of course not," he said.

"Yet you did that for Ms. Vance," she said. "Why?"

"She needed the money and I needed a favor. That's it."

"And you couldn't deliver the drugs to him directly because?" Harper asked.

"I was busy that night."

"Busy doing what?" Harper asked.

"Just busy."

"But you took the time out to meet with Ms. Vance, hear her story, and give her that money. Wouldn't it have taken less time to drive over to Dr. Dunham's office yourself and give him that Oxycontin sample?" Harper asked.

"I guess."

"So, that's a yes?" Harper asked.

"Yes." Robert was defeated. He wouldn't even try to come up with story number 1,118.

"Admit it," Harper said. "You took those Oxycontin pills in that

Oxycontin bottle you gave to Ms. Vance, you replaced those pills with high-grade heroin, and you gave them to Ms. Vance to deliver that night. You knew Ms. Vance was exposing herself to high risk in doing what she did, which was why you paid her so much money to deliver the drugs. Admit it."

He wouldn't admit it, but that wasn't the point in asking that question. Harper would get the theory of the case out there and see how he answered.

He started to laugh nervously. "And where am I going to find high-grade heroin?" he asked. "I don't know anybody who would have access to something like that."

"That wasn't the question," Harper said. "I wanted you to admit you replaced the Oxycontin pills that Ms. Vance delivered with high-grade heroin."

"And that was my answer. I don't know a soul who would have access to high-grade heroin. So, no, I didn't do that."

"I'm not even going to try to prove that, because it would be impossible to prove a negative," Harper said. "I don't know who you know and don't know, but I will note that you're a very wealthy man with connections, and one of those connections might just be a drug dealer with access to high-grade heroin."

Kevin stood up. "Motion to strike that statement. It calls for speculation, it's prejudicial and has zero basis in fact."

"Sustained," Judge Watkins said. "Ms. Ross, one more stunt like that, and I'll call a mistrial. Fair warning."

Harper nodded. She almost crossed a line that would be a basis for a mistrial, and she knew it. She was risking it, but she apparently wanted the jury to know what her thoughts were. "I'm sorry, your honor."

She finally took a deep breath. "I have nothing further for this witness."

At that, she sat down, and Kevin stood up. For the next hour, he tried gamely to rehabilitate Robert with soft-ball questions, but, in the end, it seemed this witness helped our case much more than that of the state.

By the time Kevin was done with Robert, it was time to call Sally Wallace, Dr. Dunham's office manager.

I looked over at Mom. "I think we got this," I said. "Harper was conducting a master class on how to corner a witness."

Mom looked over at Harper and smiled. "I told you I trusted Harper."

I called Sally to the stand, and she approached, raised her hand, was sworn in and I approached and got to work.

"Could you please state your name for the record?" I asked her.

"Sally Wallace."

"And you were the office manager for Dr. Dunham, isn't that true?"

"Right. I am."

"And what was your understanding about Dr. Dunham and his philosophy of treating pain?"

"He was against prescribing drugs to combat pain. No drugs of any kind. He treated patients with natural methods only," she said.

"What was his method used to treat his patients for pain?" I asked her.

"He used a special technique, one he invented. It was very effective, too. He had patients clamoring to see him."

"And what was this special technique?" I asked.

"He used a combination of radio and sonar waves to pinpoint the overactive nerves that cause a lot of pain in patients. That gave a lot of relief to patients with chronic pain."

"And was he getting a lot of attention for this method?"

"Oh, yes. Yes, he was. He not only had doctors calling him up, 100s a day, wanting to learn his method, but he also was getting attention nationwide. I was fielding calls from *The View,* and from magazines everywhere. *Time Magazine* was going to do a front-page profile on him and his method, along with all kinds of health magazines like *Prevention* and magazines like that. He was about to blow up huge for sure. But he died before he could really get going."

"And he wanted to train other doctors in his method?"

"Yes. We were very excited. He was really a pioneer. He wanted to make his method national because he was going to train doctors around the country on how they could also use his method."

I asked her some more questions, for about another hour, and then

Kevin stood up and cross-examined her. When Sally finally got off the stand, it was time to go home.

Mom would take the stand the next day, and I would have Harper conduct her examination. It would be almost anti-climactic, in my opinion, because Sharita and Robert did themselves so much damage. It helped that they were really bad criminals. If they were better at covering their tracks, Harper and I would have had a lot of issues.

"Okay, Mom," I said. "Tomorrow, it's showtime."

She nodded but looked nervous.

"Damien," she said. "I need to talk to you and Harper before I take the stand tomorrow. I need to talk to you both. I don't want to lie on the stand, Damien, so I gotta talk to you both."

I took a deep breath. "Okay, of course you have to talk to us."

"No, I mean, I gotta talk to you both. Let's go back to my place, because I gotta roll a joint before I talk to you guys."

Oh, boy. This did not sound good.

Little did I know just how not good it would turn out to be.

THIRTY-THREE

We got back to Mom's home, and, just like she said, she rolled a joint the first thing and took a long drag. "Sorry, Damien, I'm nervous, and this calms me down like nothing else."

I looked over at Harper and shrugged. I had no idea what she was about to tell me.

"Mom, you're making me nervous," I said. "Out with it."

"Wait, wait," she said. "I gotta let this stuff kick in." She waved the air in an effort to dispel the smoke that hung in her home.

"Olivia," Harper said. "What's going on?"

Mom shook her head. "I can't continue lying. I'm scared, Damien. I talked to Peg, she lives on the other block, and told her what's going on. She said that if I lied on the stand, I could get in trouble. She said her son lied on the stand and got put in jail for it and had to pay a fine. She told me I can't lie under oath."

I was getting annoyed. "Mom, with all due respect, of course you know you can't lie under oath. I told you that a hundred times. And it's a crime to lie under oath - a Class A felony. That doesn't mean jail, it means prison. Minimum 10 years in prison, to be exact."

She gave me a look. "Well, Damien, I had to hear it from my friend. And she told me I can get in real trouble."

"So," I said. "Go ahead, then, tell me what's on your mind."

"That blood pressure medicine wasn't blood pressure medicine, it was pure heroin," Mom blurted out. "There, I said it."

The words hung in the air as I realized the ramifications of what she just told me. All at once, I realized I had lied to the jury about what I planned on proving. I was wrong that this whole case was an elaborate set-up and the prosecutors and cops were dirty. Nobody planted drugs to frame my mother. Nobody had to. My mother lied to me, again, and to say I was pissed was an understatement.

She started to ramble on. "I didn't do the junk, though, I don't do it. It belongs to Annie Shaw, she lives around the corner, and her son Jimmy's on the junk. Annie found it in her house, Jimmy was in rehab, so she gave it to me so Jimmy won't find it and fall off the wagon."

Harper was surprisingly calm about Mom's confession. "Okay, Olivia, so you actually possessed heroin when the cops came in and you put it into that Nifedipine bottle. Is that what you're saying?"

"Yeah, but I was just holding it for Annie."

"And why didn't Annie flush it down the toilet?" Harper asked.

"Well, see, Annie knows high-grade stuff when she sees it. She knows when something is worth a lot of money. Guess she did her research on junk, because her son's a junkie. A recovering junkie now, I guess. But Annie knows that stuff had a good street value, thousands of dollars. And she thought she could sell it if she got hard-up for money."

Harper nodded, following Mom's whole wacked-out scenario. "And so Annie didn't want to destroy it and didn't want it around her house, because she was afraid her son would find it, so she gave it to you for safe-keeping?"

"Yeah. That's what happened. Listen, Annie was there for me when I needed her before. She was dating this one guy, a cop named Dinkleman. I got a DUI one time, and she convinced Dinkleman to help those charges get dropped. I owe her my life, because if I got another DUI, I'd be sent down the river, the big house. My license was suspended at that time, and it would have been my third DUI, so you do the math. Annie helped me get that dropped. I owe her my life."

"Welp, I guess we're screwed. We could have called Annie to the stand to explain away the heroin, but you never told us there was an Annie, so we didn't put her on our witness list." Harper shook her head.

"Oh, no, I wouldn't have let you call Annie to the stand. I wouldn't want her getting into trouble."

"Better her getting into trouble than you going to prison for life because you happened to be holding her heroin when the cops busted in," Harper said. She was finally starting to get annoyed. I didn't blame her.

"Mom," I said, as calmly as I could. "You mean to tell me I lied to the jury? In my opening statement, I made a big deal about how you were framed because drugs were planted in your medicine cabinet, and now you're telling me you were guilty all along?"

She shook her head. "No, I never gave Tracy drugs. I never did. I swear. He shared his drugs with me."

"Bullshit," I said. "Bullshit. You lied to me about possessing drugs. How can I ever believe you didn't give drugs to Tracy? How can I ever believe you weren't lying all along? You probably gave Tracy those drugs and lied to me and everyone else because you didn't know you could be found criminally liable for doing something like that. Once you found out you were subject to criminal liability, you came up with a cocka-mamie story about the cops planting drugs and your taking antibiotics, which would cause a false positive. For all I know, you gave Tracy heroin, you were doing it too, he died, and you lied to me when the cops came around and arrested you. How do I know that's not the case?"

I took a deep breath, realizing everything was making more sense in this case. All along, I wondered exactly why the cops and the state would be framing Mom.

Nope, no frame. Mom really did possess heroin and Mom really did drop a dirty UA. The cops and the state had every right to charge her the way they did.

That didn't mean Robert didn't kill his brother, though. It just meant I would look like a liar because of what I promised the jury I would prove, and that, in turn, meant the jury would take everything else I put forth with a grain of salt.

"Well, Mom, our case is going south now. Dammit, what were you thinking? You let me lie to the jury. Now the jury won't believe anything else we're saying. Did you not think about that, Mom?"

"Damien, don't yell at me. I'm sorry. I didn't want you to think I did this."

I sighed. "But you did it, didn't you?"

"No, I didn't. I told you, I didn't. I never took that junk and I never gave it to Tracy, either."

Harper was sitting in a chair, not saying a word. She finally spoke, though.

"Damien," she said, "I believe Olivia. Remember, we sent that sample of Oxycontin into a lab, and it tested as pure heroin. I still think Robert Dunham killed his brother in that way. It's been an unfortunate coincidence that Olivia also had high-grade heroin in her medicine cabinet and had antibiotics in her system, which caused a false positive, but-"

I looked over at Mom, who was taking another puff of her joint.

"Mom, you have to come clean, totally clean. That UA wasn't a false positive, was it? I'm putting an expert on to talk about false positives, but I have a feeling I'll have to call him off, too." I shook my head. "You have to come clean, Mom, you have to come clean."

"Damien, I don't do that junk."

I raised my eyebrow. "But you take Oxycontin when it's offered to you, don't you?"

She looked at Harper, on whose face was an expression I couldn't discern. "I was having a bad night and Tracy offered me some of his hill-billy heroin. I don't do no real heroin, I know what kind of crap those drug dealers put in those street drugs. But Oxycontin, if I can get ahold of that, I'm gonna take it. Tracy offered some to me and I took it that night. But, I swear, Damien, he gave the drug to me, not the other way around."

"Mom," I said, "those hillbilly heroin pills you took were actual heroin. You do know that, right?"

"Yeah, I know that now. I know somebody put actual heroin into those capsules. I thought I felt weird when I took it, weirder than when I've taken Oxycontin before."

"Mom," I said. "What's the whole story? The real story?"

Mom looked at Harper desperately. "Harper, I didn't do nothing wrong. I swear, I didn't. See, Tracy and me, we had a deal. He gave me Oxy every week in exchange for me having sex with him. I swear, I don't do horse and I never have. I swear I didn't give Tracy no drugs. I swear."

Ah, so the truth was FINALLY coming out. And it wasn't pretty.

"So, Mom, you were prostituting yourself to Tracy in exchange for Oxy. Is that what you're saying?"

She nodded. "I guess, if you want to put it that way. Me, I just thought of it as him giving me drugs and me giving him sex. I mean, I'm not no prostitute. I don't take money for sex, only drugs."

I stood up. "Mom, that's the very definition of prostitution. You take something of value in exchange for sex."

Harper was calmer. After all, it wasn't her nutso mother sitting in the living room with us. "Olivia, so, you're saying the night Tracy died, he shared his Oxy with you?"

"Yeah."

Harper looked at me. "So, the Nifedipine bottle really did have pure heroin in it, and Olivia actually did have heroin in her system when she dropped a dirty UA." She stated the obvious, but I needed to hear it in her words.

"No, I didn't do horse that night, I did Oxy."

"Yes, but, Olivia, those Oxy pills Tracy gave you were replaced by pure heroin. That's what this case is all about, remember?" I said.

"I know, I know, I keep forgetting," Mom said.

"But somehow the cop on the scene never saw signs Mom was high," I said, remembering my cross-examination of Officer Conrad. "No dilated pupils, no weird behavior, no odd syntax. Nothing."

"Yeah, but the cops came the next day when Olivia woke up," Harper reminded me. "They were on the scene at 10 AM the day after Olivia and Dr. Dunham got high. Obviously, the high and the signs of her being high had worn off by then, but the drugs remained in her system. So, we could re-call Officer Conrad to ask him more about signs Olivia was high, but grilling him won't necessarily show anything dispositive, let alone something that would help us out in this case."

I nodded. "That's true."

Harper cocked her head. "Okay, so you took heroin with Tracy that night, yet nothing really happened to you." She raised an eyebrow. "Nothing happened to you. So, it probably wasn't the purity level of the drug that killed Tracy. If it were, Olivia would have probably also died, or, at the very least, been put into the hospital."

"Yeah, nothing happened to me, except I floated around the room for several hours, but, other than that, I was fine."

Harper narrowed her eyes. "Let me see your file," she said to me. "I need to take a closer look at all of Dr. Dunham's medical records."

I had subpoenaed Dr. Dunham's medical records to see if there was any health issue that would have caused his death. I didn't really see anything in the records, however. They were extensive and I had reviewed them thoroughly.

Harper looked through the records closely. "There's something missing here," she said. "There's something missing. I just know it." She checked her watch. "Dammit, why do I think there's something missing in these medical records?"

"What's missing?" I asked her.

"I don't know," she said. "I just think there's something in Dr. Dunham's background that would have explained why Dr. Dunham died. I mean, if that heroin was that strong and that pure, Olivia would have also been adversely affected and she wasn't. What if Dr. Dunham was allergic to heroin and Robert Dunham knew that? What if-"

She shook her head. "What if Dr. Dunham took heroin earlier in his life, almost died, the doctor found out he was having an allergic reaction and this was covered up? He was rich, his family was rich, they would have had the means to cover it up if something like that happened. What if he checked into the hospital under an assumed name when that happened?"

"What assumed name?" I asked. "We've never uncovered any kind of assumed name he might have used over the years."

Harper sat down after reviewing every single record with a fine-toothed comb. "An alias..."

I looked over at my Mom, who was looking like she was thinking about something. "Try this name," she said. "Tracy Wheeler. That was the name he gave me when he tried to pick me up that one night in that bar."

"Really? You never told me that, Mom," I said. "It would have been helpful to know that he sometimes went under a different name."

"I didn't think about it until Harper just started talking about him using an assumed name, but that rang a bell."

Harper was immediately on the phone with Anna. "Anna, I need to see if you can find any kind of medical records for a Tracy Wheeler. DOB 1/19/63." She nodded her head. "Thanks." She looked at me. "Anna will call back if she finds anything."

Five minutes later, Anna called back, confirming Harper's hunch.

"I see," Harper said. "Send them to me PDF." She got her iPad out, and looked at it. "Thanks."

She apparently got into her email, and then snapped her fingers at me. "Look. Right here."

I looked at the PDF, seeing that a Tracy Wheeler, with Dr. Dunham's DOB, had a serious medical issue when he was only 15 years old. He had been brought into the ER, unresponsive, and it was found he had taken heroin. It was also found that he had gone into anaphylactic shock, and the medical records indicated that Dr. Dunham had an allergy to the drug.

"Did the autopsy miss this?" I wondered aloud.

Harper nodded. "Probably. Look at this." She pointed to some medical journal articles that indicated that anaphylactic shock was typically not detected by a post-mortem examination. The study showed that fatal anaphylaxis was often not detected because of how rapidly the person died, and because the person often died of shock and not asphyxia. The conclusion was that just because an autopsy didn't find anaphylactic shock was the cause of death didn't preclude it as the actual cause of the person dying.

"But I'll bet Robert knew his brother was allergic to heroin," I said. "I'll bet he was one of the only ones who knew this. The family covered this incident up."

"Dr. Dunham almost died once before from taking heroin," Harper said. "And Robert had to make a bet that the heroin would be fatal this time because he knew his brother's history."

I nodded. "Looks like I'm going to have to re-call Robert to the stand, or you will. You can ask him on the stand about his brother's previous incident with taking heroin. He'll lie like always, but we need to get the evidence on the record anyhow. If you don't ask him about that, there's no way to get that piece of evidence into the closing argument." Closing arguments were restricted to facts put into evidence, which meant that if we never brought this up, we couldn't use it as an argument. "But I doubt the judge will let me re-call him. I know the rule on that, and a witness can only be re-called if another witness brings in evidence that contradicted the earlier testimony."

Harper nodded. "We can bring Olivia to the stand, have her state that Tracy went by the name of Tracy Wheeler when he met her, and then use that as an excuse to bring Robert Dunham on to ask him if he knew about the alias and then use that to open the door."

"No, dammit," I said. "That won't work. We didn't ask Robert about Tracy's aliases, so Mom's testimony won't be contradictory to anything he said on the stand. We'll just have to re-call Dr. Warren. She performed the autopsy, and, at the time she was giving her testimony, I had no idea that anaphylactic shock was even in the realm of possibilities. I reserved the right to call her in my own case-in-chief, which means she was not technically released from the court after the state called her in its case. That's the only way we can get this piece of information into evidence, assuming the judge won't allow me to re-call Robert Dunham."

Harper nodded. "That's good thinking. We'll bring in Dr. Warren as our witness and ask her about the anaphylactic shock thing. We can get her on the record as stating it's difficult to detect anaphylactic shock in a post-mortem exam, and that means we can probably get this new theory into our closing argument. It won't be as good as us asking Robert if he knew his brother had used an alias or if he knew his brother almost died of anaphylactic shock caused by exposure to heroin, but it is what it is."

I looked at Mom. "Well, Mom, you screwed things up with your lying. You caused me to lie in my opening statement. You caused me to lose my chance to press Robert on whether he knew his brother had a history of a severe allergic reaction to using heroin. If we lose this case, it's on you and only you. If you would have been honest with me from the start, things would have gone much smoother. Thanks a lot."

Harper put her hand on my shoulder. "Damien, don't beat her up too much. It's unproductive. At least she finally came clean and we have another avenue to explore. We have another theory on what happened here, and, in my mind, Robert Dunham looks guiltier than ever. He was the best person to be in the position to know his brother had an allergy to heroin and was in the best position to know just how to kill his own brother. If Olivia never came clean on what she did, that she took a heroin pill just like Dr. Dunham did, then we never would have thought of this angle. So-"

I nodded. "Lemons, lemonade, I know. But still. Damn you, Mom."

THIRTY-FOUR

The next day, I conferred with the judge. "I have new evidence I need to ask Robert Dunham about," I said. "So, I need to re-call him." I knew the judge probably wouldn't let me re-call Robert, but I had to try.

"No can do," Kevin said. "You had your chance. You know the rules. You snooze, you lose, brother."

Judge Watkins shook his head. "Mr. Williams is right. You cannot re-call a witness unless you need the witness to rebut testimony of a later witness. That's not the case here, is it?"

"Well, actually, my witness, my defendant, Ms. Ward, will testify that Dr. Dunham used the assumed name of Tracy Wheeler when he tried to pick her up in a bar where they met. I would like to ask Robert Dunham about whether he knew his brother used an alias."

"And where will you go with that, brother?" Kevin asked me. "So Dr. Dunham used a different name. So what?"

Judge Watkins nodded. "I'm inclined to agree with Mr. Williams. You can re-call Robert to ask him if he was aware his brother used an assumed name, but that would be the only thing you can ask him. You can't ask him anything else, so is it worth it to you to get him back on the stand?"

I took a deep breath. "No. I suppose it wouldn't."

"Okay, then," Judge Watkins said. "I'm going to call the jury in and we're going to get the show on the road again."

I looked over at my mom, silently cursing her. I could have had the chance to grill Robert on the anaphylactic shock incident, but there was no way I could do that.

Then I got an idea. "Your honor, I would like the opportunity to bring Dr. Littman on as my own witness. Dr. Littman and Dr. Warren. I put them both on my own witness list, just to be safe." That was a practice of mine – every one of the prosecution's witnesses showed up on my own witness list, just in case I needed to call them as my own witness.

Judge Watkins nodded his head. "Any objections, Mr. Williams?"

"None, your honor," Kevin said.

"Permission granted. Let's bring in the jury."

I took a deep breath. Perhaps Dr. Littman knew something about the Tracy Wheeler anaphylactic shock thing. I wouldn't be surprised if he knew about that. After all, he had to ask Dr. Dunham about drug allergies, and if Tracy was honest, he probably told him about it.

I tapped my fingers on my table as the jury filed back in. I would call my mother to the stand first, and then call Dr. Littman and then Dr. Warren.

Then I thought better of it. Crap. If I called my mother to the stand, she would contradict everything I promised the jury that I would deliver. Everything. The UA was correct, and the cops really seized actual heroin from her home. She would testify that Tracy was dead when she woke up, and that Tracy actually gave her drugs, not the other way around, but everything else she would say would be directly contradictory to the evidence promised in my opening statement.

I felt nervous when the jury was seated and waited for my evidence to resume. What to do? I felt I had drawn a lot of blood in my examination of Sharita and Robert Dunham. I felt like I put reasonable doubt in the minds of the jury that those two were actually behind the killing of Dr. Dunham. If I put my mother on the stand, and she admitted the truth, the jury would reasonably conclude she was lying about everything else.

Better not call my mother and let the jury forget all I had promised to show. Better to do that then to call my mother to the stand and have Kevin hammer away at her about her lies.

Judge Watkins looked at me. "Counselor, call your first witness," he said.

I took a deep breath. "The defense calls Dr. Littman."

My mom poked me in the side and I gave Harper a look. I think Harper understood, because I saw her whispering to Mom as Dr. Littman took the stand. Mom was sitting at the defense table, shaking her head rapidly and pointing at me, and Harper was apparently trying to get her under control.

Dr. Littman approached the stand. He was aware he was on my witness list so was prepared to testify on my behalf. I didn't think he was prepared to testify first, however. But he didn't seem too ruffled by the change in plans.

I knew Dr. Littman probably didn't know Tracy Wheeler was a thing, but I wasn't sure. Nevertheless, I needed to get that piece of evidence into my closing argument, and asking Dr. Littman about it was the only way I could do it.

Dr. Littman was probably around 80 years old, with white hair, and looked like he had seen it all. He had a gruff demeanor but I liked the guy. He seemed like somebody who wouldn't BS anybody.

He sat down, was reminded he was still under oath, and I got to work.

"Dr. Littman," I began. "I know you testified earlier on behalf of the state, and you testified you did not see any indication that Dr. Dunham was a drug user. You also testified that Dr. Dunham did not have any underlying health issues. Just to remind you."

He nodded his head. "That's right. I've been seeing Dr. Dunham for the better part of 30 years, and I've never known him to have so much as a high blood pressure reading. But you have my records so you know that."

"I do," I said. "Have your records. But I wanted to ask another question. Were you aware Dr. Dunham was allergic to heroin? That consuming heroin would have caused him to go into anaphylactic shock?"

He furrowed his brow. "No, I wasn't aware of that. I did a complete medical history of Dr. Dunham when he came to me. He never indicated he had an allergy to heroin or to any other drug for that matter."

That was fine. I figured Dr. Littman probably didn't know. I just wanted to ask the question to get it into evidence. "And were you aware that Tracy Dunham once used the alias of Tracy Wheeler when he had a previous medical incident?"

"No, I wasn't aware Dr. Dunham had an alias."

I nodded. "I have nothing further for this witness."

I looked over at Kevin, who was looking at me suspiciously. I didn't blame him – I never brought the issue of anaphylactic shock up to him, because I didn't know it was a possibility. Thank God I figured it out before I got to my closing argument, though.

Next up was Dr. Warren, the Medical Examiner. I would reinforce the anaphylactic shock angle by asking her if that was a possibility. I needed her to establish that anaphylactic shock was often missed in an autopsy.

She came to the stand, a tall redhead in high-heels and a dark wrap-around dress. I always found her attractive, but she was all business and never gave me, or any man, the time of day. Nobody was better at her job, however.

Dr. Warren approached the witness stand, sat down, was reminded she was still under oath, and I approached her.

"Dr. Warren, when you testified for the state, you stated you found the toxicology test you did on Dr. Dunham showed he had high-grade heroin in bloodstream at the time he died, correct?"

"Yes, that was my testimony."

"You also said that, other than the heroin in his system, your autopsy was unremarkable."

"Correct."

"And that was why you concluded that Dr. Dunham died of a heroin overdose, correct?"

"Correct."

"Now, if Dr. Dunham had actually died of anaphylactic shock, brought on by a severe allergy to heroin, that would not be something you could have detected in your autopsy, correct?"

She nodded. "That would be correct. Death by anaphylactic shock can often be undetectable in a post-mortem examination. If I would have been aware that this was an issue, however, I would have looked for evidence of anaphylactic shock more closely, but I was never made aware that the deceased had severe allergies. And, often, even if a medical examiner is looking for evidence of anaphylactic shock, it is still missed."

"And why is this?"

"Because an individual dies so suddenly when they are in the throes of anaphylactic shock, and because the person dies of shock, as opposed to asphyxiation. Death in this manner is sometimes detected, but, more often than not, there are no macroscopic findings of anaphylactic shock even if that was ultimately the cause of death. Unfortunately."

"So, then, if the deceased, Dr. Dunham, died because he had a severe allergic reaction to the heroin consumed, that wouldn't have necessarily been something you would have concluded, then?"

"Correct."

"I have nothing further."

Kevin didn't have any questions for her, and she was excused.

I sat down. I looked over at my mother. I took a deep breath. Gut check time. If I called my mother, I would have to do it now. Otherwise, I would rest, and there would be no chance for my mother to tell her story.

"Counselor, call your next witness," Judge Watkins said to me.

I looked at my mother, realized that calling her would open a can of worms I didn't want to deal with, and stood up. "The defense rests," I said.

At that, my mother tugged desperately on my sleeve. "Damien, I want to tell my story. I want to tell what happened that night."

Judge Watkins looked at my mother, then at me. "The defense rests?" he asked.

"Yes," I said, projecting confidence in my voice. "The defense rests."

He nodded. "Very well. We'll take a 15 minute recess, then we'll get to closing arguments." He banged the gavel and the jury filed out for their recess.

After the jury was out of the courtroom, along with the judge, Mom let me have it. "Damien, what the hell are you doing? We went through my testimony, again and again and again. You've been beating me over the head about what I'm going to say on the stand, and you don't even call me? What's going on?"

"Mom, I thought about it. I made a snap decision. I thought about how the prosecutor would have tore you apart on cross-examination. I just think it's best the jury forget about what I promised them in my opening statement, and if I put you on the stand, there would be no way for that to happen. The jury would have been reminded of exactly what I hoped to show, because the prosecution would ask you questions designed to remind them of just that. Not only that, Mom, you would've had to admit you really were high on heroin that night, albeit you didn't know it was heroin, and you actually did have heroin in that blood pressure medication bottle. I didn't want that coming in, so, Mom, I decided it best that I don't call you. And that's all."

"But Damien, I don't think you showed I didn't do this. I could have told the jury in my own words I didn't do this. Now they won't hear that from me."

"Yes, Mom, that's true, but they also won't hear you were taking drugs that night and you also possessed heroin that night. Let's just let the testimony of Robert and Sharita be what the jury remembers." I sighed. "Mom, again, if you would've been honest with me from the beginning, everything would've been different. But you lied so you might have to live with the consequences. This is why I always need my clients to tell me the truth right up front. So things like this don't happen."

I looked over at Harper, and she nodded. "You did the right thing," she said to me. "I would have made the same call."

I smiled. Harper and I often thought alike, and I knew she would agree with me.

Now it was just a matter of closing argument.

No pressure.

THIRTY-FIVE

Kevin gave his closing argument, which was essentially duplicative of his opening statement. He hit the same high points he hit before, except he made reference to the testimony solicited from Officer Conrad, et. al.

"You heard the testimony of Officer Conrad. He gave the defendant a urinalysis, which showed she was high on opioids at the time Dr. Dunham died. You heard the testimony of Dr. Thomas Smith, who testified the drugs seized from the defendant's medicine cabinet were pure heroin in pill form. The same kind of heroin found in Dr. Dunham's blood at the time of his death."

He smiled his million-watt smile at the jury. "Let that sink in for a moment. The same kind of heroin found in Dr. Dunham's body at the time of his death was found in the defendant's medicine cabinet. The same kind. Now, you can maybe think that Dr. Dunham came over to the defendant's home and supplied her with the drugs, and he took them himself, but then why would those drugs be found in the defendant's medicine cabinet? That makes no sense, ladies and gentlemen. No sense at all. The evidence clearly shows the defendant gave Dr. Dunham drugs when he came to her home.

Dr. Dunham's wife testified that Dr. Dunham left her house the night of October 12, and he was sober and fine. This is another piece of the puzzle and shows he did not get the drugs any place else except for at the defendant's home. The defendant had the drugs in her medicine cabinet, she did the drugs with Dr. Dunham, and Dr. Dunham died. It's as simple as that.

And all that nonsense about Robert Dunham paying Sharita Vance to deliver heroin to his brother..." He waved his hand at the jury dismissively. "What a crazy story that is. There's no evidence any of that happened. They both denied it, and Robert Dunham said he knew nobody who could supply him heroin for the nefarious deed. Let alone finding somebody to put heroin into a pill form and carefully enclose the heroin pills in a foil packet that looks like a typical Oxycontin pack. And Sally Wallace testified that Dr. Dunham was working hard on an alternative method of treating pain, but so what? The defendant couldn't definitively link Dr. Dunham's work with his murder. She didn't link those two at all."

He prattled on for about fifteen more minutes, and then it was my turn.

I looked at my mother, feeling angry again that she lied to me for so long. If she went down, it was her fault, and hers alone. I had the chance to press Robert Dunham about the anaphylactic shock thing, and I couldn't. I inadvertently lied in my opening statement about what I would prove. And I couldn't put Mom on the stand because I knew it would've opened up a can of worms.

My back was against the wall, but it was go-time. I really had no choice but to give it my all.

However, I had to admit my arguments and facts were much weaker than I thought they were in the beginning.

I decided just to hammer away at Sharita and Robert and hope for the best. No point in going anywhere else in my closing argument.

"Ladies and gentlemen of the jury," I said, "I want you to focus on two things and two things only. One, Dr. Dunham was a threat to the pharmaceutical industry in general and to Robert Dunham in particular. Dr. Dunham was about to explode huge with his alternative pain management technique and his technique was a threat to the opioid industry. The second thing I want you to focus on is that Robert

Dunham hated his brother and, as a majority shareholder in a pharmaceutical company that had a portfolio of drugs that were 80% opioids, he was personally threatened by Dr. Dunham's pain management technique.

On the first point, you heard the testimony of Sally Wallace. You heard her testify about Dr. Dunham's pain management technique. You heard her talk about how *Time Magazine* would feature Dr. Dunham as a cover story. *Time Magazine*. A cover story. That's huge. Dr. Dunham was also in talks with the television show *The View*. Other industry magazines such as *Prevention* were going to do cover stories. In other words, Dr. Dunham was about to become a very big deal. But he died before he could really show his technique to the doctors around the country who were interested in learning it.

On the second point, you heard the testimony of Sharita Vance and Robert Dunham. Just to remind you, Sharita Vance was paid $50,000 to deliver some pills that were ostensibly Oxycontin to Dr. Dunham. $50,0000. She admitted that was the arrangement and so did Robert Dunham. Neither of them denied it. You heard testimony that Robert essentially blamed Dr. Dunham for the breakup of his marriage and the estrangement from his kids, because Dr. Dunham had an affair with Robert Dunham's wife, Naomi. You heard evidence that Dr. Dunham was in the process of suing Robert Dunham because Robert Dunham caused Dr. Dunham to be cut out of Earl Dunham's will, because Robert Dunham was whispering in Earl Dunham's Alzheimer's-riddled brain that Dr. Dunham was plotting to killing him. The two brothers didn't like one another and that's an understatement.

I submit to the jury that this is what happened. Robert Dunham wanted his brother out of the way. Dr. Dunham, with his pioneering pain management technique, would cost Robert Dunham a lot of money in lost opioid sales. If Dr. Dunham's technique blew up as huge as it seemed it would, then it had the potential to become the standard of care for doctors around the country. That, in turn, would mean opioid sales would decline precipitously in this country. Robert Dunham's company, Osiris, depended upon opioid sales. It was 80% of what Osiris sells. 80%. And Osiris was in merger talks with a much larger company, Aestus, and Aestus was concerned that Osiris had such a nondiversified portfolio, a portfolio that was threatened by Dr. Dunham's pain management technique.

So, Robert Dunham killed his brother. His brother knew Sharita Vance had an arrangement to where she supplied Dr. Dunham with Oxycontin on a weekly basis. All that Robert Dunham had to do was replace the Oxycontin with pure heroin, have Ms. Vance deliver the pills for the usual $500, and there you go. Dr. Dunham consumes the pure heroin, thinking it's Oxycontin, and dies because he is not used to taking heroin. Robert Dunham had the motive to kill his brother, several motives, in fact. He had the means - he's the majority shareholder of a pharmaceutical company. A drug company. And he had the opportunity - he paid Ms. Vance $50,000 to deliver the lethal dose of heroin.

You may also recall that Robert Dunham was caught in a lie. Specifically, he claimed not to know that his brother was working on an alternative pain management technique, but, yet, he indicated in a letter he signed that this wasn't the case. In this letter, he wrote the following: 'While I understand your concern that my brother, Dr. Dunham, is working on a procedure that will greatly lessen the value of Osiris, Inc., in that Dr. Dunham is working on a pain management technique that has the potential to reduce the usage of opioids in this country, I can assure you that this will not be a problem in the future.'

Let those words sink in for a moment. I can assure you that this will not be a problem in the future. Why was he assuring Aestus of this, and what did he mean that Dr. Dunham wouldn't be a problem in the future? He preposterously claimed he didn't write those words, yet he signed the letter. He signed the letter. That's all you need to know. He owned those words when he signed the letter. And he indicated that Dr. Dunham wouldn't be a problem in the future.

Also, there was the potential that Dr. Dunham died of anaphylactic shock, because he was allergic to heroin. Admittedly, his primary care physician had no knowledge of it, and the autopsy didn't show it, but Dr. Warren, the Medical Examiner, explained that anaphylactic shock was not something an autopsy could pick up."

I wanted to tie the anaphylactic shock with his brother, and explain that only Robert Dunham would know his brother was allergic to heroin, but I couldn't. I couldn't because Mom lied to me for too long.

"Ladies and gentlemen of the jury, the state didn't prove its case against my client. It just didn't. The evidence against her was all circumstantial. So, my client possessed heroin and dropped a dirty UA that showed she had opioids in her system. What does that really prove? Dr. Dunham could have just as easily given the defendant the drug as the other way around. Dr. Dunham could have picked up those drugs from literally anybody. And there is plenty of evidence he got those drugs from his brother.

There is just too much doubt in this case for conviction. And remember, the state has the burden of proof in this case, and they must prove their case beyond a reasonable doubt. Beyond a reasonable doubt. Which means that if you have doubt that my client supplied the fatal dose of heroin to Dr. Dunham, you must acquit.

Thank you very much."

At that, I sat down. The judge gave his instructions on the elements on what the state had to prove and the jury was dismissed.

All we could do was wait.

THIRTY-SIX

arper and I arrived back at my home after we hung out for several hours, waiting for the jury to return, only to be told they would not have a verdict that evening and were going home.

Mom promptly freaked out when the jury foreman announced they couldn't reach a verdict that night, and I had to talk her off the ledge.

"Damien, what do they mean, they can't reach a verdict? They're going to find me guilty, aren't they?"

I felt like telling her that if the jury returned a guilty verdict, she had nobody to blame but herself, but that was just rubbing salt in the wound. "Mom, calm down. Juries typically take a long time to reach a verdict, especially in a murder case where there's lots of evidence. Like this one."

"But Damien, I didn't do it. I didn't do it. Dammit, Damien, you should have put me on the stand. I would have told them what happened."

"And your testimony would have directly contradicted my opening statement. You think they would believe a word you said on the stand?"

"That don't matter, you should have put me on."

And so it went.

I was happy to be back at my house, but everything seemed strangely quiet. Gretchen was sitting in the living room, reading a book, and she looked up at me. "Amelia and Nate are in their rooms," she said. "I haven't fed them yet."

It was only 6 PM, dinnertime, when I got home, so I didn't mind that Gretchen hadn't yet gotten the kids dinner. "Thanks for watching them," I said, giving her her usual per diem. "Hopefully this will be my last big case for awhile, and I can slow down and be with the kids more often."

She smiled as she took the money. "Thanks, just let me know what you need."

I nodded and turned to Harper, who came home with me. I didn't know, but it seemed she was still out of sorts and needing some kind of support. My support. We had grown close over the past few months, and she had expressed to me how much she valued our friendship. I felt the same.

"Well, I guess I better get the kids out of their rooms and get some chow in here. I think I'll call GrubHub and see if they can bring something over."

"Sounds good," Harper said. "I better call Rina and Abby and let them know I'll be home later." Rina and Abby were 14, so Harper often left them home alone when she had to.

I went to Amelia's room, where she was sitting on the bed with headphones on, reading a book. She took off the headphones when I came in. "Hey, Dad," she said.

"Hey, kid," I said. "Dinner in a half hour."

"Cool."

"Your brother's in his room, then?"

She shrugged. "I guess. Last I checked, he was in the bathroom. For a long time. I don't want to even think about what he's doing in there. Gross."

In the bathroom for a long time.

He was at that age.

I went downstairs and found Harper sitting on the couch. She was reading the GrubHub "menu," apparently trying to decide what to order and where to order from.

"I saw Amelia, and she told me Nate was in the bathroom. For a long time." I shook my head and smiled. "He's at that age."

Harper furrowed her brow. "You better check on him."

"Why? Trust me, when I was his age, I was also in the bathroom for a long time, and I didn't want anybody checking on me."

She shook her head. "You just should." She pointed at her arm. "My hair's standing on end."

"Okay," I said. "I'll knock on the bathroom door and tell Nate to be ready for dinner in a half-hour and we'll just order something for him from the GrubHub thing. I don't want to disturb him too much."

"Just go," Harper said in an urgent voice. "Please."

"Okay, okay," I said, going upstairs to the bathroom. It was the bathroom that everybody used, because Nate's room didn't have an adjoining bathroom.

I knocked on the door. "Nate, buddy, just wanted to let you know GrubHub will be here in a little bit. We're probably getting Chinese. I'll order you some Orange Chicken, what do you think?"

I didn't hear anything on the other side.

"Nate? It's Dad. Did you hear me?"

Silence.

All at once, my heart started to race. "Nate, answer me! Nate!"

I opened the door. It was unlocked.

Then stopped in my tracks.

Nate was lying in the tub, covered in blood.

THIRTY-SEVEN

All the way to the hospital, I obsessed. I questioned myself. *I should have never taken Mom's case. I should have taken that sabbatical. I should have given Nate those anti-depressants. I shouldn't have assumed he was happy just because he seemed like he was.*

Harper drove to the hospital, tailing the ambulance that was screaming down the street to the nearest hospital. I was next to her, and my mother and Amelia were in the backseat. Harper put her hand on my knee.

"It'll be okay. We managed to catch him in time. The paramedics said we got him in time," she said calmly.

I shook my head. "No. God, I pray he makes it through, but Harper, even if he does, he's not okay. He's not okay. I don't know what happened. He seemed like he was happy. He seemed like he was happy." I put my head in my hands. "What happened?"

"Dad, I know what happened. Nate and Austin, they had a fight. I know they had a fight, because they weren't talking on the phone anymore," Amelia said from the backseat.

Just what I was afraid of. Nate's happiness depended too much on external factors, so it was very fragile.

What made it all worse was that Austin and Nate were on the same basketball team. Austin's mother gave them rides all the time. I gave them rides, too, and I had gotten to know Austin a little bit over the past few months. I liked the kid.

But if Austin and Nate had a falling-out, Nate probably wouldn't want to be on the team anymore. He was that kind of sensitive kid. He wouldn't want to be around Austin anymore, so he probably would just quit the team.

In other words, Nate's world was falling apart. It would be up to me to help him stitch it back together.

We got to the hospital, where I went to the ER desk and explained who I was.

"You'll have to wait in the waiting room," the front-desk clerk said to me. "They're working on him right now. We'll let you know when you can see him."

I nodded, feeling numb. Harper was right next to me, her arm around my back, but I could barely feel her. I was rolling around my self-recriminations, over and over and over.

This was my fault what happened.

My fault.

I sat down on the seat, and Harper came back at some point with a sandwich and a cup of coffee. I looked over at Amelia and my mother and saw they were already eating their own sandwich and were both drinking pop.

"You have to eat, Damien," Harper gently said. "We've been here for three hours, and you need to eat."

Three hours? How could that be? It seemed like we just got there.

Time had no meaning.

I looked at the sad sandwich and realized that, in spite of myself, I really was hungry. I took a bite, and then another, and, before I knew it, the sandwich was gone and I was hungry for more.

Harper handed me a couple of bags of chips, and I ate those and drank a coke. It seemed like I was in a haze and the food and drink was bringing me back to reality.

"Thanks," I said.

I looked up at the desk and decided to see what I could find out. "My son, Nate, he was brought in here a few hours ago," I told the woman, who, I think, was a different person than before. She looked similar to the last woman, but not exactly the same.

"Nate Harrington?" she asked.

"Yes, Nate Harrington," I said.

"I was just getting ready to send somebody out to speak with you. He had emergency surgery and a blood transfusion, but he's out of surgery and in a recovery room. We're going to admit him to the hospital. We're just waiting for a bed to open up."

I felt a great sense of relief and apprehension rolled into one. "Thank you," I said.

I followed her back to a series of rooms separated only by curtains. In one of the rooms was Nate in a bed. He looked so tiny. He was hooked up to an IV, and I saw his wrists were heavily bandaged. He was apparently sleeping, but I sat down next to him anyhow.

I took his hand, his tiny little hand, and kissed it. I gripped his little hand in mine so tight, I was afraid I would break it somehow. "Nate, buddy," I said to my sleeping son. "I'm so sorry. I'll be there for you, I promise. Your grandmother's case is done, and I'm going to take off as much time as you need me to take off to make sure you're okay. I know you probably can't hear me, but I love you, buddy. I love you and I can never lose you."

I put my head down on the bed next to him and closed my eyes.

I lost track of time, again, because, before I knew it, a doctor in hospital scrubs informed me that a bed had opened up. They were admitting Nate and needed to transfer him. "Please wait in the waiting room, and we'll let you know when Nate is transferred to a regular room," the doctor said.

"Thanks," I said. I went back to the waiting room, where Harper, Amelia and Mom were all asleep in various chairs. The television overhead was still playing something. It looked like a news program of some sort. There were a few others also in the waiting room and almost everyone was asleep.

I looked at the clock and realized why everyone was asleep - it was 4 AM.

I went to Harper and nudged her awake. "Harper, do you mind taking Amelia to your home? And I hate to ask you this, but-"

She nodded. "I'll take both your mom and Amelia to my house. I have enough bedrooms that they can stay with me as long as they like. Don't worry, we have it handled."

"Thanks," I said. "I have to wait here for Nate to be transferred to a room, and then I'm going up there to sleep in the hospital chair. He needs to see me when he wakes up."

"Of course," Harper said. "And if the jury comes back, I'll handle it. I'll tell the judge what happened and I'm sure it will be okay."

She understood, and I loved her for it. "Thank you." I put my hand on her shoulder. "I have to go."

She roused Amelia and Mom and I helped her herd them back to her car. The night air was heavy with fog and it was still pitch-black outside, although I knew dawn was just around the corner.

"Thank you again," I said to Harper after everybody was buckled in.

"Don't mention it," she said. "You'd do the same for me."

She was right about that.

I would do anything for her.

THIRTY-EIGHT

The next day, Nate slept until around noon and I was there when he woke up.

He looked like he had no idea where he was or how he got there.

"Dad," he said, looking around the room. "What?"

"Nate, you're in the hospital," I said. "I found you in the bathtub. You were...hurt. I brought you here."

I knew he was slightly drugged up, as much as a child of his age could be. "Dad, I'm sorry. I'm so sorry. I know you don't want to deal with me. You have enough going on with grandma."

"Shhhhhh...don't apologize. Don't ever apologize for something like this. I love you, buddy. Your grandma's case is over. We're just waiting for the verdict. I won't leave your side, buddy. I'm here to stay."

He smiled weakly. "You don't have to stick around, Dad," he said to me. "I'm okay."

"No, you're not," I said. "You're not okay, but you will be. I promise you, you will be."

He stared at the ceiling, looking like he was counting some non-existent dots.

"Dad, I'm gay," he finally said after a long, long pause. "I really liked somebody but he doesn't like me back. Not right now, anyway. He did like me back but he doesn't anymore. I don't want to be on the team anymore. He's on the team, and he turned all the guys against me. He's been spreading rumors about me, and I just don't want to be around any of them."

I took his hand in mine. "Son, I love you no matter what. Thank you for confiding in me. I'm sorry you got your heart broken and I know it hurts. I don't really know what to say except to let you know I'm here, I'll never leave, and I love you just the way you are."

He smiled a slight smile. "I love you, too, Dad, but I'm really tired." He closed his eyes.

I sat back in my chair and fell asleep myself.

A few hours later, I got the text. Not guilty. Harper and my Mom, now free as a bird, were going to be heading over to the hospital and wanted to take me out to dinner.

I looked over at Nate and smiled. "Looks like I'll be gone for a few hours, but I'll be right back, I promise."

He was asleep, so he didn't really hear me.

He was physically fine, thank God.

But he was far from okay.

Also by Rachel Sinclair

For information about upcoming titles in the *Harper Ross Legal Thriller* series, sign up for my mailing list! You'll be the first to know about new releases and you'll be the first to know about any promotions!!!!
http://eepurl.com/hBqhtr

Johnson County Legal Thrillers (Kansas City, Missouri)

Bad Faith

Justice Denied

Hidden Defendant

Injustice for All

LA Defense

The Associate

The Alibi

Reasonable Doubt

The Accused

Secrets and Lies

Until Proven Guilty

Emerson Justice Legal Thrillers (Los Angeles)

Dark Justice

Blind Justice

Southern California Legal Thrillers (San Diego)

Presumption of Guilt

Justice Delayed

By Reason of Insanity

Wrongful Conviction

The Trial

Milton Keynes UK
Ingram Content Group UK Ltd.
UKHW040715201123
432908UK00002B/402